OPERATION: PLEIADES

BOOK II: RELICS

By
Vijaya Schartz

Triskelion Publishing
www.triskelionpublishing.com

Published by Triskelion Publishing www.triskelionpublishing.com
15508 W. Bell Rd. #101, PMB #502, Surprise, AZ 85374 U.S.A.

First e-published by Triskelion Publishing
First e-publishing August 2004

ISBN Ebook 1-932866-21-3

ISBN Print 1-933471-54-9

First printing by Triskelion Publishing
First printing November 2005

CHAPT ER ONE

Montreal, March 2023

"Hit me, damn it!" Jake's lungs bellowed in and out as he fought for much needed air.

Celene Dupres dropped-kicked to his face and followed with a double kick to his rib cage, forcing him into a corner then she pulled back. It wouldn't do to defeat her teacher and best friend in front of his whole stable. *Honor, Respect, Loyalty*, declared the banner on the wall.

The other residents of the gym fell silent around the two fighters. Not even the rhythm of a skipping rope, the bounce of a punching ball or the thump of a big boy punch could be heard. Only the squeak of Celene and Jake's rubber soles on the gleaming parquet echoed in the vast room, punctuated by their yells and high jumps.

Through the plexiglass of his black headgear, Jake looked suddenly older and now breathed heavily. Celene stopped and bowed in surrender. Jake stared at her in disbelief then broke eye contact and shrugged. He removed his helmet to wipe the sweat off his face.

"You shouldn't hold back, girl. I trained you to win, not give up. Never apologize for your superior skills."

Celene bit her lips. "Sorry, Jake." She knew she couldn't keep losing to the dear man, even to save face, but she respected him too much.

The students released the breath they had been

holding and shuffled back to their own training. Jake, the kickboxing legend of Montreal, remained undefeated.

Celene bounced back on slender tan legs, still sparring with an imaginary adversary as she followed Jake to the co-ed locker rooms. "I'll try harder next time, hey?"

Jake set his helmet on the wooden bench. "Don't hold your punches. If it becomes a habit, you lose your edge in a real fight." He slumped onto the bench, leaned back against the metal lockers then smiled. "For a skinny girl, you fight like one of those damned nano-enhanced freaks that pop up in the gym these days."

Celene pulled off her red gloves and headgear, shaking loose her long auburn hair. "Nothing that fancy, Jake." She winked at him. "I just had the best teacher for the past eighteen years."

"That long? Hell, I was your age when you came to me, twenty-six. You should think about teaching."

"Sorry, Jake. Not me. Montreal is where I live, but I like to come and go. Too many places to see, too many mysteries to unveil... I could never commit to lifelong students. I need the dust of a dig site, the wonder of discovery." As she picked up her towel from the bench, she uncovered her phone earpiece. It flashed blue. She'd missed a call. "Do you mind?"

Jack shook his head then removed his chest protector. Celene donned the earpiece and tapped it twice to call back.

From the other end came a warm male voice. "Hi, Angel."

Celene winced at the static. "Dad! How do you

like Ukraine? How's the dig coming along?" She started unlacing one shoe.

"We found the motherlode!" her father yelled, as if to compensate for the bad connection.

Celene waved to Jake who ambled toward the showers. "You found the crash site?" She pulled off her sock and her elastic ankle brace and massaged her right ankle, still tender from a recent sprain.

"That and more." The excited voice came in spurts. "The ship was not completely destroyed on impact. We have bodies. Big, ugly, muscular alien bodies with dark skin hard as a shell, part human, with no hair and smooth artificial plates instead of skulls."

"Anaz-voohri bodies?" That changed everything. Celene sat up, her ankle forgotten. "I want to see that up close."

"There is also a bank of crystal shards with pictographs and writings on them," her father blurted out. "I'm sure each of these shards contains a load of information. We don't know how to read them, though. We'll need a translator."

"This is so exciting! You are going to be busy, hey?"

"We've got a bunch of relics to catalog. Archeology museums all over the world are going to fight over these alien artifacts."

"Congratulations, Dad! You deserve this break. You've been working so many years for this."

"So, when can you take a look at the bodies? You could stay a while and gather samples for the lab. We'll also need your language skills to decipher the writing on the crystals. The symbols resemble those you studied at the Anasazi ruins in Arizona."

"What?" Celene blanched. She felt something stir deep inside her. "So the Anaz-voohri are really related to the Anasazi abducted eight hundred years ago?"

"Without a doubt. Told you this was big. You've got to hurry. So far I've kept this under wraps, but as soon as the Global Government agencies hear about it, they'll be buzzing all over the place. Hell, they may even want to take over if what we found is too important. I don't trust those guys."

Celene's mind reeled with the possibilities. "Can you imagine? This could lead to the cure for the filovirus plague and the hemorrhagic fevers. The Anaz-voohri are immune. Samples of their DNA should jumpstart the fight for the cure."

"Exactly." Her father paused and Celene could almost hear him smile with pride. "Professor Armand Dupres, Nobel Prize. It has a nice ring don't you think?"

Celene laughed at her father's dreams of grandeur. "Still, be careful, Dad. Some fringe groups say hybrids have infiltrated the highest levels of government and are keeping tabs on us. Maybe the Anaz-voohri don't want us to learn their technology. Many believe they want us all dead!"

"Don't listen to that ridiculous gossip," Armand Dupres scoffed. "Each generation must have its witch hunt. Don't worry your pretty little head. They could have destroyed us a long time ago if they wanted to. Just get on the next plane. I'm sending you the map and the satellite coordinates. Here goes."

Fishing her epad out of her gym bag, Celene

punched a few keys. A map and digital numbers appeared on the screen. "Got it."

"I'll send you pictures of the hieroglyphics later. Love you, Angel. See you soon."

"Love you, too, Dad. Be careful."

After hanging up, Celene called her office at Montreal Concordia University, the world-renowned center in forensic archeology research. She occasionally taught field classes there and participated in government-funded research. She asked her assistant to cancel all her appointments for the next week. Her private treasure hunting clients would have to wait.

One more call to ask her neighbor to keep an eye on Isis, her Siamese cat, cost her a pair of tickets for the Montreal Canadians hockey game tonight at the Molson Centre. But Celene couldn't use the tickets anyway. From her epad she booked a flight to Munich with a connection to Uzhgorod in the Carpathian Mountains, then she hit the showers.

* * * * *

During the long Lufthansa flight over the North Pole from Montreal to Munich, comfortable in her jogging sweats, Celene watched the hockey game on pay-per-view on her epad. She was careful not to stand up and cheer each time the Montreal Canadians scored a goal.

Still euphoric from her team's victory, Celene consulted her notes on Anasazi cryptographs and compared them to the hieroglyphics her father had sent her. She found significant differences despite the uncanny resemblance. The language had evolved over the centuries spent off-world, but somehow Celene could feel the meaning of the words just beyond her grasp, as if the knowledge was locked in a secret compartment of her brain. She felt so close to unlocking its secrets, she knew she would decipher the language eventually.

Reclining her seat, Celene settled back for a nap, envisioning her favorite dream of a small tropical beach. Palm trees swayed in the gentle trade winds, and *hula* dancers undulated to the sounds of *ukuleles* and steel guitars. In all her travels, she'd never been to Hawaii, but she felt a strange fascination for its sandy shores.

She woke up in a cold sweat no thanks to the nightmare that had plagued her for the past eighteen years. Once awake, she could never remember the dream, only the malaise and the helpless terror it left behind. During her childhood, her father seemed to understand her fright and always comforted her on those scary nights.

Now wide awake, she pushed the disturbing feeling away. She rejoiced knowing she would see her father soon. The dear man had spoiled her since childhood. Her loving family had given her happiness as far as she could remember, although Celene had no memory of her first eight years.

Often Celene had questioned the fact that there were no baby pictures of her in the house. She was told the flood that forced her parents to move to Montreal had destroyed every last photo album. She always suspected her parents were hiding something about her past, but when she asked, her father denied it. In an attempt to re-open her childhood memories, Celene had recently tried regression under hypnotism, but that did not work either.

When her mother had fallen into a cave and died on a dig site in the Pyrenees, Celene had cried for days. Her father wept like a child and hugged her so tight Celene couldn't breathe. He claimed her mother had been murdered, but he couldn't prove anything. Ever since, Celene and her father had held on to each other for emotional support.

Celene later took up forensic archeology, foreign languages and anthropology at Concordia University. Then as an adult, after following her father on many dig sites, she became an archeologist in her own right. She accepted a research position at Concordia after returning from an important dig in Russia three years ago.

The plane landed in Munich which was covered by a blanket of snow. Thanks to her flawless German, Celene explained to the suspicious customs employee why she had funny-looking knives, brushes, and vials in her backpack. Then she had to hurry to catch her connecting flight to Uzhgorod.

It took only one hour for the smaller craft to reach Uzhgorod located at the border of Slovakia and Ukraine. Although Europe had long ago become a united country, ethnic groups still took pride in their separate identities. Celene changed into her snow gear in the narrow washroom of the plane. After landing, she followed the horde of chatty tourists dressed in colorful parkas through the prefabricated Uzhgorod terminal, to the carousel where she retrieved her pack.

After donning her white faux fur coat and hat, Celene wove her way through the crowd of tourists carrying skis and snowboards. She stepped outside to retrieve the old Hummer waiting for her in the parking lot. She found it loaded with several gas tanks and a cardboard box filled with food and drink for the trip. She thought the Hummer a rather crude and polluting vehicle, but that's all the travel agency could find on short notice in such an isolated place. Celene clipped her epad to the dashboard and followed the satellite navigation system as she drove out of the charming town, past the red brick cathedral under reconstruction flaunting its whitewashed onion dome.

Celene could hardly tell that three years ago a cataclysm had leveled the area and destroyed most of the buildings in central Europe, killing millions. Speculations about the source of the deadly electromagnetic field still puzzled scientists. Some even said the Anaz-voohri had hit the area with an alien weapon to declare war upon the human race, but no other strike followed. The survivors had rebuilt the small town of Uzhgorod with international funds thanks to an outpouring of solidarity. Now, simple inns and restaurants were able to welcome eager tourists to the area.

Outside Uzhgorod, winter blanketed the mountains. Celene took the southeastern road along the railroad tracks and traveled deep into the Carpathian mountain range. The camp lay far from the ski lodges, almost a hundred miles inside the wild life reserve. It would take four to five hours to reach the site through rugged mountain roads.

Halfway there, Celene left the paved road to take a shortcut of rocky gravel trails. The trail narrowed so much in places, she feared the Hummer would not fit, but it managed. As she ascended the mountain, the snow-covered forest of beech, maple and sycamore gave way to spruce. Celene could now feel the scarcity of oxygen as she breathed in the thinner air. The pale afternoon sun lay low when she reached the vicinity of the dig site. According to her guidance system, she gauged the camp must lie on the other side of the closest peak.

She drove the Hummer up a rocky incline. Soon, the trees disappeared and the trail steepened. The Hummer lurched dangerously, then the trail simply ended. Frustrated, Celene stopped the vehicle. She checked the phone reception on her epad and called her father.

"Angel? Where are you?" He sounded happy.

Celene's spirits soared. "I'm really close according to the satellite guidance, but I'm stuck on the peak."

"Our peak? Why didn't you take the road? It's in much better condition. How far are you from the top?" He sounded so close.

Celene looked at the summit to evaluate the distance. "Only a few hundred yards."

"Leave the vehicle and climb on foot. You are young and strong. The camp is just over the top on the other side. You can't miss it."

"All right. I'll see you in a bit."

Celene grabbed her pack, secured it on her back

over her fur coat so she could use her gloved hands for climbing, then she proceeded on foot uphill. Despite her excellent physical shape, her muscles felt stiff from the cold, and her furry boots slipped in the snow. The decrease of oxygen due to the high altitude made her feel winded.

She took her time on the dangerous ascension. While climbing, she heard unusual sounds, faint and far away. She didn't think they were bears. Since it was winter they should be hibernating in their caves. Wolves? Lynx, maybe? She knew the mountains teemed with all sorts of wild animals that had been hunted for centuries. Just recently, though, the whole Carpathian range had become a wildlife reserve. She felt it was about time man stopped killing innocent creatures for sport. As an animal rights activist, Celene rejoiced at this small victory.

When she crested the top, Celene stopped to catch her breath and smiled as she found an edelweiss. She plucked the furry snow flower that had come to represent the area, like a symbol of hope and endurance through the long winters.

From the top Celene had a perfect aerial view of the dig just below the tree line. The woods looked bare all around it as if a fire had cleared the area at the time of the crash, and the trees had never grown back. A dozen white tents surrounded the central find, with vehicles and supply crates in plain view. The blue portable washrooms contrasted brightly against the snow.

Fishing into her backpack, Celene retrieved her epad and snapped a shot of the golden alien ship half-sunken in the dirt. The structure looked like a flattened dome, with ports around the central ridge connecting the upper and lower halves. Her father had good reason to be proud of this find. It was the motherlode. It looked like one of the ships first sighted in the 1950s, but this one had crashed recently, more like three years ago, according to the growth of the surrounding vegetation.

Could this be related to the cataclysm? Could this crash have provoked the devastating electromagnetic field? Or had the vessel fired upon the land with an alien weapon and crashed afterwards? Or, if the disaster was of natural origin, had it brought down the alien craft? So many questions. Celene burned to solve the mystery.

Careful not to sprain her ankles, Celene climbed downhill. She lost sight of the camp when she reached the tree line, but soon she could see it again. From a distance, she recognized the hulking figure of her father, dressed like an Inuit with his furry hood, busy labeling artifacts on a table outside one of the tents.

"Dad!"

Armand Dupres turned and waved back.

Celene hurried across the expanse to meet him. In the same instant, she heard a distant roar. Then a battle cry pierced the quiet woods, followed by the screams of a charging horde of commandos in white camouflage gear. Soldiers irrupted into the camp, phase-guns zipping deadly beams of green fire that sizzled through the air.

Celene saw her father fall and heard him cry out. She wanted to go to him, but some survival instinct stopped her.

Inside the tents, men and women screamed in pain and horrified fright. A few escaped and ran in every direction, only to be caught and massacred. None of them fought back.

Adrenaline surged in Celene's blood as her martial arts training took over. She heard Jake's voice in her head. *Still your mind, focus, evaluate the enemy. Never start a fight you cannot win. Control your impulses.* Celene hid behind a tree. What could she do unarmed against what, fifty commandos? In this she was helpless. She watched a second wave of soldiers emerge from the woods, the black muzzle of their phase-guns contrasting with the snow and their camouflage gear.

When Celene saw her father move, she realized he was still alive. Against reason, she ignored the phase beams slicing the perimeter and dropped her backpack so that she could crawl toward her father. She wormed around bodies with blistered faces and charred wounds that smelled of burnt flesh. Her heart hardened in her chest like a lump of ice. The chaos and savagery around her did not make any sense. When she finally reached her father, she dragged him under a table and cradled his head in her arms. Armand Dupres stared into nothingness.

"Dad, I'm here!"

"Angel?" A thin trickle of blood oozed from the corner of his mouth. "Save the relics," her father managed to say feebly.

"Dad, please don't leave me." But Celene knew such a wide chest wound from a phase-gun could only be fatal.

"Run now, Angel. Save the relics, for me, for humanity…" Her father's blue eyes fluttered then closed, and she felt his lifeless body go limp.

Celene wanted to scream at the injustice and vent her rage, but she suddenly realized she crouched under a table in the middle of carnage. The phase fire had ceased. The commandos now searched the tents for survivors. She could hear a plane approaching. Why was she still alive? Because she was a woman? No. She could see women among the victims.

A soldier passed by, kicked the foot of her dead father and ignored her, as if she was not even there. Something unusual was happening to Celene. She felt strange, out of synch. Why was she not afraid? Somehow, she felt safe. Finally, Celene gently eased her father's head to the ground. To her amazement, she could not see her arm holding her father's head. She couldn't see her body at all!

Was she dead? Was she a spirit now? That would explain her invisibility. Heart beating fast, Celene scanned the clearing in vain to see if she could find her dead body lying on the ground among the victims. No, she wasn't dead. Not that Celene feared death. She only feared the place of her childhood nightmares. She pinched her cheek and it smarted. She was not dreaming either. How unfortunate.

Celene must have become invisible somehow. She'd heard of genetic research on invisibility for military purpose, but no one had succeeded yet. Or had they? In any case, how could this possibly happen to her?

Commandos ran from the deafening sound of a military transport helicopter hovering overhead. The large cargo bird alighted in the clearing in a cloud of powdery snow. A man wearing an officer's uniform immediately climbed out and dusted his pants then readjusted his gold-rimmed glasses. She thought it strange. Who wore glasses in this day and age? The pilot killed the engine and the twin blades slowed their thumping then stopped. Celene heard the officer addressing the commandos in a clipped voice. "Load everything on board!"

Hope flared when Celene recognized the only surviving member of her father's team. She almost ran to the tall elderly scientist then stopped. Something felt wrong. Emile Blanchard, her father's best friend and colleague, walked unhurriedly toward the stocky commanding officer. The commandos following Blanchard seemed to treat him with deference. Far from devastated by the sight of the killing grounds, Emile smiled and bent his skinny frame to shake hands with the officer who laughed and slapped his shoulder.

Celene seethed inside but did not dare make a sound. Why would Emile Blanchard have her father and his team murdered? For what? Money? Professional jealousy? And who were these executioners?

More confident in her invisibility cloak, Celene moved about, careful not to attract attention, but she left footprints in the fresh snow, so she kept to the hard snow and bare rock. The soldiers brought empty crates out of the plane and started packing the relics. Each crate bore the seal of the Moscow Archeological

Museum. So that's where the artifacts were going!

Celene knew she needed to pay a visit to Sergei Ivanovitch, the conservator of the Moscow Archeological Museum. She wondered if he still pined for her since their short affair three years ago. Celene had broken her relationship with Sergei at the end of her assignment in Russia, when she wanted to help dig the people of Central Europe out from the debris of their cities. Sergei, indifferent to their plight, demanded that Celene commit to him, renounce her career, her travels, and settle down in Moscow.

Not ready to give up her freedom, Celene wanted to help people whenever she chose. Besides, she loved her career and travels. Romantic entanglements always complicated things. Since then, they'd remained friends, nothing more.

Footsteps crunched the snow behind her. Celene moved to avoid a collision. The soldier carried two irregular shaped crystal shards in deep shades of amber and aqua. About ten inches long, they glinted in the fading sun like huge broken gems with beveled edges. The soldier inserted both into protective foam pillows before laying them into the crate.

The relics! Celene couldn't carry them all, but when the soldier turned his back, she snatched one of the shards, which disappeared from view as soon as she slipped it into the deep pocket inside her coat. At least she could start studying it and discover why her father thought they were so important. Celene started to like this invisibility trick. How long would it last? She hoped not forever.

She watched soldiers drag bodies out of the tents,

line them up on the ground then store them in black
body bags that they loaded on the cargo bird. As she
watched the zipper close over her father's face, Celene
mouthed a silent goodbye and blew him a kiss. She let
her tears flow for the gentle archeologist, but inside she
boiled. If she survived, Celene intended to exact
revenge on these heartless savages.

One hatch to the alien ship lay open but two
sentinels stood in the doorway. Celene itched to get
inside the ship. She doubted she had any chance
getting through the guards, even with her being
invisible. Soldiers came out of the alien ship, carrying
all kinds of strange equipment, consoles, metal boxes
and crates. Others paired up to carry large red body
bags stamped with biohazard symbols. She guessed
they probably the alien bodies. They seemed taller,
bulkier and heavier than human bodies.

Celene wanted to peek into the red bags, but too
many soldiers surrounded them. She struggled to
control her frustration. She should be the one
examining the alien remains. She knew where to find
them later, though. She'd look for them at the Moscow
Archeological Museum, along with the relics and the
human bodies. She hoped Sergei would help her return
her father's corpse back home, where she could give
him a decent funeral.

A soldier walked up to Emile Blanchard and the
commanding officer. Unseen, Celene approached them
to listen to their conversation.

The soldier saluted. "What should we do with the
device?"

Before the officer could answer, Blanchard spoke.

"I would like to study it further and get it to work. The perfect place for that would be…"

"Don't say anything top secret," the officer cut off. "Not all the soldiers here have top clearance. The less they know the better. I'll let you study that thing wherever you see fit. We'll talk about it later."

"Thank you." Blanchard heaved a deep sigh. He looked relieved.

When Celene stepped on a branch that cracked underfoot, she stiffened and remained still. The officer turned his broad face toward Celene and stared straight at her with silver gray eyes through the glasses. The round patch on his chest displayed a blue constellation and the lettering ORION. Celene had heard of ORION, a Global Security Sector agency, but she knew very little about it. Something to do with protecting the planet from alien attacks.

Could the man see her? Something felt wrong with one of his eyes as it glinted in a ray of sunlight. His steely stare remained fixed through the glasses. He walked toward Celene and looked around. No. He couldn't see her, but from the set of his square jaw and the intense expression on his well groomed face, Celene suspected he could feel her presence. Did he know about invisibility? A shiver raised the small hairs along her spine.

The officer then shrugged and directed his steps toward the plane with Emile Blanchard following close on his heels. Celene wondered if she dared sneak inside the transport and stay with the relics. She decided against it. She had no idea how long this invisibility miracle would hold. If discovered, she knew she would be killed like the others. These people did not want witnesses and had no regard for human life. So she watched the cargo bird take off, knowing she would catch up with it in Moscow.

A group of soldiers dismantled the tents, erasing all traces of the campsite, phase fire, or human presence. They shoveled dirt and snow to bury the naked ridge of the alien ship unearthed by her father's team, as if to make sure no one would ever find it again.

Silently, avoiding the soldiers left behind to decontaminate the site, Celene retreated to the woods. She retrieved her backpack at the edge of camp and climbed toward the top, her boots leaving fresh tracks in the snow. When she reached the crest, she finally dared to look back. No one followed her. The camp had all but disappeared. She could not see the outlines of the wrecked spaceship anymore, only a natural mound of dirt and snow in a clearing.

Running down to the Hummer, Celene realized she could now see her booted feet in front of her, but she had no time to stop and think about the phenomenon. Sliding into the driver seat, she kicked the vehicle in gear and rushed down the narrow trail. Mountain shadows soon brought darkness. Celene drove with the lights off using the glare of moonlight on the snow to guide her way and trusting her satellite guidance system. With a little luck, she would reach Uzhgorod airport in time for the latest flight to Moscow, where she must ask a favor from Sergei Ivanovitch.

But could she trust anyone after what happened? The soldiers' crates bore the stamp of his museum. What if Sergei was involved?

CHAPTER TWO

Moscow, next morning

Around three in the morning, eyes burning from crying and from lack of sleep, Celene landed at Domodedovo, Moscow's fastest growing airport. During the flight, she had reserved a room online at her favorite hotel in town, the Metropol located across from the Bolshoi Theater. Moscow had suffered little from the cataclysm of 2020, due to its eastern location.

After renting a hydrogen-converted black sedan at the airport, Celene drove the fifteen kilometers to the heart of Moscow. The many lights of the city were reflected crisply in the Moskova River, but tonight Celene could not appreciate its beauty. Too many thoughts tumbled about in her mind; the violent death of her father, the fact that she became invisible at the site. And why would Emile Blanchard, a man she considered an old friend, conspire with assassins to murder her father and his team? She couldn't let him get away with such ruthless killings.

As she drove toward the heart of Moscow, Celene replayed the massacre in her head. She also wondered what happened to her and even started questioning her sanity. For the best part of an hour she had been invisible, then without knowing why or how once she was out of danger, her body reappeared. Could she have hallucinated the whole scene?

Wanting it to have been a bad dream, she even voice activated a call to her father while waiting for a green light. At the other end, his phone rang several times then someone picked up the call. Celene's heart leapt with hope. Against all odds, maybe this had all been a nightmare after all, and her father was alive and well.

"Hello, Dad?"

Muffled voices and background noise followed. Celene heard things falling, like panic at an unexpected event. After a few seconds she felt a silent presence at the end of the line, faint breathing, then the phone went dead. The streetlights blurred through her tears as she reached the Metropol Hotel.

Exhausted, in her filthy clothes, and in serious need of a few hours of sleep, Celene left the car with the valet at the door. She picked up her key at the desk, went straight to her room, and drew a bath.

* * * * *

When Celene awoke, she checked herself to make sure she could see all her body parts, in the flesh as well as in the mirror. She looked quite normal and felt relieved. Outside the window, a pink dawn pierced the haze from the smokestacks of Moscow's industrial suburbs. The wind had shifted, choking the city with heavy smog. Celene called Sergei's office and left a brief message. Although no one knew she'd witnessed the massacre, she knew she had to be careful.

Surfing the Net, Celene searched for any kind of

information on ORION and the symbol she saw on the murderers' uniforms. Her search brought up stargazers' sites and legends of Greek mythology about the god Orion trying to catch the Pleiades, the seven abducted sisters who eventually became the seven stars of the constellation.

The Pleiades also happened to be the star system of the Anaz-voohri. She wondered if there was a coincidence between the two. The graphic representation of Orion's constellation matched the symbol on the soldiers' patches. She wondered about the connection.

Further inquiry into military covert operations brought up a conspiracy theory site. According to this unofficial source, the government agency ORION had the task of removing any alien threat from the planet. Celene thought she might be on the right track. They would want the relics but why kill innocent archeologists? She saved the information for further reference.

Taking the alien shard out of her backpack, Celene held it up to the window. The relic felt light in her hands as it refracted the morning sun's rays into rainbow colors. This particular crystal had a pale blue tint, like an aquamarine gem. Others from the pictures her father had sent had more intense coloring, like topaz, ruby, amethyst, even obsidian black. The many inscriptions precisely engraved into one facet looked somewhat familiar. Celene burned to study their meaning.

Wrapping the shard in its protective sleeve, she slipped it back into her bag. Depending on how much she trusted Sergei, she might want to show it to him. She threw her white faux fur over navy sweat pants and sweater, grabbed the backpack, then walked out of the room. At the hotel front door, she hailed the valet.

Morning traffic in Moscow didn't compare with Montreal. From her previous trips, Celene knew the metro would be crowded, but the streets harbored more pedestrians and bicycles than cars. No fancy Dial-a-Bikes here, the new anti-gravity motorcycles that were all the rage among the wealthy Canadians. The few vehicles seen in town this morning used obsolete fossil fuel. Russia still had far to go to meet the global anti-pollution standards. The drivers honked their horns profusely and ignored the speed limit. Celene parked the black sedan near the front steps of the Archeological Museum just as the security guard unlocked the tall glass door to the public.

Instead of following the visitors to the ticket counter, Celene took the brass elevator marked "private" to the upper floor offices. Glad for the relative warmth, she removed her gloves. On the top floor, at the end of the long marble hallway, she nodded to the blonde secretary who looked at her with some surprise then smiled.

Celene felt underdressed. She had not packed for city life. She greeted the secretary in Russian and asked to see Sergei Ivanovitch. The girl pushed a button on her desk and announced the visitor. The door to Sergei's office opened automatically. Celene walked in.

Sergei turned away from the view at the window to face her. "Celene!" He came to her with natural grace, tall and smiling, elegant in a black cashmere sweater. His dark hair and eyebrows enhanced deep aqua eyes in a somewhat pale face. "I received your message. What a wonderful surprise." Sergei's winning smile still had some power over her, but Celene controlled her feelings. For both their sakes, they could only be friends. He took her hand and kissed her fingertips. "Are you free for breakfast? You seem to have lost some weight. I must feed you."

A famished Celene smiled back. "I'd love some borscht."

"I know exactly the place. Right across the street. It's almost as good as your cooking, but not quite." He smiled then grabbed his coat from a peg, took her arm through her furry sleeve and walked her toward the elevator. "What brings you to Moscow?"

"A mystery." Celene had rehearsed what she would say but hesitated. "My father seems to have disappeared in the field."

Sergei held the elevator door for her. "Where? Is he in trouble? How do you know?"

Touched by his genuine concern, Celene wanted to trust him but didn't feel she could reveal the whole truth. "He doesn't answer his phone. I talked to him two days ago. He had found something big in the Carpathians. We were supposed to meet here with his findings, but I haven't been able to reach him since I left Montreal." Her eyes misted as memories of her father tightened her throat. "It's not like him. I fear something bad happened to him."

Sergei looked grave as he held the door again while they exited the elevator. "He said he found something big? I haven't heard about any big find around here in years." They left the museum, walked down the front steps, then crossed the cobblestone street. "What kind of find was it?"

Celene closed her coat tightly against the chill. How much could she tell? "Something to do with the Anaz-voohri."

Sergei glanced at her sideways. He cleared his throat but remained silent as they entered the restaurant. The dark interior in brass and red leather smelled of onions and boiled meat. Soft violin music seeped from hidden speakers. Celene guessed the crystal chandelier was probably clear plastic. They removed their coats and left them on a peg by the door. The owner came out of the kitchen to greet Sergei with a wide smile and a hug, then he led them to a secluded booth in the back, at the end of the long window.

Sergei let Celene sit first then took a seat across from her. Through the lacy curtain, Celene could see the street and the museum on the other side. Sergei ordered borscht for both of them then sighed as the man moved away. "I hope your father is all right."

"Thanks." The word stung.

"Everyone talks about these aliens, but to my knowledge, we have never seen one yet, dead or alive." Sergei leaned against the back of the red leather booth. "Do you really believe they are descended from an Anasazi tribe abducted eight centuries ago?"

"I do. Their writing is so close to that of the Anasazi, it's frightening. I can almost understand it."

They remained quiet while the server filled the water glasses.

After the man left, Sergei finally blurted, "How did you get samples of alien writing? The Global Government keeps them under wraps."

"Dad sent me a few pictures before I lost contact," she said, glad she didn't have to lie.

Sergei lay back against the red leather with a genuine smile. "How can I help?"

Celene answered the smile in kind, hoping she could trust Sergei. "Maybe you can tell me if his artifacts have arrived. Did he reserve a temporary storage room or vault at the museum for his find? Maybe under his friend's name?"

Sergei fished his epad out of his pocket. "Let me check the museum files." He punched a few keys. "No, not under his name. What's his friend's name?"

"You know him, Emile Blanchard. He was here with us three years ago."

"Blanchard, right. Nothing under that name either. In fact, we haven't provided storage units in our facility to anyone in months."

"Are you sure?"

"Positive." Sergei closed his epad and reached for her hand. "You know I would do anything for you, Celene. Anything."

Here it came, the Slavic charm in all its seduction. The irresistible smile, the open heart asking to be skewered, the selfless male ready to help a damsel in distress... Three years ago, it would have melted Celene's brain cells, but she vowed to never fall for Sergei's dramatic wiles again. Taking control of her feelings, she smiled with indulgence. "You haven't changed at all."

"Ah, but it seems to me that you have." Regret lingered in his voice.

"You're right, Sergei. I'm not twenty-three anymore. I have grown up in the past three years."

"Right." Sergei looked into her eyes with sadness then lowered his gaze.

The waiter brought a steaming cooking pot and set it on the table with two large bowls and a ladle. Celene inhaled the aroma of beet, cabbage and meat. She reached into the pot with the ladle and filled both bowls with hot stew, noticing parsnip and carrots.

Sergei dropped a dollop of sour cream into each bowl. "Is it true Americans think borscht is supposed to be served cold?"

"Some do." Celene dug into her stew.

Smiling, Sergei watched her, shaking his head. "Americans are strange."

After a few spoonfuls, Celene slowed and her mind focused on the food. She could taste the navy beans, crunchy celery, bits of peppercorn, leeks, and chunks of Kielbasa sausage. Definitely a good recipe. As she ate, she started to feel better.

"I guess you were hungry." Sergei dabbed at his mouth with a napkin. "So, what can I do to help?"

Forcing herself to let go of the spoon, Celene gathered her thoughts. "Can you find out from the airport if the shipment is still in transit? A bunch of crates with the museum's name on them should be easy to spot. Wherever the artifacts are, my father cannot be very far." It was not a complete lie. His body would be with the loot.

Sergei gave her a patient look, as if indulging a

child, then dialed his phone. After a short conversation in Russian, he turned to her and smiled. "You better hurry if you want to see those crates, or your father, if he is anywhere around them. As we speak, they are being loaded onto a cargo plane bound for London."

"London?" *What was in London?* "Can you find out where the plane is now?"

"Hangar fifty-three." Sergei paused, contemplating her. "Your father must be in a hurry to get these artifacts out of the country. Not that I can blame him. We tend to protect our national treasures. It's all we have left to sustain our national pride."

Celene had no time for long conversations. "Can you stop the shipment from leaving the country?"

"I don't have that authority." Sergei seemed reluctant to say more. "Government approval would take at least two days."

"Then I have to go now." Celene spooned the last drop of borscht in her bowl, licked her lips then rose. "Sorry, Sergei. Hope to have more time to chat next time."

He stood and held her at arm's length. "Now I remember why I agreed to cease to be your lover and become your friend. You always have to leave in a hurry." His sad smile tore at Celene's heart.

She gave him a hug. "It's the nature of my job. Thanks for everything."

She rushed out of the restaurant and ran to her parked sedan, barely avoiding a collision with a moped.

* * * * *

Through the lacy curtain of the restaurant window, Sergei watched as Celene climbed into her rented sedan and took off. He fished his communicator out of his pocket. "Emile Blanchard." He waited.

"Allo?" A male French voice sounded impatient at the interruption. .

"I just wanted to warn you to expect company," Sergei whispered.

"*Merde*! This is a bad time for surprises. Who is coming?"

"Celene. She picked up your trail. She's worried about Armand and decided to track the relics. She just left the restaurant across from the museum."

"*Putain de merde!* How did she find out?"

"I'm not sure. Somehow she knows about the crates from the museum. That's why she came to me. I couldn't refuse to help her without blowing my cover. I gave her the hangar number."

"You've got to be kidding! Why didn't you give her a false number?"

"Sorry. I had to show good faith." Sergei looked around the room. None of the other patrons paid attention to his conversation.

"*Nom de Dieu!* It's not my business to judge, but the boss will not like that at all. I hope the kid doesn't get in the way, because if she does, we'll have to take care of her, too."

"Please make sure she doesn't get hurt. She's too cute to die."

Blanchard grumbled. "I'll do my best. She's not responsible for her father's activities, but we have to keep our eyes on the big picture."

"I know, my friend. Good luck."

"Thanks for the warning. *Au revoir.*"

Sergei closed his communicator and slipped it back in his pocket. He re-arranged the napkin on his lap and resumed eating his borscht.

As he finished his bowl, a tall blond man in his thirties entered the restaurant and waved at him. Sergei waved back and smiled.

The man came directly to Sergei's booth and sat across from him, smiling all the time.

Without a word, the man dug into his coat pocket and came up with a phase-gun under the table. He pointed the weapon at the unsuspecting Sergei. The phase fire zing went unnoticed against the background music of the violins. The blond man rose and left the restaurant. A stunned expression on his face, Sergei stiffened then collapsed, his head falling into his bowl. A patron noticed and called the owner's attention. Too late. Sergei was no more.

* * * * *

Within twenty minutes, Celene reached hangar fifty-three at Domodedovo Airport, where the cargo plane should have been, but it had already left. She spotted the large plane taxiing up the runway, too far away to catch up with it. Feeling powerless, she watched it take off. She had failed her father. But Celene wasn't ready to give up yet. If she did, her father would have died for nothing.

At the cargo terminal, she approached a loading employee on a cigarette break, and tried not to inhale the smoke. The man obviously enjoyed looking at her. His smile boasted a few missing teeth. The fact that she spoke fluent Russian impressed the man even more when she asked about the cargo plane.

The man hesitated but obviously couldn't resist a chance to converse with a pretty girl. "It's going to stop over in Berlin first, then on to London."

"You know the flight number?"

"Sure. K507."

Celene graciously thanked the man and smiled. If she booked a direct flight to London, she might get there first and wait for flight K507. After dropping off the rental car, she purchased a ticket for London.

While waiting to board the plane, she remembered receiving an invitation to an archeology gala at the British Museum. When was it? She had not planned to attend at the time, but now it might be a good place to gather information about the relics and the mystery surrounding her father's violent death. Perhaps Emile Blanchard, the murderous betrayer, would attend. A visit to the museum's website confirmed the event for tonight, so Celene RSVP'd online then made a hotel reservation from her epad.

Half an hour later, as the British Airways Boeing lifted in the hazy morning sky, Celene stared out the porthole and made a solemn vow. She wouldn't stop her hunt until she retrieved the relics and brought her father's assassins to justice. And she would make sure that, even in death, the sweet man received credit for this important find that could solve the mystery of the 2020 cataclysm and give humanity a fighting chance against the Anaz-voohri threat.

CHAPTER THREE

Anaz-voohri temporary mooring in deep space, 2023

In the head spacecraft, berthed in the center of the swarm, Captain Kavak, exalted leader of the Anaz-voohri people, rejoiced. A good day indeed! Relaxing against the back of her reclining chair, she took a gulp of the deep blue cordial from her fluted glass.

What better way to celebrate than to enjoy the sweet drink of blueberries and rum, a divine beverage she'd acquired on her last Earth voyage. The alcohol warmed her insides, and she almost smiled as she stretched, letting the silvery fabric of her long gown caress her muscular body.

With her thumbless hand, Kavak touched the glowing petroglyphs of the console on the side of her chair. She hated her birth deformity and often hid her hand under her long sleeves, but centuries of cloning had taken their toll on the race, and physically perfect Anaz-voohri had become rare.

The face of a young male appeared on the giant screen of her private room. He bowed. "Exalted leader, how may I serve?"

"Commander Wasaw," Kavak took a quick sip then set down the flute. "I have important orders for you."

The young man's ridged skull glowed with

excitement. "What can I do for the glory of our race?" He looked rather handsome, with the trace of a jawbone despite the typical narrow chin and wide forehead. Could he be a perfect specimen?

"The time has come to return to Earth for our ultimate mission." Kavak didn't mention she would seize the opportunity to replenish her stock of blue cordial. Her propensity for the human drink need not be advertised among the lesser ranks.

Wasaw's cranium lit up wildly. "The planet of our ancestors awaits!" Religious awe hung on his words as he repeated the ritual greeting of the fanatics.

Kavak scoffed. "I'll never get used to the fact that some of us still revere our human ancestors." Kavak recoiled with disgust at the thought of hairy humans, with eyebrows, lashes, fur on their head and sometimes on their cheeks and body as well. "If you ask me, these ancient Anasazi must have been an ugly, pitiful lot."

On the wall screen, Wasaw's lips pressed together and his eyes narrowed slightly. He squared his wide shoulders under the glimmering cape. "My grandfather was one of the chosen Anasazi, and I carry most of his genetic makeup."

"Right. Good thing you don't look like him." Kavak scoffed.

In her mind, Wasaw was all Anaz-voohri, with wide almond eyes and glowing black irises. But he also looked virile, an obsolete quality in a society that couldn't reproduce anymore, except through cloning. Could he produce the seed for the future generation? Kavak made a mental note to have him tested. "I want your vessel to start monitoring the secret Sipapuni cave immediately. Since your late grandfather was the official guardian of the cave, I now give you that responsibility."

Wasaw seemed to glow as his enthusiasm returned. "So, the time has finally come."

"Indeed." Kavak allowed herself a half smile. "The second Pleiades sister, the one named Celene, is awakening into her powers. Our sensors indicate that she is in the proximity of a crystal shard."

"How did she come to possess one of our shards?"

Picking up her fluted glass, Kavak paced her quarters. "Her father did his job and provided it for her. It seems, however that Armand Dupres did not survive. Probably some stupid human feud. His marker ceased emitting." Kavak sighed. "It's just as well. He had become sympathetic to the human cause. As a hybrid, he should have dedicated himself to expanding the glory of his betters." She waved away the thought. "Celene's programming will soon guide her to the canyons, so get ready."

"Where is she now?"

"Check your screens." Kavak sent him the map where small colored triangles traveled. "Her marker indicates that she is on her way to the nation called Great Britain, a small island despite its name. So are the other crystals from our wrecked ship."

"How long before sister Celene reaches the cave?"

"Probably a few Earth days. Report to me as soon as she does."

"Aye, exalted leader. Is the human female aware of her mission?"

"Of course not. If she knew she worked for us, she

might rebel. But that wouldn't matter anyway. She has no choice but to obey her DNA programming."

"I will not fail, exalted leader. This sister will perform perfectly, not like the last one."

"Shut up, Commander." Kavak hated to be reminded of her only defeat. The first Pleiades sister, Maya Rembrandt, had misfired early, then overcame her programming and destroyed Kavak's favorite ship. Kavak had barely escaped with her life. She raised her voice and her brown skin darkened. "You know we must not fail. We cannot afford to lose this little blue planet. The survival of our superior race is at stake. Our numbers have dwindled so much, we barely have enough people to man all our ships. Besides, without a planet to call home, no race can prosper in the universe, let alone conquer other civilizations."

"If all fails, we could still level the planet, as a few of our generals suggested." Did Wasaw foment against her with generals? No. He was just young and spoke his mind.

Kavak shook her head. "We saw what happened three years ago when one of our ships crashed. Too much destruction would jeopardize the fragile ecological balance of the planet. We do not have that luxury. We need a planet in working order, and we must preserve the cloning facilities established on Earth by our hybrids to hatch our new generation of Anaz-voohri warriors."

"Of course, exalted leader." Wasaw's casual tone bordered on disrespect.

Kavak had to control her temper. If she acknowledged his lack of reverence, she would have to kill him, and she could ill afford to lose even one member of her military force, certainly not a perfect specimen. "There is more than one way to win a war, Wasaw.   Billions of ants cannot overcome a technological giant."

A mischievous glint lit Wasaw's dark irises. "If I remember our history, it seems that we did overcome our own masters, back on the planet of our abductors. Weren't *we* the ants against a technological giant? Weren't *we* the inferior slaves then?   And still, we won."

"Make no mistake, Wasaw."   Kavak hovered in front of the screen.   "The proud day when we rose and butchered those who enslaved us, the day we left them lamenting in the rubble of their destroyed cities, we already were the great people of the Anaz-voohri. We were highly evolved warriors in every military field – ship engineers, medical wizards, biological warfare experts and cloning specialists.   We were a superior race in our own right, with none of the weaknesses of our human ancestors."

"Yet," Wasaw smiled, "everything we own we stole from other races, including our fastest ships and our deadliest weapons."

"Careful, Wasaw." Kavak bristled. "Your youth is a poor excuse for insubordination.   I might take offense."   Kavak forced herself to relax and sit back in her chair. "The swarm is sailing off today. We should be within Earth range in a week.   Set your ship to monitor the cave and let me know as soon as our little puppet enters it."

"We will succeed, exalted leader."

The traditional phrase before a battle made Kavak smile. "I certainly hope so. The first sister was wasted and that reduces our chances of final victory." Kavak shook her head and sighed. "Wasaw, you'll never make a decent warrior. The philosophy of your grandfather has spoiled your mind circuits, but you may be adequate for procreation."

Wasaw's cranium glowed. "Am I to believe I have been chosen to generate offspring?"

"Visit the lab ship at the first opportunity, and we'll test your samples."

"Aye, exalted leader." Wasaw saluted and signed off.

By Kokopelli's flute, how dared this young pup doubt the superiority of his people? Kavak took a gulp of the blue cordial. She knew the old legends to be true, of course. But she didn't like to be reminded that she came from a mere five hundred human Anasazi abducted from Earth eight hundred years ago. After the gods of their tribe lifted them to heaven, the poor bastards had believed their fate would be one of bliss and wonder. How humiliating it must have been when they realized that their abductors were only a more advanced race in search of fresh humanoids to clone disposable soldiers.

Touching the glowing petroglyphs on her console, Kavak straightened the back of her chair and composed herself to address the swarm. "Prepare to move at once. Swarm formation, battleships on the outside, science vessels and supply cargos at the center. Maximum speed. Destination: Earth."

* * * * *

London, same day

Celene paced in front of the cargo schedule board in Heathrow airport. Where was flight K507, supposedly carrying the alien relics from Moscow? Did it stop in Berlin as scheduled? It should have landed over an hour ago, and still no estimated arrival time. When the screen finally updated to show that flight K507 had been canceled, Celene felt crushed. What now? She made her way toward the information desk, avoiding the forklifts that moved pallets of shrink-wrapped equipment back and forth through the open hangar. The lanky woman in grey uniform at the desk gave her a blank look.

"What happened to flight K507?"

The clerk shrugged. "Bad weather? Engine problems? Who knows? Since the 2020 disaster, German airports are not reliable anymore. We'll have more details later."

Had the crates switched destination in Berlin? In her frustration, Celene almost bumped into a forklift loaded with fragrant cardboard boxes of pineapple from Martinique. Around her, small electric trucks pulled metal containers toward the loading docks where eighteen-wheelers waited. A loaded train pulled up to the quay that bordered one side of the structure, the vibration on the rail tracks shaking everything inside the transit terminal.

Through the chain-link fence separating the public area from the aisles of stored cargo in transit, Celene watched conveyor belts carrying crates with colorful labels from Madrid, Dakar, Goa, Mexico, Rio de Janeiro. She knew many of these places. Most of them held memories of her father.

Unable to cross the fence, Celene squinted to scan the aisles of cargo piled up by flight number, type, point of origin and destination, but she could see no crates resembling those from the Moscow Archeological Museum. Since Sergei said the shipment was bound for London, it would show up sooner or later, but where? The relics must be on another flight, maybe landing at a different airport, at a military base, or on a secret government landing strip. She had to find out.

Whom could she trust? Celene knew a few people in England. Leaving the cargo claim area, she stepped outside in the cold drizzle and hailed a cab. When one pulled up, she called, "To the British Museum," then threw her pack on the luggage platform and hopped in. She usually stayed at the hotel across the plaza and hoped they'd received her last-minute reservation.

The driver flipped on his counter and took off. Celene always felt nervous driving on the left side of the road, so she never rented cars in the islands of the old commonwealth. She made a few calls to distract herself from the scary traffic. None of her friends from Oxford or Cambridge had heard about a shipment of artifacts from Moscow.

Most of her colleagues in the archeological community happened to be in London for tonight's charity gala at the British Museum. The scheduled speakers included a few big names in archeology circles. During the event, rare pieces would be auctioned to benefit an archeology institute for young

Londoners.

At a loss in her search for the relics, Celene hoped tonight would bring some kind of information. After the fiasco at Heathrow Airport, she felt desperate for a clue. Any clue. And if Emile Blanchard had followed the relics to London, he might show up at the event. Celene had no idea how she would react if she came face to face with Blanchard, but she must be there. Rumors and news moved fast after a few drinks whenever so many experts gathered.

After checking in at the hotel, she realized she had nothing to wear for a gala night. She spent the rest of the day shopping on Oxford Street, where she found a formal black dress and a suitable pair of high-heeled shoes that would not kill her feet. Used to hiking boots or sandals, she rarely wore fancy footwear. She also purchased an evening pouch large enough to carry the shard.

Celene had not brought any jewelry on this trip, except for an ancient Mayan necklace of silver and turquoise, a present from her father for her eighteenth birthday. She wore it like a talisman. Tonight, most ladies would flash rubies, diamonds or emeralds, but the antique necklace would have to do.

Back at the hotel, Celene took a bath then slipped on her new purchases. Used to comfortable pants and boots, she felt exposed in the little black dress, but it looked perfect on her. The spandex silk hugged her small breasts in a flattering low neckline then flared slightly at the hip. The uneven hem, short in the front and long in the back, flirted with her slim tan legs. Not pretentious, just classy. Although Celene never wore makeup, thanks to her natural tan from working outdoors in tropical sun or snow, this special occasion called for a little color. She applied a touch of deep burgundy to her full lips.

When she stepped back from the mirror, she liked the look. It set off her large emerald eyes. She pulled up her long, auburn hair and gathered it loosely on the top of her head with pins, letting a few artistic strands hang down to frame her high cheekbones. Dressy enough. Even the necklace looked more valuable with her hair up. A drop of musk between her breasts added the final touch.

A glance through the window told her it had stopped drizzling. Good. Not trusting the hotel personnel, she stuffed the alien shard in her evening bag, a tube-like sheath of black silk she had chosen for that purpose. It fit perfectly. Throwing her white faux fur over her shoulders, Celene left the hotel and stepped into the brightly lit street, careful not to twist her ankles on the uneven cobblestones.

Across the plaza, the British Museum looked like a Greek temple to human history, with massive columns along the façade. White and black Rolls-Royces lined the sidewalk. Guards in red uniforms stood at attention on each side of the front steps as lords and ladies exited the vehicles and climbed toward the entrance.

Many of the ladies sported flashy hats with feathers and scarves, an English fashion Celene never understood. The miracles of gene therapy to prevent aging made it almost impossible to tell a rich woman's age, but wearing a hat definitely betrayed the older generation. Their respectable husbands, less vain, looked like their grandfathers. Thank heavens the members of the House of Lords did not wear their horsehair wigs anymore. Old King Charles had abolished the silly practice.

Arriving alone among the fancy crowd, Celene felt a little self-conscious. No one asked for her invitation. She caught the movement of a tiny lens above the door and remembered something about the security system, scanning the arriving guests and checking them against the ID database. She hoped the shard in her purse would not trigger an alarm or be mistaken for a weapon. She expected any minute to see a uniformed valet politely ask her to leave the premises. When it did not happen, she concluded the shards did not record as metal or explosives on the scanners.

Once inside the marble foyer, Celene left her white fur at the coat check. A chamber music ensemble played Vivaldi while the elegant guests mingled. Monumental flower arrangements on pedestals exuded exotic scents of jasmine and orange blossoms. Spotlights on the ceiling, as well as tall gold-framed mirrors on the walls, gave the austere foyer a festive sparkle. Celene recognized a group of British colleagues climbing the marble stairs to the second floor. She caught up with them, happy not to be the odd one anymore.

Chatting gaily as they had not seen each other in many months, the friendly group reached the vast Egyptian Antiquity Hall sheltering the event. Celene hardly recognized the familiar place. Oriental rugs on the marble floor and tapestry hangings between the statues of pharaohs and sphinxes muffled the echo of voices. Servers circulated trays of finger food and stem glasses filled with wine and bubbly. Celene accepted a canapé of smoked salmon and chutney, and a glass of champagne.

This type of event always made Celene uncomfortable. She listened to the chitchat of her small group while scanning the room. Hopefully, she would recognize someone useful to her quest.

In a corner, between a statue of Akhenaton and a stone sarcophagus under tempered glass, a bartender in a striped vest served black label Scotch to gray-bearded Lairds in black kilts and frilly white shirts. Celene wondered whether or not they wore underwear, since tradition required they did not. She shuddered at the thought. She didn't want to know.

Rows of empty padded chairs faced a small stage at the far end of the vast hall. The stage, decorated with tropical ferns, would probably serve for the speeches and auction later, as attested by the lectern and the discreet bank of speakers hidden in the flowerpots.

Ravenous, Celene went hunting for caviar on blinis and petits fours, miniature French pastries she particularly enjoyed. Of course, she had to try the chocolates, too. She settled outside the hall on a velvet bench, where she could set her glass on the wide banister and listen to Vivaldi while watching the foyer entrance from above. No matter how hard she tried, Celene could never play the social butterfly for long. She felt tempted to get out her epad to read or do some work while waiting for Emile Blanchard to show up, but she refrained. It might attract unwanted attention.

Just when she thought the evening would be a total

waste of time, Celene spotted a new arrival who made her blood gel. The man sported a different look, in a flashy parade uniform with a battery of colorful metal bar decorations on his breast pocket. But Celene recognized him immediately. It was the officer who had orchestrated the massacre in Ukraine and stolen her father's relics. She'd know his arrogant stance, buzz cut, square jaw and cold, fixed gaze anywhere. She had come for the traitor Emile Blanchard but had found the ORION officer instead. What was he doing here tonight?

Stay calm. Celene remembered Jake's voice from her training. *Never show your emotions to your enemy.* She struggled to control her rage and pasted a vacant smile on her face as she rose. Then she picked up her glass and sipped from it while casually watching the ORION man ascend the stairs among a group of deferential lords.

When the military man reached the landing, she felt the urge to kick him in the throat. As if he guessed her thought, the man's piercing stare behind spectacles drilled through her. In that instant, fear gripped Celene's chest as it had at the dig site. Did the ORION officer know she had witnessed the massacre? Blood rushed to her head. She felt shaky and light suddenly, as if her body would lift off the floor. Her hand holding the glass shook and became almost translucent, as if she would become invisible again.

No. This couldn't happen! Not here, not now. Did fear or danger trigger her invisibility? Celene felt in and out of phase like a hologram with a faulty feed. She had to stop this, calm her mind. In a supreme effort, she convinced herself she was in no immediate danger. As she relaxed, her body regained its normal density.

The ORION man turned away to shake someone's hand then walked with his group toward the Antiquities exhibition hall. Had he noticed what happened to her? Had anyone? Did she hallucinate? If not, how did she do that?

When the officer walked away with his entourage, Celene thought of following him, but she didn't trust herself to remain calm. She felt relief at his disappearance, but she found it difficult to breathe, as if the dot of a phase-gun heated her nape. Then she recognized the uneasy sensation. Someone was watching her!

Celene spun around and stared straight at her observer. Twenty feet away, a tall oriental man wearing a tan Italian suit and black silk shirt leaned against the wall in an easy stance, sipping a drink from a square glass. Who was he? An ORION hit man? Had he seen what happened to her? Was he watching her for personal or professional interest? He looked Chinese, with a curtain of wavy black hair framing a serious face. What a magnificent specimen of raw animal sex appeal. His splendidly muscled frame turned away from her gaze, and the very gesture made her ache for his attention. She hated herself for that weakness but could not help it.

Although troubled by her emotional response to the handsome Chinese, Celene needed to find out why he watched her, so she walked toward the mysterious man who made her pulse quicken. Careful, there. She felt light-headed. Was it the aftermath of her near invisibility, the champagne, or the adrenalin? She wanted him to look at her, she wanted to gaze into the depths of his wide, almond eyes. Even from a distance, he looked dangerous, like a Bengal tiger, never to be tamed.

It took no effort to smile when she reached him. "My name is Celene Dupres, archeologist." She extended her free hand.

With a surprised and slightly embarrassed smile, the stranger faced her in a graceful motion. "Armand Dupres' daughter?" She detected a hint of Mandarin accent. When he took her offered hand in a warm grip, his dark gaze made her legs feel like pudding. "Kin Raidon, avid collector, at your service."

I wish.

"You said something?" His open grin bothered her as he caressed the magnificent jade medallion of an exquisite dragon on his muscled chest. Could he read her feelings?

Celene felt herself flush. "And what do you collect, Mr. Raidon?"

"Please, call me Kin. I specialize in Anaz-voohri artifacts. Found any lately?" His enigmatic expression made the question sound even more dangerous.

Celene cleared her throat. "Those relics are rare and most of them have been appropriated by the Global Government. I know of none available for purchase at the moment." She paused. "Why were you watching me earlier?"

His dark brown eyes glinted with flecks of gold. "Maybe I was watching the same man you were watching."

"I wasn't watching anyone." How unsettling to discover she had been so obvious despite her efforts to look natural.

"Yes, you were." Kin nodded in the direction the officer had gone. "He noticed you, and attention from him is never a good thing."

"You know the man?" Celene felt elated at finally learning something useful.

Sipping on his drink, Kin seemed in no hurry to answer. "His name is Jason Carrick, a powerful and ruthless collector. He always gets what he wants, one way or another."

"A collector?" Celene tried to sound casual. "Rather unusual for a military man."

Kin's dark eyes narrowed. "Men of action can appreciate art, too, you know?"

"And what in heaven is wrong with the man's eyes?"

"One of them is made of glass. A battle wound against a hybrid." Obviously, Kin knew much about Jason Carrick.

"Hybrid? As in half-alien, half-human?"

Kin shrugged. "That's his story."

Celene had to take a chance. She looked around to make sure no one stood close enough to hear. "How much do you know about the organization called ORION?"

Kin's face remained guarded. "Not much. They are rather secretive. Are you one of those conspiracy theory nuts?"

Celene did not like the insinuation. "I could take

offense, but you know what? For some reason, in the last few days some of these theories are starting to make sense to me. How far do you think Jason Carrick would go to get what he wants?"

Kin sighed. "Whatever it takes."

Celene lowered her voice. "Even slaughtering a team of innocent archeologists?"

Kin remained very still then nodded gravely.

"And what about you?" Celene held his gaze. "How far would you go to get what you want?"

"You ask too many questions." As if to soften the blow, he chuckled, all charm. "It all depends on what I want and why." He sipped on his drink. "As for alien relics, to me they are only a way to learn more about the universe, not a witch hunt to seek and destroy."

"Not like ORION, you mean?" Celene didn't believe for a minute Kin was a collector. He didn't look the type, too smooth, and too handsome to have time for collecting. This man must have an active social life. "Have you ever seen Anaz-voohri relics up close?"

Kin looked around casually then nodded. "Have you?"

This might not be the best place to talk about it, but Celene felt desperate for information. "Were you really watching Jason Carrick?"

"Affirmative."

Amplified voices suddenly came from the auction hall. "Then we should go see what's happening at the auction. You are missing it, by the way, Mr. Avid Collector."

When Kin offered his arm to walk back inside the

Egyptian Antiquity Hall, Celene felt like a queen. Her hand tingled, resting on his sleeve. His close proximity sent heat waves through her body. He smelled of rum, vanilla and spice. A heady combination. Was he friend or foe? In order to find out, she must get close to him, and the prospect delighted her.

On stage a young woman from Sotheby's explained the origins of an eighteenth century music box and started the bid at ten thousand pounds. Kin and Celene sat on an isolated bench, far away from the last row of chairs so they had a full view of the audience and could talk quietly without disturbing the auction.

"Why are you watching Jason Carrick?" Celene whispered.

"It's personal." Kin's intense expression and the tightening of his jaw left no doubt about the seriousness of his motives. "He killed my parents."

"I'm sorry." Celene knew how he felt.

Kin's expression lightened and his jaw relaxed. "And what about you? What is your business with Carrick?"

Celene hesitated, but deep inside she wanted to believe Kin told the truth. "He killed my father and stole his find."

"You mean Armand Dupres is dead?" Kin looked so stunned he couldn't possibly have been involved in the killing. "The media didn't mention it."

"No one knows, yet. You knew him?"

Kin shook his head. "I knew his work. What happened?"

Now certain that Kin couldn't be working with Carrick, Celene just blurted out the truth. "Jason

Carrick and his ORION goons assaulted my father's Anaz-voohri dig in Ukraine, killed everyone and stole the relics."

"How do you know?"

"I was there. I saw it all. My father's best friend, Emile Blanchard, was in league with Carrick. Good thing they didn't see me. I escaped."

"Hard to believe Jason Carrick would let anyone escape." Kin's velvet gaze penetrated all the way to her soul. "Do you have any proof other than your word?"

Discreetly, Celene pulled the zipper of the tube handbag hanging from her shoulder and let Kin get a glimpse of the shard inside. "That's one of the relics from the dig."

Kin stared at the relic then looked up at Celene with an expression of renewed respect. "If what you say is true, then you can bet the rest of the relics are somewhere in London. Carrick must have them in a secure facility."

"Maybe he can lead us to them?"

"Right you are, Sherlock." Kin winked. "Did you say us?"

"Aren't you going to help me?"

His grin widened and he stretched his arm behind her, on the backrest of the bench. He looked like a tiger playing with a mouse. "What's in it for me?"

Anything you want, Baby. But instead, Celene said, "Don't you want Carrick to pay for his crimes? Once he is in jail, isn't it all the same to you?"

Kin chuckled. "I wish it were that simple. But yes, I will help you, and I have a few friends who can help us as well."

In that instant, for the first time since her father died, Celene felt perfectly safe. Somehow she knew that soon, the world would make sense again.

CHAPTER FOUR

As Kin Raidon studied Celene sitting next to him at the auction in the Antiquity room of the British Museum, he felt at a loss. Ignoring the buzz of the auctioneers, the waiters circulating trays of food, and the rare Egyptian statues lining the walls, he had eyes only for Celene.

The girl seemed too smart, too beautiful and too curious, a dangerous combination for a target in his line of work. Her black dress revealed delightfully firm breasts. Her full lips seemed to beg for a kiss. When she gazed into his eyes with such hope and trust, he wanted to protect her from the jackals who would soon hunt her. And he gladly would, if only for a time...

Never had Kin felt so helpless in his life, not even as a teenager when he was shot and watched his parents executed before his eyes. He never panicked, even when the scientists at the Center for Evolutionary Medicine in China injected him with experimental strands of recombinant DNA, the nano-technology that made him a killing machine. Back then, he knew exactly who he was and what he would become.

The unusual aura he'd noticed around Celene under Carrick's stare puzzled him. It almost looked as if she would disappear, not unlike the nano-enhanced ability that allowed him to blend into shadows. Did Carrick see it, too? Had he figured out what Celene was? Too many uncertainties…

Kin could not concentrate as Celene's musky perfume heightened his testosterone to dangerous levels, an unfortunate side effect of his genetic altering for aggressiveness. He'd always harnessed his intense sexual urges on the job before, no matter how strong. But right now, all the nano-controls in his brain seemed to crash under the power of the auburn-haired beauty. Could it be that when he escaped the CEM compound before the end of his training, he missed an important point in mastering the kind of emotion he now felt for Celene?

At least he could still conceal his feelings behind a placid mask of casual confidence. As his target, Celene must never know what he really felt for her. Kin would make sure this unforeseen weakness did not interfere with his mission. The survival of the human race depended on his efficiency.

"Don't you agree?"

Jarred out of his thoughts, Kin covered his surprise with a smile. "Sorry, I was lost in the contemplation of your beautiful eyes. They remind me of dark jade, my favorite stone." Through his screamer implant, the first specimen of a highly experimental hearing device, Kin could hear her heartbeat quicken and her breath catch in her throat.

Celene blushed at the compliment. "Thank you."

Kin patted the medallion on his chest. "In China, jade is considered good luck."

"Is it your family crest?" She touched the exquisite jade dragon and brushed his pectorals through the black shirt in the process. "Ming dynasty?"

The caress tested Kin's self-control and the sensation almost overwhelmed him. "Yes, Ming. A family heirloom." He couldn't tell her that the dragon's eyes contained miniaturized receptors and recording devices that kept him in constant contact with Mythos Mission Control.

"I don't see you participating in the auction." She frowned. "Unusual for a collector."

"I only collect alien relics. Is yours for sale?"

She looked offended. "Not a chance."

Kin could think of several people in the room who would kill for such a treasure. "Who else knows you have this?"

"Just you." Her candor made her even more desirable.

"Good. Make sure it stays that way. I'd hate to see you end up dead for a piece of organic crystal."

"Organic?" Celene looked surprised. "I didn't get a chance to analyze it yet."

"The Anaz-voohri mix organic DNA with electronic components to store information." As she seemed fascinated, he added, "I know a place where we can examine your relic, if you like."

"Your place?" Was that eagerness in her eyes?

Kin laughed to hide his embarrassment. "Not quite." He knew too well what would happen if she came to his place. He couldn't take the chance of losing control of his superhuman sexual impulses. "Like most Chinese, I am a very private man, but the lab I offer has all the equipment you need, and it is safe from prying eyes. I can vouch for it." He would have said anything to take Celene away from the crowd and be alone with her, if only to work together. The Mythos lab would be deserted at this hour. "It's where I work, if you will."

"And what kind of work do you do?"

Why did she have to ask such direct questions? "All right, Miss Curiosity." He willed himself to relax into an easy smile, a familiar technique. "I study alien artifacts and alien technology, mainly." The half-lie did not strain his brain centers. Kin felt almost in control of his emotions again. "Would you like to go now?"

When Kin touched her smooth hand, he noticed she didn't wear any rings. As she watched Jason Carrick, who now embarked in a bitter contest over a Sonoran painting of Anasazi ruins, he caught her reaction to the gaudy work of art. "Amazing how the value of these paintings skyrocketed since the Anaz-voohri scare of 2015."

"I know." Celene turned to face him. "Most of these works have no artistic value whatsoever. Can't they see that? I don't get it." She sighed. "I would love to go with you, but I don't want to lose sight of Carrick."

Kin made his voice soft and persuasive. "Don't worry. I've ways of keeping track of him. We can pick up his trail later." He rose and offered Celene his arm then shuddered at the squeeze of her slim hand through the tan sleeve of his Armani suit. God, the woman had a way of arousing his nerve centers.

As they descended the stairs, he felt as if all eyes turned to them. Kin didn't care for the scrutiny. No professional killer did. In the foyer, he went to claim their coats and slipped the white faux fur on Celene's lean shoulders. He noticed the deceptive frailty of a slim athlete. He liked that in a woman. Closing his eyes briefly, he delighted in her musky perfume and found his heightened sense of smell to be both a blessing and a curse. *Damn!*

Once outside in the chilly night, Kin asked a valet to hail a taxi. After giving the crossroads address to the driver, he helped Celene inside the car then scooted back on the leather seat, secretly berating himself. Taking Celene to the Mythos lab would precipitate her death warrant. No regular citizen saw that place and lived to tell about it, but with Celene already marked for death, it did not matter. Besides, his mission required that he help her study the relics and decipher their meaning before... He didn't want to think about what he must do next.

*   *   *   *   *

Celene leaned against the backseat of the cab and smiled. Was it the champagne? It seemed like a long time since she'd relaxed and let a stranger guide her through a foreign city. The last time had been with Sergei in Moscow, before the European cataclysm. But even that did not compare with what she felt now. She thought Kin was the sexiest man alive who had eyes only for her, and he would help her fulfill her promise to her dead father. He seemed to understand, and even foresee her needs, and offered the right information and the right kind of help at the most opportune time. "Do you believe in coincidences?"

Kin shook his head. "No."

Giddy, Celene tilted her head back. "I am starting to consider the possibility of predestination."

He laughed. "That's a giant leap of faith for a scientist."

"I know, but when the right person comes along, it seems that everything falls into place by magic. It feels like a dream, like now."

Gazing out the window, Celene noticed that the deserted part of town where the cab took them looked like an unlikely place for a scientific lab. Capricious gusts of wind along dark alleys blew garbage along the sidewalks while blackened brick buildings with broken windows. Kin seemed perfectly at ease as he directed the nervous driver and made him stop in front of an abandoned building. He paid the man.

When the door opened automatically, Kin helped Celene out of the car. Once on the sidewalk, she looked around, expecting marauders to attack.

"Hope you don't mind the neighborhood." Kin looked perfectly calm. "This used to be an industrial suburb. The rent is cheap and the neighbors mind their own business."

Celene felt suddenly foolish. What if she had walked into a trap? She felt light-headed again. Her shape seemed to waver and lose some of its consistency. Would she disappear again?

Kin grabbed her wrist, and his intense gaze pierced her. "Does this happen to you often?"

Responding to her martial arts training, Celene kicked his hand. When he let go of her wrist, she almost lost her balance on her high-heeled shoes.

"Don't ever grab me like that again!" She willed her shape to remain visible and it seemed to work.

Kin grinned and shook his hand. "Sorry. I didn't mean to scare you." He licked a drop of blood from his fingers. "Can you disappear at will, or does it happen by accident?"

"I don't know what you are talking about." Somehow Celene felt her invisibility episodes should remain her secret.

"Like this." Kin suddenly seemed to shift and change color, like a chameleon.

Celene could still see his shape, but his color blended with the street shadows. To the casual eye, he had become indistinguishable from the background. Only when he moved slightly could she see a blur. "What kind of trick is this? What are you? An alien?"

Kin returned to his usual coloring. "I am only human, like you. So, you haven't studied your gift, yet? I assume it's something new, then."

Celene readjusted her high-heeled shoe. She didn't want to have this conversation with him. Maybe she could run away, but where? Although frightened, she struggled to maintain her shape. She didn't want him to see her fear.

"Let's go inside. It's not safe out here." How could he look at ease in such a neighborhood?

Far from reassured, Celene glanced around and saw shady silhouettes converging toward them. No sense asking for help from muggers armed with knives and guns. Suddenly, a closed room with Kin sounded like a much safer place. "All right. Where is it?"

Kin led her into an alley and stopped in front of a

rusty door. When he pressed his palm to the metal, the heavy door opened quietly, as if recognizing his handprint. Celene followed him inside and watched the door close automatically. It had no lock or handle, and she suspected it would not respond to her palm-print. She felt trapped in a poorly lit stairwell going down.

Kin offered a reassuring smile. "Let's go downstairs. There is something I want to show you."

Frustrated for getting herself in a situation where she had no control and little choice, Celene followed him. She desperately wanted to believe in Kin's good will, but how could she trust anyone when her world had just fallen into chaos? "What was that ninja trick outside?"

"It's called blending into shadows." Kin didn't look at her as he kept descending the stairs.

"A ninja is a paid assassin. Is that what you are?"

"You ask too many questions."

At the bottom of the long stairwell, a door opened to his push, a bright light illuminating the dingy stairs. It felt comfortably warm down there. Beyond the threshold, they entered a clean facility with banks of computers and large wall screens.

"Wow!" Momentarily stunned, Celene felt her previous fears wash away. Kin had told the truth. The state-of-the-art equipment made the research lab at Concordia University look like an amateur's garage. "This is some lab."

Kin flashed an enigmatic smile as the door closed behind them.

Celene flushed under his gaze and hated herself for it. She couldn't help but find him irresistible. And unnerving. "Who is paying for all this?"

No answer from Kin. On the large screens lining the walls, maps showed pulsing dots, red, green, and blue, like tracking devices in various parts of London.

Curiosity got the best of Celene. "Is this what I think it is?"

"Yes." Kin pointed to a red dot inside the British Museum. "This is Jason Carrick. I bugged his epad yesterday. Told you I could find him easily." Kin punched a few keys on a board and a close up of the auction room in the museum showed an x-ray view of Carrick sitting among the buyers.

Kin had not lied about following Carrick. If Kin was Carrick's enemy, Celene hoped to consider him her ally, at least in theory. Despite his strange powers and rough manners, Kin seemed like a good guy after all.

Celene took off her fur and threw it on an armchair. "Well, may I use this incredible equipment to analyze the shard?"

Kin swept the room with one arm as if to invite her in. "That's what we are here for."

Unzipping her black silk purse, Celene took out the relic and laid it on the tray of an electronic scale. Computerized density scans revealed the crystal to be organic despite its mineral aspect. No specific density variations were noted inside the shard. The engravings covering one facet looked like a list with microscopic inscriptions. Celene found it difficult to concentrate when Kin's breath caressed her neck as he bent over her shoulder to watch the small plasma screen.

Celene pointed to a petroglyph. "See? Here is a star system. It looks like the Pleiades, the system the

Anaz-voohri came from, but this other character says something else. It looks like it's stating something like an important job, a task, a mission."

Kin's expression closed. "It would translate as Operation Pleiades."

She looked over her shoulder. "Any idea what that could be?"

Kin shook his head as he removed his coat. Obviously, he knew something but remained silent.

Thinking aloud helped Celene concentrate. "All these petroglyphs must represent file names, not the information itself."

"Yes." Kin hovered behind her again, his voice close to her ear. "Maybe this is not meant to be examined by sight but needs to be introduced into a decoding device."

The idea made sense to Celene. "What kind of decoding device?"

"Probably some sort of computer that can extract the information. Each shard could be like a data chip or a memory bank."

"Then there must have been a decoding device on the alien ship." Celene found Kin's proximity distracting. She held her head in her hands to think more clearly. "Now that Carrick has buried the spaceship and controls the area, how can we extract the information? My father used his last breath telling me these relics are important to the future of humanity. I must figure out what they mean."

"I know of no device that could possibly read these crystals." Kin sounded close behind her. He paused. "Not even among the alien technology we have gathered over the years."

"What do you have?" Celene faced him and met his dark gaze. "Can I see it?"

Kin chuckled at her eagerness. "We'll see. In any case, it's not here."

"And this is only one shard. There must have been at least twenty of them on the ship." The amount of data the relics must represent made Celene dizzy.

"Then we'll have to find out where Carrick is hiding the other relics. If we had a device to read them, can you translate the text?"

"With enough information and cross-references, I should be able to." Celene returned to the study of the shard. "Operation Pleiades. Could this be referring to the Greek legend?" She remembered the story from the website and took on her teaching voice and rhythm. "Abducted by an unwanted lover, the seven sisters committed suicide. Then Zeus made them into stars to shine forever in the sky, ahead of Orion who hunts them but can never quite catch them."

"There are many legends about the Pleiades, but they are just that, legends." She noticed even when he spoke in a neutral voice, Kin sounded sexy.

Celene pointed at more petroglyphs. "These could be the names of each star in the system. What do we call them?" Punching a few keys on an online keyboard, she read the screen. "Alcyone, Celaeno, Electra, Maia, Merope, Sterope, and Taygete." A sudden realization gripped Celene's chest. "Celaeno. Would that be the same as Celene?"

Another coincidence? She was named after one of the seven sisters. Celene shivered at the thought that

Jason Carrick, like the god Orion, would hunt her if he knew she'd witnessed her father's massacre.

Kin's tan skin seemed to pale slightly but his face showed no emotion as he casually erased the screen.

Unruffled, Celene kept thinking aloud. "You know, the old Anasazi based their calendar on the Pleiades, so did the Aztecs. Some believed their ancient gods came from that star system and would some day return."

"Not gods!" Kin's outburst echoed in the empty lab. "These were bloodthirsty aliens, requesting human sacrifices. They abducted the Anasazi, manipulated their DNA to turn them into savage warriors, and now their descendants, the Anaz-voohri, this aberration of humans crossed with soulless machines, have returned. I fear this time they intend to wipe out the human race."

Surprised by Kin's vehement reaction, Celene softened her voice. "Why? They could have destroyed us long ago."

"I believe they want to preserve the planet for themselves."

"That's a big assumption." But the thought made some sense to Celene. "How would you know that?"

"The evidence we collected so far points to it."

"We?" So, Kin wasn't alone in his crusade. "What evidence? And who are your friends?"

"It's classified."

Celene considered the sophisticated equipment around her. Of course, it would take extraordinary funding to finance such a facility. Could this be a Global Government secret facility? But ORION was also a branch of the Global Government. So why was

Kin watching Jason Carrick? Celene felt a headache coming.

"If you've done all you can do with that shard here tonight, I'll get you back to your hotel." His patronizing ways reminded Celene of Sergei. She controlled the urge to lash out.

Before leaving the room, she glanced at the wall screen. Carrick's red dot still pulsed at the British Museum.

A taxi waited at the corner when they emerged from the alley. During the ride back, Kin's close proximity gnawed at Celene's common sense. Of course they could not talk because of the driver. Although usually levelheaded, she caught herself entertaining the possibility that Kin might want to accompany her to her room. What would she say?

When the taxi stopped in front of her hotel, she expected him to move, but he remained seated. "Have a good night. I'll call you if I hear anything about the relics."

Hiding her disappointment, Celene bent over to give him a small kiss on the cheek, but he moved back guardedly and offered a handshake. Humiliated, Celene did not take his hand but rushed out. She didn't look back as she heard the car door close and the taxi drive away. Running into the lobby, she rushed upstairs to her room.

Mad at being rejected, Celene paced her hotel room. She wouldn't be able to sleep. Planting herself in front of the full-length mirror, she used her frazzled state of mind to mimic the fear that had induced the disappearing phenomenon previously. If she could control this thing, as Kin did, maybe she could use it at will.

Focusing to create that particular sensation in the pit of her stomach, Celene watched her reflection in the mirror waver. As she let the process take over, she became totally transparent. Much better than Kin's ninja trick! Not even a blur when she moved. Calming herself and willing herself to reappear, she saw her image in the mirror solidify in seconds. She repeated the process several times back and forth, each time more rapidly.

After changing into black stretch pants, a sweater and quiet shoes, she emptied her backpack and set it on her shoulders. Then she made herself invisible and stepped out of her room. Once outside, she crossed the plaza in the direction of the British Museum.

As attested by the traffic in front of the edifice, guests came and went as the gala continued. If Carrick was still there, she could learn much by following him. She was positive that sooner or later he'd go take a look at his newly arrived relics, and when he did, Celene would be there. Empowered by her fresh knowledge and the success of her new gift, Celene felt ready to face anything.

CHAPTER FIVE

Blending into the shadows of the dimly lit street, Kin kept his gaze on his target a hundred feet ahead as he tapped the jade dragon on his chest.

A voice from Mythos mission control came from his ear implant, "Icarus? Report. Over."

"This is Icarus," Kin whispered. "Closing in on target by foot. Maintain silence until I contact you."

The target, a black cloak thrown over his parade uniform, marched ahead with a definite sense of purpose, his steps echoing on the concrete sidewalk. Suddenly the stocky man stopped and looked back. Kin froze and slowed his breathing to diminish the sound, a ninja technique that had often saved his life.

Could Carrick sense him following at a distance? The man seemed frighteningly aware for an unaltered human. Kin took comfort in that notion, unaltered. According to his file, Carrick had refused to submit to DNA tampering and even denied himself an eye implant to wear a stupid glass eye. He had the reputation of a purist when it came to race…more of a fanatic, really, with an ego the size of Big Ben.

Careful not to make any sound, Kin congratulated himself for changing into comfortable black clothes. Stealth required agility. When Carrick resumed walking, Kin breathed normally again. What did the filthy general seek in this part of town? Kin knew the truth behind the façade. Carrick looked so clean, so neat. His ascension to head of ORION in 2015 gave him an army of supersoldiers carrying alien phase-guns. If not watched closely, Carrick could some day control or even take over the Global Government. That would be a sad day for the planet.

Kin took his work seriously. Mythos wanted him to make sure Carrick did not turn ORION into a dragon that could devour its masters, and Kin would see to that. His other important target, Celene Dupres, might prove more difficult.

Celene... Why did she have to be one of the seven Pleiades sisters? The Anaz-voohri implanted a timed device in each girl during the abduction twenty years ago. Kin could not imagine Celene would ever pose a threat to humanity, but she did. Deep inside her DNA slept an alien mechanism. When triggered, it would loose on the planet this innocent, beautiful woman. And the devastation she would inflict could kill millions. The time and manner of the release remained unknown, but Kin hoped the shards from the Anaz-voohri vessel would reveal that knowledge.

Celene's budding power of invisibility could only mean that the time drew near when she would have to use that power to accomplish her gruesome mission. Unfortunately, the fact that the Pleiades sisters knew nothing of their purpose could not change their fate. They must be identified, their threat evaluated and eliminated by whatever means possible.

Kin felt terrible about dropping Celene at her hotel so abruptly earlier tonight, but duty came first. Besides, despite his strong attraction to the girl, he didn't want to get involved. It would complicate matters too much. His relationship with Celene must remain strictly professional. He didn't want to flinch when he had to terminate her at the end of the job. If he hesitated, the astute girl might take advantage of his weakness. She'd already surprised him with her quick reflexes when he'd inadvertently grabbed her wrist. It had taken all his nano-control not to counterattack as he was trained to do.

Never had Kin missed a kill, and he had killed many. At first, he'd killed for revenge after his escape from the Center for Evolutionary Medicine in China. Then he'd killed for money, but a few of those jobs helped a good cause. That was years ago. Now he let a higher authority decide who lived and who died. Kin only killed for Mythos, a secret organization monitoring the men in power and eliminating anyone who presented an imminent threat to humanity at large. Financed by wealthy businessmen and protected by powerful politicians, Mythos did not trust military leaders such as Jason Carrick.

Feeling unusually high-strung, Kin thought he heard someone behind him but relaxed when his heightened night vision showed no one else along the deserted street. Still, he felt his concentration slip away. Not a good thing. Taking a slow breath to quiet his thoughts, he refocused his mind on his target, who steadily took him farther away from the British Museum. Why didn't Carrick take a cab, or even the subway?

It started to drizzle again. Kin froze when a lone

car sped up the dark street. Only in stillness could he escape scrutiny. Otherwise, a keen eye might detect his shadowy blur. As soon as the car taillights disappeared around a bend, Kin resumed his hunt.

Since Celene told him of Carrick's ruthless murders at the dig site, Kin had decided to find the relics before the man monopolized their information. Carrick had control of the alien ship and, consequently, the only known decoding device. If he deciphered the shards first, he might want to control the knowledge and use it as leverage to gain more power. Mythos couldn't let that happen. Nor could Kin.

His personal score with Carrick, however, would have to wait. Back in China, the son-of-a-bitch had ordered the execution of Kin's parents. It had taken strong emotional control on Kin's part not to execute Carrick on sight when he took the mission, but he'd learned to master his anger. And now Carrick had murdered Celene's father, as well. But just as Kin had renounced killing Carrick to become his shadow, he would have to accept terminating Celene. Deep inside, however, he'd give anything to have the two tasks reversed.

As the rain intensified, Kin hunched his shoulders against the cold shower. Straight ahead, Carrick kept looking back. Kin could still smell Celene's perfume, probably on his neck where her hair had brushed earlier. He hoped Carrick's unaltered sense of smell wouldn't detect it.

After following a high wall topped with barbed wire, a private park judging by the tall trees, Carrick stopped. His gaze swept his surroundings. He ascended the few steps leading to a quaint, four-story building with whitewashed walls and widely spaced windows. Kin hid behind a buttress to regain his shape then punched the coordinates into his epad. No official site, secret or otherwise, came up at this address. Nothing came up at all. Strange. Someone had to live there.

Did Carrick have a secret home in London? Kin could not imagine the man who had spent his military life in barracks and officer's quarters would have a use for a home, except to store his impeccably pressed uniforms. It was the wrong neighborhood anyway, too far from ORION local headquarters. Visiting a woman? Doubtful. Not on the day he received a new shipment of alien artifacts.

Blending into shadows again, Kin stepped closer and directed his epad to assess the security system around the building entrance. Discreet but efficient. Movement detector lights, cameras, infrared heat sensors, X-ray scanner, handprint, and eye print recognition…way too sophisticated for any apartment building. His heartbeat quickened, and Kin made a conscious effort to slow it down. This could only be one of Carrick's secret caches.

Despite his camouflage abilities, the security system would detect Kin's presence if he approached the door. He tapped his medallion and whispered, "Mythos? Icarus here. I need a full team for an emergency raid." He watched Carrick open the door then Kin looked up at the ten-foot garden wall. Cameras swept the perimeter. Timing his jump between sweeps, he leapt over the high wall protecting the building's private park.

* * * * *

Celene watched the blur of Kin's shadow leap over the wall and clear the barbed wires. She couldn't help but admire his amazing agility. Kin must have superhuman genes, like the nano-enhanced freaks Jake talked about at the gym. Even Celene couldn't jump like that. She wondered what else in Kin's physiology had been improved. Still mad at him for excluding her from the hunt, Celene found comfort in the fact that he had not noticed her. She had followed Jason Carrick all the way from the British Museum after the auction, and while she could make out Kin's blur in the night, obviously he couldn't see her at all.

Celene followed Carrick inside the building. Confident in her invisibility, she felt strangely invulnerable. Although the place looked like an apartment building, she noticed no list of names outside, no concierge desk, no mailboxes in the lobby. No one lived here. The state of the art security system did not discover Celene's presence. Somehow, she knew that would be the case. No electronic device could detect her in invisible mode, although she couldn't explain how it worked or how she knew all this.

Jason Carrick glanced around nervously and Celene couldn't tell whether he was excited or worried. Once inside, the man stared straight through her as if he could feel her presence. Could his partial blindness heighten his other senses? Since no alarm went off, he probably attributed his unease to paranoia.

Past the two small brass elevators, Carrick crossed the lobby toward what looked like the door to a maintenance closet at the far end of the hall. The small door opened on an enclosed courtyard, circular in shape and brightly lit by floodlights. A dozen armed sentinels lining the perimeter saluted when Carrick emerged.

Four stories above their heads, like a lid over the enclosed yard, Celene saw a milky glass dome. It looked like the dome could retract and open to allow a large helicopter to land. The painted markings on the concrete confirmed the courtyard as a helipad. That must be how Carrick had smuggled the relics into London. He had flown them right into his den.

Guards stood beside several closed doors around the yard. When an elevator door slid open at Carrick's approach, Celene followed him inside. The two armed sentinels in the freight elevator saluted then resumed their stance, phase-gun at the ready, finger on the trigger. Celene flattened herself against the side and tried not to breathe. What if she lost her balance and bumped or touched anyone? In such close quarters she could easily be discovered. But the soldiers didn't even blink as they stared straight through her. Celene noticed the ORION badge on their chests and sleeves.

The elevator descended several floors. So, Carrick had an underground fortress. How clever. Easy to seal the doors, bombproof, probably shielded and undetectable from land or from space…the perfect hideaway.

The sliding door opened on a well-lit underground facility. Celene followed Carrick through a succession of broad metallic tunnels, all painted stark white and built like a pipeline, reinforced by metal beams with giant protruding bolts. A black rubber mat covering the floor muffled Carrick's heavy footsteps. At regular intervals, bolted metal doors on both sides of the tunnel bore painted numbers, some red, some blue. Soldiers guarded some of them.

When Carrick stopped in front of a door with a red four-digit number, Celene held her breath. Was it the one hiding the relics? The sentinel moved aside to let Carrick peer into the eye scanner. The door opened with a grinding sound and Celene followed Carrick inside.

The square vault had been carved into the rock and smelled of saltpeter, a white grainy substance that covered the rock-walls. Exposed wires fed a camera over the door and a single bulb overhead. Rather primitive, as if Carrick had adapted an old facility for his purpose. The place must have served various functions over the years. Bomb shelter during the Second World War? Nuclear shelter for high-ranking officials?

There, in the middle of the floor, Celene recognized the crates with the stamp of the Moscow Archeological Museum. The relics from the dig! She felt her heartbeat quicken. But she couldn't possibly take all that stuff with her. She'd only brought her backpack. The relics that mattered at the moment were the crystal shards. Celene watched in silence as Carrick opened the crates one by one and examined the objects inside., She waited to see which crate held the shards.

How could she steal the relics under Carrick's

scrutiny? Even if she was invisible she couldn't do it in front of him. She must let Carrick lock her inside the vault, then wait for someone to open it again. What about the infrared camera? It could probably record in the dark. As long as she remained invisible, Celene knew the device couldn't sense her heat, but would it detect her flashlight? Maybe not if she sheltered it with her body.

Just when she thought the crate containing the shards might be in another vault, Carrick uncovered the crystals. He seemed fascinated by them and Celene feared he would take them, but instead, after a cursory inspection, he replaced the lid on the crate and left the vault. Celene felt her heart drop when the door clanged shut, leaving her alone in the dark vault. Someone outside the door must have flipped the switch. She did not dare regain her visible shape for fear of triggering an alarm.

Careful not to make any undue noise, Celene interposed herself between the camera and the crate and turned on her flashlight. When no alarm sounded, she started to unload the shards one by one. Keeping them in the protective wrapping from the crate, she carefully slid them into her bag. Then she transferred a few objects from other crates into the empty one, so it wouldn't feel suspiciously light. The later they discovered the missing shards the better her chances to get out of London unhindered.

Once finished, Celene turned off her flashlight. Now, she just had to wait for someone to open the door, but how long would it take? Doubt constricted her throat. She hadn't thought of bringing any food or water. What if no one visited the vault for weeks? She willed away the fleeting fear. Certain no one would come tonight, she decided to lie down and catch some sleep. But would she remain invisible while sleeping? If she lost her cover, would the infrared camera pick up her body heat and sound the alarm?

* * * * *

In the vast English garden of the facility, hiding behind a prickly bush, Kin stood perfectly still to blend into the shadow of the wall behind him. Rain dripped down his body and chilled his muscles. Five feet away, three Dobermans yelped as they sniffed the wet ground, obviously confused by his watery smell but unable to see him. The dogs turned around at the sound of a soft whirr and left in the direction of the building. Kin recognized the familiar buzz of an approaching stealth helicopter. The quiet bird flew in silent mode, all lights out. The Mythos chopper Kin expected. Slowly releasing his breath, Kin whispered, "Icarus here. What do you see from the sky?"

A friendly male voice came through his screamer implant. "Got you, but your target disappeared. Probably underground, shielded by heavy metal. There is light under a large plexiglass dome."

Kin could see the milky glow above the building. "An enclosed courtyard? What's underground?"

"Nothing but a 3D network of gigantic metal pipes. It seems connected to various other networks, subway tunnels, sewers. From here it all looks like a subway storage facility or such."

"Brilliant camouflage." Kin moved one foot from a muddy puddle. "They probably have several escape routes as well. How can I get inside from here?"

"Ventilation shaft among the bushes, twenty feet away at nine o'clock."

"Roger. See you inside."

Kin ran silently on the lawn, careful not to alert the dogs. He snagged his sweater on the naked thorns of some rosebushes and silenced a curse. When he found the shaft entrance, he had to cut the metal locks with his laser while the chopper veered then shot at the milky glass dome. Somehow, the projectiles ricocheted, zipping through the air into the garden. Kin flattened himself on the ground. They'd have to launch something bigger to break it.

When he saw the small bomb drop toward the glowing dome, Kin turned off his ear screamer. Dirt, glass and gravel flew overhead. Then he saw the black-clad Mythos team slide down the cables dropped from the helicopter. The light rising from the courtyard, revealed the men wore gas masks. Grenades exploded as they dropped into the building's central courtyard.

Kin entered the ventilation shaft and slid down the service ladder to get inside before the alarm sealed all the access ports. The shaft shook from secondary explosions, and pebbles fell on his head through the grille above. When he reached the ventilator blades, he understood why the shaft didn't have better protection. Anyone attempting to get through would end up as hamburger meat.

But Kin knew how to remedy that. He aimed his laser and traced a circle close to the center of the turbine, then another circle close to the edge. The severed blade pieces went flying deep into the shaft, sounding like a battery of pots and pans hitting metal pipe. The ventilator still ran, but it had lost its blades.

Kin hauled himself through the hollowed crown and ended up in a narrow conduit where he had to crawl. The ventilation tube, just wide enough for his body, followed the ceiling of a tunnel, but the openings along the conduit were too small to allow him to get out. He felt wet and muddy.

Glancing through each opening, Kin watched the soldiers run along like ants rushing to the surface to fight their attackers. Alarms wailed, and red lights pulsed in each tunnel. Kin tried not to make any noise as he crawled forward.

When the conduit branched out, Kin followed a quiet tunnel, probably a storage area. When he realized the size of the facility, he wondered how he would ever find what he came for.

After making certain the tunnel he followed was deserted, Kin took out his laser and cut an opening through the metal conduit. The cut out plate dropped onto something soft, then Kin lowered himself silently onto the rubber floor. Switching to shadow mode, he followed the metal walls noiselessly, alert for any activity coming his way.

Kin stopped in front of the first door and tried to determine what lay on the other side, but his scanners could not penetrate the heavy steel. Would he have to cut open each door to find out which vault contained the relics?

* * * * *

As the explosion shook the walls of the vault, Celene's senses came to full alert. On the other side of the metal door she heard sirens, then the muffled drumming of running feet in the hallway. Had the security cameras detected her presence? That would not explain the explosion. An accident with explosives? When the soldiers' steps faded away, she wondered whether the guard at the door had left as well.

She wondered if Kin could have caused the alarm. She'd seen him leap over the garden wall. Did he single-handedly attack the facility? Somehow she pictured him better at stealth than waging a full-blown attack. So, who targeted the ORION facility? She was positive it had to be someone bent on stealing the relics.

This did not augur well for Celene. Security would seal the exits. Someone would come to check on the relics or take them away. They would notice their disappearance, but this could also give her a chance to escape in the commotion. Would her invisibility keep her safe?

CHAPTER SIX

Celene's heart leapt. Someone behind the door probed the metal, knocking on it. She quieted her breath and stepped to the side, ready to escape as soon as the door opened. When she heard the strident whine of a laser and saw the metal starting to glow, she stepped further back and covered her ears. A razor-thin line cut the heavy steel like flimsy foil. Soon, the metal cut out fell inside the vault in an ear-chattering clang, but no one barged in. Then she saw it, the blur of movement she had come to recognize as Kin when camouflaged. She thought of revealing herself then changed her mind. What if it was some other ninja?

The blur spoke. "Who's there? Show yourself."

A wave of relief washed over Celene when she recognized Kin's voice. How did he detect her? She wanted to trust him, but could she?

Kin made himself visible and sniffed around. "Celene?" His black pants and sweater were soaked with mud. "I'd recognize that heavenly perfume anywhere. What are you doing here? Do you have the relics?"

Reluctantly, Celene answered, "Only the shards," but she remained invisible. She hadn't thought of washing off the musk since the gala earlier. How dumb.

"Then let's get out of here. I know a way out. The stuff must be heavy. Need help carrying it?"

Although he couldn't see her, Celene stepped back, protecting her backpack. "That's all right. I can manage."

Kim shrugged. "As you wish." He turned into a blur and took off.

Celene followed Kin's shadow through the deserted white corridor. The shards weighted her back, but she found their presence reassuring. When Kin stopped and flattened himself against the metal wall, she did the same. From the turn in the tunnel ahead came deliberate footsteps. Celene shuddered when she recognized Jason Carrick coming toward them. He stopped in front of her and stared at the white metal wall through his thin-rimmed glasses.

Celene didn't dare move.

Carrick extended one hand as if to touch her. Celene shifted imperceptibly to avoid his touch. Then Carrick's good eye widened. "That perfume...I know who you are, Miss Dupres. So, you have powers of invisibility? Of course...you are one of the Pleiades sisters!" He called around. "Guards! Close this corridor!"

Celene kicked Carrick in the solar plexus. As he collapsed she saw Kin's blur hit the man on the head. Carrick fell to the floor unconscious, and Celene ran behind Kin's shadow along the corridor. At the sound of more running footsteps, they both flattened against the wall. The ORION soldiers passed them by, then Kin and Celene resumed their escape.

Celene heard Carrick screaming a string of colorful

curses further down the corridor. She touched Kin's shadow. "Why didn't you kill him?"

"No time to explain now." Kin picked up the pace. "Just run." He led her to an opening in the ventilation shaft on the ceiling and hoisted himself through the hole. "Grab my hand."

Celene fumbled, trying to grab a shadow, and marveled at how solid Kin's arm felt despite his ethereal state. Quickly they scrambled along the ventilation shaft, then up the ladder. When Kin became visible, Celene dropped her invisibility as well.

Soon, they emerged on the surface. The rain had stopped. Floodlights illuminated the grounds, helicopters flew quietly overhead, and the assault team held the premises. The soldiers in black wore no distinguishable badge or identification. They saluted Kin like a ranking superior.

"Who are they?" Celene fought the urge to disappear. Instead, she brushed the conduit dust from her black stretch pants and readjusted the weight of the bag on her shoulders.

Kin seemed perfectly at ease. "These are my friends." He approached one black-clad man. "Any losses?"

The soldier shook his head. "Just a few scratches."

"The ORION men?"

The soldier grinned. "They'll sleep like babies until morning. We are gassing them like rats in their tunnels."

Kin slapped the man on the shoulder. "Take the seized goods to GSS to be catalogued and photographed."

The soldier nodded. "What about the frozen bodies we found in the morgue?"

Kin glanced at Celene then back at the soldier. "Human? Alien?"

"Both." The soldier shifted uncomfortably as if the bodies bothered him.

"Send them to the GSS lab." As if on second thought, Kin added, "Make sure they remain frozen."

Celene couldn't help asking, "Is Armand Dupres among the bodies?"

The soldier glanced at Kin in surprise. When Kin nodded, the man saluted Celene. "I believe that name is among the bodies we identified, Ma'am."

"Thank you." Celene felt relieved.

"I'm sorry." Kin motioned Celene toward a waiting silver Bentley.

Celene pushed away the sadness that threatened to engulf her and followed Kin to the car. The chauffeur held open the door. Celene set her backpack containing the relics on the car floor and went in. Kin talked briefly to the chauffeur outside, then he sat beside Celene. The vehicle exited the grounds through an iron gate, its headlights revealing a deserted back street.

As they drove through the sleepy London neighborhood, Kin sighed. "What the hell did you think you were doing, going alone into the lion's den? Why didn't you tell me?" Kin sounded more worried than angry. Did he fear for her safety?

But Celene felt righteous about her adventure and would not let him treat her like a kid. "For the same reason you took me to my hotel and went after the relics yourself. Did you intend to share the loot?"

"I did. I just didn't want you to get hurt." Kin squinted. "But did *you* intend to share?"

Celene had no answer to that. She felt her father's find was hers by right.

"That's what I thought." Kin gazed out the car window. "Now that Carrick made you out, he will hunt you wherever you go. You won't be safe anywhere. We are going to have to hide you and give you protection."

The memory of the moment when Carrick recognized her made Celene shudder. "What did Carrick mean, calling me one of the Pleiades sisters?"

Kin cleared his throat. "Well, you were right about the connection between Operation Pleiades and the Greek legend."

"How do you mean?" Celene felt almost afraid to find out.

"Twenty years ago, seven little girls were abducted from earth then returned to various adoptive families two years later." Kin paused and stared at her, as if to make sure she understood. "You are one of these little girls."

"I am?" Celene remembered the day when she awoke on her eighth birthday with total amnesia. She recalled the lack of family pictures, supposedly destroyed in a flood, her inexplicable childhood nightmares. It all started to make sense. "Is that why I have no memory of my early childhood?"

Kin nodded.

"My God, that means I am adopted!" The fact that her known father and mother had pale blue eyes while hers were emerald green should have alerted her scientific mind long ago. Her gold, easily tanned skin should have been a clue, too, but somehow Celene must have blocked out those important details. She never thought of questioning her family ties.

Kin took her hand gently. "During the time you spent off-world among the Anaz-voohri, they manipulated your DNA. I bet you never had a sick day in your life, you were a gifted student, a perfect athlete, and now you have this incredible power of invisibility."

Celene, who had always taken her learning abilities for granted, now realized how easy her life had been. Early on, she truly believed anyone could achieve anything if they just applied themselves, and she had judged her classmates unfairly. Suddenly, she felt ashamed. She'd never struggled for anything, physically or intellectually. "Why did they give me these abilities?"

Kin's jaw stiffened. "We don't know for sure." He turned his dark gaze on her. "But you should use them to help the human race against the Anaz-voohri."

It was Celene's turn to look away. "I'm still not so sure their intentions are evil. My father seemed to think they were too evolved to want to harm us."

"The best way to find out is to decipher the shards. All we have to do is find or build a device to read the relics. Or we could return to the crash site, but once Carrick finds the shards gone, he'll make sure we can't get to it. One way or another, we must make sense of the petroglyphs."

Celene nodded but her head swam with contradicting thoughts. She stared blindly at the dark empty streets passing by. *Who was she? What was she?* She felt perfectly human, but how would she know the difference? She had to find out for herself, but how?

Kin let go of her hand and laid his arm on the top of the car seat behind her. "Listen. Much is at stake, and our best chance of success is to help each other. Once we find a way to read the relics, you have the knowledge to decipher them, and I have the means to help you and protect you while you are studying them. So why don't we decide to trust each other, at least until the job is done?"

Celene saw the logic in his offer, and besides, he had such charisma. "All right, but no more going solo on your part either. Promise?"

"Promise." His radiant smile had a soothing effect. "Where did you learn to fight like that? Impressive. It took guts to infiltrate the vault alone. I thought you couldn't control your invisibility yet."

"It came quite naturally." Celene enjoyed his praise. "It's awesome."

"Awesome is the word. Even I couldn't detect you. But you wavered a bit, and then I recognized your perfume."

Celene made a note never to wear perfume or use scented soap again. It could be her undoing. "So, why didn't you kill Carrick back there in that tunnel?"

Shifting in his seat, Kin seemed to relax. "Carrick is a necessary evil. We do not approve of his techniques, but he serves a purpose. No one wants him dead more than I do, but the truth is, we need him alive, for now."

"But why?"

"It's classified."

Pondering the ramifications of Kin's statement, Celene decided she would rather see Carrick dead, but she would not argue. Kin made a formidable ally, and she would try not to antagonize him. "Now that we have the relics, what's next?"

"You are packing, so am I. We must leave London before Carrick awakens. I'll arrange for a plane."

"To where?"

"Some place where you can pursue your study in secret and safety."

"I want to go home to Montreal first." Suddenly the grief Celene had locked away overwhelmed her. Her chest tightened and tears blurred her vision. "I want to give my father a decent funeral." She heard her own voice tremble.

"But that's the first place ORION will come looking for you."

It did not matter to Celene. "I'll go invisible if I have to, but this is important to me. Besides, I can start my preliminary study of the relics anywhere. Can your friends organize a funeral?"

"All right." Kin squeezed her shoulder. "But promise never to leave my side, invisible or not."

"You have my word." Celene rather liked the prospect of spending time with Kin. She felt safe around him. He'd just rescued her and she welcomed his protection. His close proximity sent her reeling with uncharted emotions, but she welcomed them, too. She leaned her head on his shoulder. He smelled like a wet forest in the fall. Feeling safe against his chest, she allowed herself to cry for the loss of her father.

* * * * *

On the private jet from London to Montreal, Celene found it difficult to concentrate on her Anasazi language files and even more difficult to ignore Kin sitting next to her. She caught him observing her when she pretended to doze off, but when she tried to make eye contact, he usually turned away or even left his seat.   A team of bodyguards accompanied them, supposedly to protect Celene, but she would have preferred some privacy.   She couldn't talk to Kin openly about her research, as not all the soldiers on the transport had the proper clearance.

During the long flight, Celene often thought of her adoptive father traveling in the cargo hold. The poor dear man never suspected his friend of treason. Celene wondered where Emile Blanchard had fled. And what was his connection with Jason Carrick?   Even Kin hadn't known when she asked.

Before landing, Celene changed into her black dress for the funeral, but she would wear her boots and faux fur. There would be snow in Montreal.

The jet landed on a snowbound Canadian Air Force base on a cold and cloudy afternoon, in the vicinity of Montreal. While Celene and Kin exited the plane down movable stairs, military personnel rushed to open the cargo hold. They unloaded the coffin covered with a Canadian flag, red and white with the maple leaf in the center.

Kin's friends had taken care of all the details. A hearse and several unmarked cars waited on the cold tarmac, but no crowd had gathered to welcome home the fallen hero. In Celene's heart, her father was a hero who had died for his ideals. The soldiers slowly loaded the coffin into the hearse.

Celene and Kin's luggage went into the trunk of a black electric sedan, then the chauffeur opened the door for them.

In the falling dusk, the small cortege proceeded toward the cemetery where Celene's adoptive mother had been buried years ago. Celene regretted that none of her father's friends could attend, but Kin had insisted. If Emile Blanchard had ties with ORION, other friends of Armand Dupres could be involved as well, so only Kin's companions attended the quiet ceremony. Celene wished Jake, her teacher and friend, were here, but Kin forbade that, too.

Despite that fact, Celene felt a sense of closure at allowing her father to repose there. That's what he would have wanted. As night fell, they gathered by the orange light of the nearby street and a few candles.

Someone handed Celene a white rose, and she dropped it on the descending coffin. The delicate flower fluttered down the frozen laser-cut pit and landed quietly on the black lacquered wood. "I love you, Father," Celene whispered, and in that instant, it started to snow.

After the condolences of the priest and the few bodyguards, Celene stepped into the black sedan. Kin sat next to her.

"I need to go to my apartment to fetch some decent clothes and take care of Isis."

"You live with someone?"

"My Siamese cat."

Kin looked uncomfortable at the idea. "Let's hope ORION will not be waiting for us there. I don't like it."

"Aren't they still asleep from the gas? It's only for the night."

Kin grunted his assent. "Whether it's a hotel or your apartment, I can't let you out of my sight, agreed?"

"Agreed." Celene felt rather grateful for the company.

"On second thought," Kin scoffed, "Carrick would never think you'd be dumb enough to return to your apartment, so it might be just the perfect place to hide, but only for tonight. We fly out at dawn."

Kin gave orders to detach sentries on Celene's street. Two men found a vacant apartment in the building across the street and established an observation post there. Celene admired their efficiency. They seemed to have connections everywhere. Who were these people?

Somehow her apartment always looked smaller when Celene returned from a trip. Her Siamese cat, Iris, rushed to the door as Celene opened it and switched on the light. Loud purring and the cat's cries of protest at her absence made her feel welcome. Celene picked up Isis and scratched the back of the cat's head. She realized how much she'd missed the unconditional love of her little companion.

Kin walked past her, dropped his bag on the couch, walked to the window and closed the blinds. Three of his men who followed them upstairs inspected the apartment with electronic devices, opening cupboards, closets and bathroom doors. As Celene started to protest, Kin held his index finger across his lips and whispered, "Looking for bugs and recording devices."

When the team finished the inspection, one man gave Kin a thumb's up. "All clear, boss."

Kin nodded. "Thanks. Stay behind the door, close enough to stand watch and far enough to give us privacy." After the team left the apartment, Kin grinned. "Now, I'd like to take a closer look at the shards you are hoarding in your pack."

Celene let the protesting Isis down and opened her pack. "Here they are." She unwrapped the shards and laid them on the coffee table. "What's the next step?"

Kin crossed his legs and sat on the rug next to her, leaning his back against the white leather couch. "Find a safe place where you can study these."

Together, they examined the gem-like crystals, all engraved with tiny inscriptions on one facet.

"Do you have an electronic magnifier?"

As Celene stood to get the magnifier, Isis leapt onto the coffee table. The cat stepped all over the shards to play with Kin's swift finger. Kin didn't seem to mind the cat's sharp claws and was winning the game. When he scratched the cat's head, she purred loudly.

Celene brought the instrument to the table and sat across from Kin. She picked up Isis and laid her on her lap. As Kin and Celene pored over the shards, their hands touched, and Celene felt that rush of untamed desire again.

Unable to concentrate on the work at hand, Celene

rose, unsettling the cat. "Are you hungry? I can make some dinner." The mundane occupation would keep her mind off Kin's proximity and her father's funeral.

"I'm famished." Kin grinned.

Celene opened the refrigerator. "I still feel gritty from that ventilation shaft. Feel free to use the shower."

"Don't mind if I do. I feel like a caveman."

The image didn't fit. Even after two hectic days and a sleepless night, Kin still looked smooth and clean cut, with hardly a shadow on his jaw. Celene nodded toward the bathroom door. "The towels are in the closet." She glanced into the freezer. "Fish okay?"

"Anything is fine with me." Kin picked up his travel bag and went to the bathroom but kept the door ajar.

Celene's ear tuned to the sounds of the running shower. Was the open door an invitation? She pulled a whole filet of salmon out of the freezer and threw it in the microwave to defrost. She preheated the oven and opened the wine cabinet. Riesling. Great! She found a nitrogen-pac of mushrooms, a jar of capers. Good thing she had lemons and onions. The French bread was hard. She ran it under the faucet and set in on the kitchen counter. She'd re-bake it in the oven for five minutes.

After buttering the dish, Celene sliced the onions, sautéed them in butter and added flour and wine to make the sauce, then she squeezed lemon juice. She loved to cook, especially for a man. It made her feel special to be able to create a delicious meal. Arranging the salmon in a glass dish, she poured the sauce, added capers and nutmeg, covered with a glass lid, set the timer for thirty-five minutes and prepared the table.

When she heard the shower stop, Celene figured she had another five minutes to pull out a frozen cheesecake and let it defrost in the microwave. Did she have time to whip a ready-made walnut salad, with carrots and greens? Filling a bucket with ice, she set it on the table with the bottle of wine. Candles would look nice, too. Might as well relax all the way. She needed a bath as well, she thought as Kin came out of the bathroom.

He looked very Chinese in traditional garb. The black silk robe, embroidered with a red dragon over black pants, opened to show his hairless pectorals and Celene tried not to dwell on it. Even after a shower, he still wore his jade medallion. How strange.

"I feel much better. You should try it, too."

"I intend to." Celene filled up two glasses with the white Riesling and handed one to Kin. "If you'll excuse me, I should be back before the salmon is done." She took her glass into the bathroom.

As she closed the door, she glimpsed Kin relaxing on the white couch, glass in hand.

"Keep that door open a crack. I want to hear you."

Celene complied. They'd made a deal to remain together at all times. She drew a quick bath, brushed her teeth, washed her hair, and scrubbed two days of grit off her face. She relaxed in the bubbles for a few minutes, sipping wine, willing the fatigue and the tension of the past few days to go away. Through the door left ajar, she heard soothing music in the living room. Kin had excellent taste. He'd chosen Chopin.

Perfect for a relaxing mood.

As much as she enjoyed the bath, Celene kept an eye on the bathroom clock. She couldn't let the salmon burn. Feeling refreshed enough, she wrapped herself in a towel, half-dried her hair, then slipped on a comfortable sage-green caftan that set off her emerald eyes.

She emerged in the living room and slipped the bread in the oven with the salmon.

Kin smiled. "It smells delicious."

"Hope you like it. It's my secret recipe."

"Somehow I didn't picture you as a cook."

"It's the French blood in me." Celene refilled the glasses. The oven timer went off, and she brought the salmon and bread to the table. *"Bon appetit!"*

They both ate as if they hadn't for days. Kin complimented her cooking and it made Celene feel warm inside. The only thing about traveling that bothered her was the food. Very few countries offered decent cuisine.

The salmon melted in her mouth, moist and perfect in taste. Somehow a full stomach helped her see things more clearly. "How do you expect to keep me hidden with an army of bodyguards around us? If anything, they might attract attention."

Kin wiped his mouth with the napkin and leaned back in his chair, wine glass in hand. "Maybe you are right. Secrecy might work better."

Celene stared at him, wondering what he was thinking. Instead, she said, "You have a dangerous job. Do you ever get hurt?"

"It happens."

"Did you ever kill anyone?"

Kin nodded gravely. "Sometimes, you have to. Our life is not a fairy tale. Some elements must be eliminated for the safety of innocent people." He looked down to his glass of wine.

Although she preferred it when Kin smiled, his broody mood made her want to reach out to him. "Where are we going tomorrow?" She kept her voice light.

"Think of a place where you would like to spend a few months. Maybe a place you've never seen."

Celene chuckled. "I don't think there is such a place, except maybe Hawaii. I've traveled for the past eighteen years."

"Well, you have the night to think it over."

"It's getting late and I feel jet-lagged." Celene yawned. "How are we going to sleep?"

Kin set down his empty glass. "You take the bed, I'll sleep on the floor."

"In the same room?"

"Can't let you out of my sight. That's the rule."

Celene nodded and secretly rejoiced at this intimate prospect. They wrapped the shards in their protective foam and stored them in the bag.

From the closet, Celene grabbed a blanket and pillows and threw them on the couch. "We can push the sofa into the bedroom, so you won't have to sleep on the hard parquet."

Isis leapt on the couch and protested vocally as Celene and Kin carried it through the bedroom door.

Celene went to the bathroom to change into her pajamas. When she returned to the bedroom, Kin seemed comfortably settled on the sofa. Celene welcomed her soft bed and her down comforter, but despite the cat purring by her head, sleep did not come easily. She could hear Kin's breathing, close by. He'd already fallen asleep. Finally, she fell into an uneasy dream, or rather the recurring nightmare that had plagued her all her life.

The six-year-old girl awoke in her bed on a summer night. The crickets outside the open window stopped chirping, and the summer breeze ruffled the curtains of her small bedroom. Suddenly she felt a presence. A strident ring hurt her ears. Blinding white light filled her room, and the stranger standing next to her bed looked like a monster, impossibly tall, with a dark cloak and a hood on his head. His skull seemed to glow from the inside, and he had large black eyes. When he reached to grab her, Celene's heart beat wildly and she screamed.

Celene jolted awake and sat up in cold sweat. Isis leapt off the bed. Celene's heart threatened to escape her chest. She'd seen a monster! She jumped when a hand touched her shoulder but calmed at the gentle squeeze. Her father? No. Her father was dead and buried.

"You had a nightmare." Kin's deep voice had a soothing effect.

Relieved, Celene relaxed against Kin's solid body. "I guess. Sorry to wake you up."

Kin sat on the bed next to her and brushed her cheek with one finger. "What was your dream about?"

For the first time, Celene realized she could

remember the nightmare that had eluded her all these years. "You were right. I was abducted as a child." She shivered against him at the memory of the monstrous alien grabbing her.

Kin was so close, she could smell his aftershave and feel his warmth. His bare chest felt so comforting, so inviting. She looked up at him in the milky moonlight and met his intense gaze. He made her feel warm all over. A wave of desire engulfed her. Could he feel it, too? Did he just bend to kiss her?

Without volition, Celene felt herself pulled toward his parted lips. His other arm encircled her waist in a powerful embrace. She felt him tighten his grip on her. She felt his breath so close, then, unable to resist anymore, she silenced all the warning bells in her head and lost herself in the mad pleasure of his demanding kiss.

CHAPTER SEVEN

Lost in Kin's kiss, Celene forgot everything else. He tasted like sweet strawberry wine, and his gentleness contrasted with his incredible strength. Held in his embrace, Celene couldn't have fled, not that she wanted to. She liked being his captive. His fingers, caught in her long hair, massaged her scalp in a way that made her head swim with overwhelming sensations she never knew existed. She wished that kiss would last forever.

Never in her life had Celene felt such desire, such passion. The spicy fragrance of his aftershave filled her lungs, adding to her disorientation, and her body burned wherever they touched. Her insides melted at the contact of his smooth muscled chest. She felt his jade medallion against her silky white pajamas, but he reached for the jewel and stuffed it under a pillow. In all this time, their locked mouths never separated, even as he proceeded to open her silky top slowly, one button at a time.

After his demanding tongue plundered her mouth, Celene felt his lips slip to her chin, then he pressed hard kisses along her jaw line, behind her ears, down the hollows of her throat. She couldn't help but throw her head back to allow him more freedom. Celene heard herself moan, surprised at the throaty sound of her own voice.

The chill of the night on her bare shoulders told her he'd slid her top off, but her body blazed anew when he reclined her onto the pillows. She felt his weight shift then he threw back the blankets and covered her in a possessive embrace. He felt so solid and warm atop her. He nibbled her shoulder, but that wasn't enough for Celene.

Her mouth now sought his skin, gently biting his earlobe. "Harder," she whispered in his ear.

His head rose slightly, and a curtain of dark hair brushed her bare breasts. Her nipples stood erect at the sensation. As his body weighted hers down on the bed, one strong hand pinned both her wrists over her head, while the other massaged one of her breasts, then his fingers tormented her nipple.

Celene arched under the caress and felt her breasts grow hard, but she could not move and loved the feeling. How did he know she would like being dominated? His weight kept her down. As she stretched and arched even more, she wished he would hurry and satisfy her, but Kin clearly intended to take his time, and Celene wondered whether she could wait that long.

When he relaxed his grip on her wrists to suckle her nipples, Celene raked his silky hair. In the moon's glow seeping through the sheer curtains, he looked like a werewolf or vampire, despoiling his prey. He was a monster all right. The sexiest monster she'd ever known.

She cried out when he bit her nipple ever so lightly, sending tendrils of heat all the way to her inner core.

The devil of a man guessed her most secret desires. Would he fulfill her every fantasy?

Celene could not think and did not want to. She wanted him, body and soul. She wanted to tame this savage beast who made her melt in his heat. But he hadn't finished his slow descent along her body; He laved her navel with an intensity that made her want to scream. "Lower," she moaned.

He laughed, and the vibration against her taut stomach sent her reeling with unfulfilled want. "You'll have to beg." His voice rumbled in a rich baritone as he pulled down her pajama bottoms.

"Beg? Oh, I'll beg." Celene would do anything at this point to satisfy her need of him. "Please," she said, but when his mouth found her most secret place, she forgot the begging to writhe under the assault of his exploring tongue. She groaned and wanted to arch again, but his strong hands pinned her hips down so tight, she felt paralyzed, unable to escape his ministrations.

How she loved a man who could give her pleasure while keeping his clothes on! Unlike her previous partners, Kin didn't give her any choice but to submit, and the very thought scared and thrilled her at the same time. Since they'd first met, she felt a special connection to Kin, but what did she really know about this man? What if he meant her harm?

All her fears vanished as she reached a climax and heard a low animal growl, hers. And suddenly Kin stopped.

"Don't stop, please."

When she felt the hot, silky skin of his erection

against her inner thigh, Celene realized he was now naked and ready. The very size and hardness of his manhood made her heart beat faster, if it were possible. A shiver of anticipation ran through her, and she reached for his member, wanting to pleasure him as he had pleasured her, but he didn't let her touch him. Instead, he covered her mouth with his and the sheer weight of his body made her moan into his mouth.

Delirious with his intoxicating foreplay, Celene expected him to take her, but he found another way to pleasure her. His strong fingers entered her and stroked the underside of her nub, sending her in a frenzy of uncharted sensations that made her roar like a panther in heat.

Just when she thought she couldn't possibly endure more pleasure, she felt his huge member push through her, and she cried out in surprise as much as delight. Never had she felt such ecstasy. Forgetting everything around her, she merged with Kin on a higher plane, as if gravity didn't exist anymore, as if her spirit had left her body and bathed in the intense joy that filled the room. Waves of pure energy traversed them both as they moved in perfect rhythm, heightening her sensations until she could not take any more of this consuming pleasure.

When Kin exploded inside her, Celene resonated to his tremulous release. He cried her name, and she held him tight until the last of the shock waves washed over their bodies.

"You were incredible," she whispered in his ear. She wanted to say more, but he laid one finger across her lips then kissed her mouth wantonly.

"Who said we are finished?"

Celene's head reeled with the possibilities.

* * * * *

Celene awoke with the remnants of a dream and tried to hold on to it, so she didn't open her eyes right away. Instead, she lay in bed trying to remember as much as possible. It was more of a vision than a dream, as if she'd actually lived the experience instead of dreaming it. She saw an Anasazi pictograph on an ancient stone blocking a secret passage. Leading to what? Celene recognized the ruins. She'd been there before, but according to her vision, something very important lay behind that pictograph, a secret cave calling to her. She must go there.

When she opened her eyes, a pale dawn flooded her bedroom. Isis purred on the pillow next to her. The sudden memory of last night made Celene flush, and she felt disappointed that Kin had left her side. She sat up on the bed to search the room. He was not on the sofa either.

She felt like a young girl after her first sexual experience. Having discovered this wonderful feeling, she wanted to hold on to it and keep it forever. She didn't just want to have sex with Kin. She wanted him for herself, and she intended to keep him for as long as she could hold on to him.

Noises in the kitchen and the smell of coffee and eggs made her stomach growl. She retrieved her pajamas strewn on the carpet and visited the bathroom, brushed her hair, gargled, then went to meet Kin.

"Good morning, Superman." She couldn't help the silly grin on her face as she sat at the table, already set with the coffee pot in the middle and orange juice in the glasses.

Kin barely glanced at her from the eggs he scrambled. "Morning."

She poured herself a cup of fragrant coffee, added hazelnut creamer and took a sip, welcoming the sweet shot of caffeine.

Kin looked somber, fully dressed in black jeans and sweater. He even had his shoes on. "So, where did you decide to go study the relics?" His business-like manner frayed Celene's nerves.

But she wouldn't let him spoil a perfect night of love. "You were quite a tiger last night. Way better than I expected."

He glanced back, as if surprised at her comment. "About last night…" His shifty gaze didn't bode well. "I'm sorry." He grabbed the toast as it popped out of the toaster and dropped the slices on an empty plate on the table.

"What?"

Kin cleared his throat as he returned to the stove. "It was very insensitive of me, after your father's funeral, and I promise you this will never happen again." The finality in his tone cut Celene like a knife.

"Why?" Celene felt lost. What did she do wrong? She couldn't imagine never making love to him again. She just couldn't.

"We have an important job to do, and I think we should keep things strictly professional between us." The man wouldn't even look at her.

"Last night you didn't seem to care much about keeping things professional." Celene tried to hide the hurt she felt.

"Last night was a mistake."

"A mistake?" Her voice cracked despite her efforts. "I thought maybe we had something special."

His back to her, Kin didn't seem to react. When he turned to serve the eggs, his expression was unreadable. He sat across from her and they started to eat in silence, then Kin repeated the question. "Where do you want to go? I have to make arrangements."

Celene hoped this cold morning after would not set the tone for the remainder of their time together. "I had a dream last night."

He sat across from her. "I know, a memory of your abduction." The way he dug into the food, he must be hungry. No wonder, after such prowess in bed.

Celene had lost her appetite. "No, another dream, more like a vision."

"A vision?"

"I'm not sure I was asleep. I saw images. I think I know where we can find another device to read the shards."

Suddenly animated, Kin gazed straight into her eyes. "Really? Where?"

His renewed interest warmed Celene who described her dream, then said, "I think the pictograph I saw on the boulder is hiding a passage to an artificial cave. Think about it. According to the drawings in the surrounding sites, it seems that aliens resided there with the Anasazi for a while, before they all disappeared. It would make sense if they had built or carved a place for them to reside, to study…"

"And read their database crystal shards."

"Exactly." Hungry again, Celene started devouring the eggs.

Kin seemed elated. "Where is that place?"

"In the canyon lands of northern Arizona," she said on a full mouth. "High among the Anasazi cliff dwellings, in the middle of nowhere."

"Perfect. Could you direct a small plane to the site?" He pulled out his epad.

"With a good map, probably." Celene retrieved a file from the cabinet where she kept her research papers and threw the folder on the kitchen table. From it, she pulled out a map with many landmarks and stars indicating various sites of Anasazi ruins. She pointed to a particular star. "This is Arch Canyon, but the ruins I'm talking about are not accessible to the tourists. Are you a good climber?"

"As good as any."

"Then that's where we should go study the relics."

The warmth Celene had seen in Kin while he talked about their search vanished as soon as she closed the folder. He became all business again and made arrangements for their trip to northern Arizona. He closed his epad. "Well, now you should go pack for a field trip. I'll do the dishes."

Celene pointed to the bag containing the relics. "How are we going to carry these? On our backs?" She'd better pack light to compensate for the extra weight. Climbing cliffs was dangerous business.

But most of all, Celene hoped the wonderful lover she'd discovered last night would soon return to her.

She missed him fiercely.

CHAPTER EIGHT

Northern Arizona

The sightseeing Beechcraft banked in the clear blue sky, then the pilot looped over the canyon. From the backseat, Celene admired the many layers of red and bluish rock, black burn, and white deposit that coursed like long ribbons along the majestic cliffs. Next to the pilot, Kin busied himself taking topographic scans of the landscape below. He had not spoken the whole trip from Montreal to an isolated gravel landing strip in the desert that pompously called itself South Rim Airport.

When Kin insisted on a reconnaissance flight before driving across the canyon lands, Celene didn't argue. In the absence of roads, with so many tributaries and connecting canyons, the satellite guidance might not be enough to avoid getting trapped in a dead-end canyon by a flash flood. In the desert, even on a dry year, a spring shower could become a hazard. Many lost their lives in the area each year, from poor planning and lack of accurate directions. These unfortunate tourists ran out of fuel, out of batteries, out of water and food and fell prey to rattlesnakes; Months later, other wilderness explorers found their bones picked clean by scavengers. Some were never found at all.

A bald eagle on the right wing seemed to race with the small plane. The majestic bird reminded Celene of her previous trips here with her adoptive father, when they'd discovered a nest. Happy times, full of hope for the future... Now that memories of her abduction started to come back, all Celene wanted to remember were the happy times with Armand Dupres.

He'd taught her to respect nature, to love the wild, and he'd given her the best gift of all; his love for archeology. It was a love that had filled Celene's life with travels, adventures, discoveries, and more successes than she could count. And to thank him for that, Celene wanted Armand Dupres remembered as the man who contributed to save the human race by finding the Anaz-voohri ship.

Celene's heart beat faster when she recognized the familiar landmark, and she pointed it out to the pilot. "That's the cliff we want to scale."

The pilot veered and started a slow descent. Kin, still glued to the scanner screen, said nothing. Since this morning in her apartment, he'd shown less congeniality than any boulder below.

As they approached the tall cliff, Kin finally looked through the window. "The riverbed at the bottom of the cliff is dry. We can drive the vehicle on the sand. I've got the topo map. It's about sixty miles from the strip as the crow flies. Much more around the canyons. Let's get back."

"You sure you don't want the full tour?" The pilot sounded disappointed.

Kin grunted. "We want to get back here before nightfall."

"You paid for the trip, you're the boss." The pilot turned the plane due west, toward the landing strip on the south rim.

When they landed, a large Land Rover waited for them at the end of the runway, loaded with equipment and supplies. Kin gave Celene the list on an epad and enumerated each item in turn. Tent, hydrogen fuel tanks, sleeping bags. Celene check-marked each item on the epad as he spotted them in the Land Rover.

"Electronic climbing shoes?" Celene looked at Kin in surprise. "You trust your life to these anti-gravity gadgets?"

"I wager you prefer the old-fashioned way." Kin sounded almost sarcastic. "We have climbing ropes if that's the way you want it."

"Unless you are afraid of a little exercise." She'd show him she was no wimp. She returned her attention to the list as Kin enumerated.

"...hooks, harnesses, water, fire bricks, spare batteries, rations, nitrogen-pacs, first aid kit, snake bite kit, blankets, cooking pot, camping gas stove. That's for making tea and warming up the soup cans." Kin paused. "I don't know how long we'll have to stay there, so I prepared for the long haul."

Celene noticed that Kin checked his phase-gun and battery clips in his black leather pack. She recognized other weapons there, knives, ninja stars and even a sword. Kin threw his pack under the blanket with the bag containing the shards and Celene's backpack. Although the weapons would insure her safety, it made Kin look suddenly ominous, given his change of attitude.

Celene hoped this time alone in the wild would allow her to rekindle the magic with Kin. She missed his congenial self, not to mention his loving attentions. By the time they finished the inventory of the car, the sun started arcing in the west. Kin plugged his scanner into the dashboard satellite guidance system and took the driver's seat. "We'll camp out on the riverbed tonight, then climb the cliff in the morning."

After a bumpy ride that didn't allow for much conversation, they reached the bottom of the Anasazi cliff as the sun set the red rocks ablaze. Long shadows already stretched on the stone walls and the riverbed. They pitched the tent in relative silence, speaking only when necessary.

"We should camouflage the car." Kin held a desert print tarp and desert netting. "I'll find greenery to pin on the meeting in the morning."

Celene nodded.

"And this," he held a small device to her scrutiny, "is an electronic net that provides shielding from electronic scanners like those on planes and satellites."

Around them, the desert teamed with wildlife. A lone coyote howled in the distance. Mountain cats growled. After the snow in Montreal, Arizona in March felt like early summer.

Celene unrolled the sleeping mats while Kin lit a campfire in the sand. The night chill forced Celene to wrap a blanket over her shoulders as they ate energy bars and drank instant hot tea from metal cups that burned her lips.

"Why didn't we use a helicopter and drop right where we didn't have to climb?" Celene set down her cup.

Kin offered a half smile. "Too obvious. That kind

of activity would attract too much attention in the area. The fewer people who know we are here, the better."

"I see." Although Celene understood the need for secrecy, she'd never trained her mind for that purpose and it still felt strange to her.

She couldn't see a cloud in the sky while the night was full of so many stars. Away from the city lights, it seemed that the stars actually twinkled. After the short dinner, Kin pointed at a constellation that Celene had recently learned to recognize. Orion. Following Kin's finger farther west, she stared at another star cluster. "The Pleiades?"

"That's where all our troubles started. The hemorrhagic plagues, the destruction of central Europe, the big blackout on the east coast, the attacks on human facilities…"

"I don't want to think about that now. Too depressing." Celene didn't want all that pressure about saving humanity on her shoulders. Whatever they would find in the cave could wait until tomorrow. Tonight, she just wanted to enjoy the beauty of the stars and remember her adoptive father.

Although they slept in the same tent that night, Kin and Celene might as well have been a hundred miles apart, but she didn't lose heart. She remained confident that her splendid warrior would come to his senses.

In the predawn, the birds started signing. Celene awoke to find a fire going. She made herself a mug of instant coffee with the hot water.

Kin had already unloaded the ropes, sorted the hooks, and now measured the cliff with his electronic gauge. As he glanced her way, his face remained as blank as a bare wall. "You said you scaled that cliff before? Which route did you pick?"

Celene pointed at a vertical fissure running haphazardly to the left of the wall. "That's the easiest, but it misses the cave entrance, so you have to climb to the very top, then rappel down to the outcrop to get to the ruins." She blew on the steam.

"Seems like a waste of time to me. Why not take the direct route?"

Celene followed Kin's pointing finger to a smaller fissure in the wall. She set down her mug and assessed the route with her electronic binoculars. The crack offered measly handholds and challenging areas with overhangs. "You think you can climb that?"

Kin scoffed. "We'll find out. Do you fear a little friendly competition?"

"Of course not!" Celene already berated herself for her prideful reaction. But if Kin challenged her, she would not back down. She only hoped she wouldn't lose face. She'd never attempted such a difficult course before.

"Then let's do it."

"What about the relics?" She retrieved her mug and enjoyed the warming brew.

"We'll leave them here. When we reach the cave overhang, we can secure ropes on pulleys and use them to pull up the shards and the equipment."

"Like an ancient Anasazi elevator? They sometimes used ropes to bring supplies to the cliff dwellings." Celene breathed easier. She didn't have to risk the shards in such a reckless climb. She would, however, show Kin what she was made of, although his agility seemed better than hers.

They buckled on their gear and checked each other's harnesses. The pull of his hand on the straps to check the buckles reminded Celene of how he'd made love to her, just two nights ago in Montreal. Now, that magical night almost felt like a faraway dream, as if it happened only in her fantasies. Kin had suddenly become a stranger. When she met his gaze, Celene only saw aloofness in his eyes, then he turned away.

* * * * *

Kin hated his mission. Killing Celene went against everything he believed. Since that fated night in her apartment, he felt distracted. His mind and his senses reacted to the slightest of her moves. Each time her jade gaze turned on him, he felt guilt at what he must do. Guilt, and something else… Something disturbing he'd never experienced before, even with Shani, his very first girl and only love. Something wrenched his gut at the thought of losing Celene. A dangerous feeling for an assassin toward his intended victim.

He inspected the cables and hooks before handing Celene a coil of climbing rope. It seemed heavy for her slim frame, but he knew she could carry it. All the equipment looked brand new. Mythos had spared no expense to make sure the mission would succeed. He felt glad Celene liked an old-fashioned climb. He didn't care much for the antigravity magnetic shoes that allowed a climber to walk up or down the steepest walls without using arm muscles. His enhanced body preferred a good workout anytime.

Before starting the ascent, Kin dragged the longest coil of rope to the bottom of the cliff then hooked one end of it to his belt. As he climbed, the rope would uncoil while the bulk of it remained on the ground. That would be the rope he'd use later to lift the supplies from the riverbed.

Celene stepped up to the sandstone wall. "I'll go first. I know where we must end up."

Kin agreed. If she fell on him, he might be able to catch her. "Shall we rope ourselves together?"

Celene stiffened. "I don't think so. I'd rather rope myself to the rock in the tight places."

"You sure?" Kin would have preferred to hold her on a leash. He couldn't afford to lose her. But when she stared at him with such defiance, he reluctantly agreed. Damn her stubbornness. The girl had guts. How he wanted to kiss her.

After adjusting her sunglasses and baseball cap, Celene started up the first few easy feet, then she tackled the base of the steep wall. As he followed her, Kin watched her climb above him and enjoyed the view. How did she manage to look so good in gray parachute coveralls and climbing boots? She'd looped her long auburn hair through the baseball hat. As she balanced her weight from hold to hold, her long ponytail swept her lower back in cadence. Kin expected her to run out of breath and stop after a while, but she kept climbing at a rate he could barely match. Could she best him? Doubtful.

The wall steepened, and soon they couldn't find any holds and had to hammer hooks in the crevices to pull themselves up the cliff. The process took time and careful placing of the hooks.

At the mid point up the cliff, the extra rope hanging from his belt started to weigh Kin down. They neared an overhang, a shelf where they might be able to rest and catch their breath. Above him, Celene hoisted herself upon the shelf.

As he looked up to make sure she was safe, the hook holding Kin's rope slipped, and he dropped a few feet then bounced and swung at the end of his rope. Adrenalin surged and his heart beat faster as he hung precariously under the overhang. Too far from the rock to plant another hook, he glanced at the faulty hook that threatened to move some more.

Kin heard Celene's cry of anguish. Was she worried for him? Suddenly he realized the hook would not hold. It started slipping out of the crevice. Through the haze of his concentration, he heard hammering sounds from the ledge above, but he couldn't see any trace of Celene. He didn't dare look down. No one could survive a fall from this height. It had to be two hundred feet.

Climbing the rope or swinging it would only dislodge the hook faster. What now?

As his mind searched for more options, Celene's head popped over the rim. She smiled as if she found the situation humorous. "Grab my rope. It's secured to the rock." She swung the end of a rope toward him.

Kin seized the lifeline and clipped it to his harness.

"Ready?"

"Okay!" He felt the pull as the line tightened and Celene brought him up inch by inch, then helped him over the ledge. For the first time since they had started

the climb, Kin looked down at the riverbed and realized
how high they had come. In his euphoria to be alive, he
wanted to hug Celene but refrained. "Thanks," he
mumbled with reluctance. "It appears that you might
have saved my life."

"Then we are even." Her smug smile troubled him.

Had he found his match? He'd never owed his life
to a girl before. The feeling humbled him and he didn't
like it. Kin unhooked himself then freed and recoiled
his short rope. "Want to take a break?"

"Not unless you need one." That smug smile
again.

"I don't."

They resumed the ascent, and half an hour later,
they emerged on the floor of the Anasazi cave dwelling.
The sun now warmed the rock face, exposed to the
south. A large circular flat stone occupied the center of
the ledge.

Kin removed his harness and watched Celene peel
off her parachute coveralls to reveal a black tank top
and a pair of khaki shorts on long, tanned, muscled
legs. Good thing Kin didn't know what she wore
underneath from the start. He'd have been even more
distracted. "Is this the right spot?"

But Celene had already walked into the shallow
cave, toward a labyrinth of small square houses built in
several layers. They resembled the many cells of a
beehive, connected by ladders, bridges, and
rudimentary stairs.

"I'll get the supplies!" Kin yelled, before looping a
rope around the grinding stone to anchor the pulley.

* * * * *

Inside the cave village, Celene was drawn to a particular area. She heard Kin's words but didn't bother to respond. She felt driven to find the pictograph she'd seen in her dream. Curiously, she didn't remember seeing it on her previous trips, so it must be hidden.

Calming her mind, she tried to recreate the scene. What could she see from the spot in her dream? Then the images surged in her mind's eye, and she knew. She hurried through the cave, up and down stairs, around grinding stones and down graveled paths, until she reached a hidden recess against the main rock, where an egg-shaped boulder blocked the entrance to some vault or passage.

The rock had a different color and texture than the surrounding sandstone. Then Celene realized that a thick layer of gray powder covered the whole stone. Ashes? Saltpeter? She didn't have her tools yet, so she brushed some of the dust with her fingers and sneezed. A pictograph lay underneath. It wouldn't do to damage the ancient paint with her fingers, so she doubled back toward the cave entrance. She needed her brushes.

When she emerged in the open, she realized Kin had secured a pulley with short ropes around the large circular stone near the entrance. The long cable hung all the way down to the riverbed, where Kin now attached several bags together to the rope.

Yard by yard, the bags ascended under the power of an electric pulley. Soon, Celene grabbed and unhooked the load, then she let the rope drop down to the riverbed, so Kin could secure another load.

Within minutes, the shards, her tools, water, blanket, food and other supplies had reached the rock shelf in front of the cave. Then she saw Kin attach his own harness to the cable to ascend the cliff.

After retrieving her tool kit, Celene didn't wait for Kin but returned to the boulder to uncover the pictograph. Enough daylight entered the cave so she didn't need a flashlight. With a wide silk brush, she removed the first layers of gray dust, sneezing profusely, until she could see vague outlines and a few colors. Then she proceeded with a finer brush to clear the picture, unveiling inch by inch the details of the Anasazi drawing.

Bright orange, blood red, ochre, gray and black dominated, with a few touches of turquoise and lapis lazuli. Celene took infinite care not to damage the ancient pigment. Focused on her work, she did not look at the whole picture, but at each spot in turn, trying to clean it as perfectly as possible.

When she stepped back to look at her handiwork, she shuddered. Fire, smoke, blood. In the forefront, a bunch of grimacing demons butchered each other while running from something.

"Good job!"

She jumped at the sound of Kin's voice. She hadn't heard him coming. The man had a way of fraying her nerves. She willed her heart to slow down. "I think there is something important behind that boulder.

Kin inspected the drawing. "A warning?"

Celene pointed to the writing that framed the

pictograph. "There lay danger...or some kind of curse." She knelt to read more writing at the bottom. "This tells the story of a catastrophic fire. Its green smoke turned people into atrociously disfigured bloodthirsty demons."

"Pretty graphic." Kin's brow shot up. "Could this be an empty threat to keep the superstitious Anasazi away from that spot?"

"Possibly. I imagine the aliens of that time didn't want uncivilized humans to enter their secret residence." Celene rose and wiped the dust from her hands with a rag.

"Are you hungry?"

"Ravenous." Celene smiled at the prospect of food. "How are we going to move that boulder?"

"Let's brainstorm while we eat."

The thin dust from the boulder now covered Celene's clothes. She brushed it off her black top and sneezed again. "This dust is rather strange. It's only on this boulder, and not on anything else."

"Maybe we should take a sample for the lab."

Celene nodded and took a vial from her kit then filled it up with some of the gray powder she'd dusted off the stone. She capped the vial and handed it to Kin. "Got a homing pigeon to take this to London?"

Kin grinned briefly as he pocketed the vial then regained his serious composure. "I made lunch. Hope you like it."

Celene secretly enjoyed teasing Kin. She wouldn't take no for an answer. How dare any man make passionate love to her then shun her. A light approach seemed the best way to regain Kin's trust and his

wonderful attentions. She noticed he'd open up a little
each time she chided him or made a joke. Someone
said once that laughter was the surest way to a lover's
heart, and Celene intended to demonstrate that fact by
winning back that difficult man.

Whatever ate at Kin could only be a silly
misunderstanding or some misplaced male pride.
Celene didn't quite understand him, but she would
force him to face his feelings for her. For she knew
darn well that no one made love with such abandon
without true feelings.

When they came out of the cave, Celene noticed
the sun already in the west. She had worked for several
hours. Surprised at the smell of roasting meat, she
discovered that Kin had made a small fire and
improvised a meal. Vegetables simmered in the
cooking pan, but the carcass roasting on the spit hadn't
come from their food supplies. "What's this?"

"I can cook, too. I specialize in wild game. This is
rabbit."

"You killed that lovely creature?" Celene hated
the idea of destroying animal life.

"Just an old male that wouldn't have lasted the
spring. I swear I didn't threaten the ecology of this
place."

"How did you kill it?" She couldn't help her
accusing tone.

"Phase-gun. Instant and painless."

At least the poor thing hadn't suffered, but Celene
couldn't keep the sarcasm from her voice. "Should I
congratulate the brave warrior for his courage at slaying
the wild beast?" She wiped her face and hands clean

with a wet towelette from her pack then discarded it in a plastic trash bag. Her stepfather taught her never to litter on ancient dig sites. She missed the dear man.

Ken snorted but his expression softened. "If you don't want any rabbit, I'll eat it myself, but I think you need protein. This could be our only chance at fresh meat for many days."

Her hunger helped her decide. "Actually, it smells good."

They sat on boxes and he ripped off a rabbit leg for her. No plates. She just bit into the meat. A little tough but very satisfying. He poured some vegetables in a mug and handed it to her with a spoon and a chunk of bread.

Celene enjoyed the camaraderie of a campsite. She had done this thousands of times with her father on small isolated digs. She noticed that Kin looked just as comfortable in the wild as he had at the fancy party at the British Museum. Personally, Celene preferred the open spaces. She felt most alive in the dust of a dig, with the anticipation of an important find ahead of her.

She ate some vegetables, a bean medley with celery and carrots, then licked her lips. "So, how do we move that boulder?"

Kin ate voraciously. They'd had no breakfast and it was mid-afternoon. "It looks like we might be able to roll it, if we can unsettle it with a lever. The hard part is to prevent it from rolling too far. The ground is sloped, so we'll have to rig it with ropes first."

Celene focused on what they could use. "Wooden blocs! Don't we have some for the car, to block the wheels on a steep incline?"

Kin rose. "That might help. I'll go get them."

While Kin went for the wood blocs, Celene found a crowbar and went back to the stone. Cursory inspection showed no seam, no space between the stone and the adjacent cave wall, but somehow, Celene knew there must be a cavity behind that egg-shaped boulder. She tried to pry the edges with the crowbar with no success. Using her epad, she calculated the weight of the stone from its size, shape and density. It weighed two and a half tons.

Kin returned with the wood blocs and several glow sticks. The light inside the shallow cave recess had started to dim as the sun moved farther west. The boulder now lay in shadow.

Celene had a few reservations. "Are you sure we can do that ourselves? Shouldn't we call your friends for help?"

"Whatever is behind this boulder is probably top secret." Kin hit three glow sticks against the rock. Instantly, they generated a soft suffused light with minimum shadows. He set them around the perimeter, lighting the boulder. "The fewer people involved, the better."

Celene nodded. The bloody colors in the drawing seemed to brighten in the light. She still wasn't sure what they would find and hoped it would include a decoding device for the shards, but something told her it would be much more. She shivered sensing a great find, and her whole being tingled with anticipation. This was what she lived for.

Kin measured the vertical length of the stone with his scanner then projected the measurements on the ground and backed up a few steps. He stopped. "If we can limit the rolling to one revolution, it should stop here." He placed the wood blocs on that spot, then arranged the ropes to slow the fall of the stone. "Now, hand me my crowbar and take yours. I want you to pry on the opposite side, then pull on the rope as hard as you can."

Her heart beating fast, Celene took the other side of the stone and mirrored Kin's position.

"On the count of three."

As he counted, Celene focused her mind to gather all her strength. On three, she pried and within seconds felt the stone give. Dropping the crowbar to hold the rope with Kin, she followed the movement of the boulder until it balanced on its tip then fell on its flank and stopped right where Kin had positioned the wood blocs.

Celene cheered and jumped for joy. "We did it!"

The grin on Kin's face told much about his satisfaction as he wiped his forehead with one sleeve.

They'd opened a tall passage with wide steps leading down. The cooler air inside the dark tunnel attested to some ventilation shafts, probably natural crevices in the rock. Grabbing a glow stick, Celene took the lead. Soon the wide steps also steepened.

Celene heard Kin behind her. "These stairs were made for people with longer legs than ours."

Soon they emerged into a vast domed room, like a half-sphere. By flashlight, the smooth texture of the sandstone looked polished by some unknown feat of technology. The dome looked empty, except for a round pedestal in the center.

Kin whistled.

"Wow!"   Heart pounding with wonder, Celene went to the pedestal that exhibited indentations carved with several petroglyphs.   She recognized a few characters from the Anaz-voohri crystal shards.   "I think we may have found our decoding device!"

CHAPTER NINE

As soon as Celene touched the writing on the pedestal, the vast empty dome lit up and glowed soft pink, as if the stone itself generated the light. But the smooth surface of the dome looked more like burnished metal. A pleasant warmth filled the cave. She stepped back and bumped into Kin. "Do you feel this?"

A gentle humming vibrated throughout the artificial cave. As Celene watched in amazement, the central area where they stood rose like a round stage two feet above the rest of the floor, leaving two wide circular steps to access it. Several cylindrical consoles arose from the ground, evenly spaced along the periphery of the dome.

Elated, Celene hugged Kin and felt him resisting her embrace. Darn, he was playing hard to get. She pretended not to notice and released him with reluctance. If she didn't know better, she'd think he found her repulsive.

He gave her an embarrassed smile. "It seems you were right. This is definitely alien technology. Let's hope you're right about the decoding device, too. While you try to figure it out, I'll go get the relics."

Celene didn't hear him leave. Now alone in archeologist heaven, she noticed no dust of any kind on the floor or the consoles. How could this be after eight hundred years? The top surface of the central panel had a few indentations and geometric depressions. It felt soft and warm to her fingers, almost like skin. She shivered at the feel and touched the sun symbol for light. The light went out, leaving only the glowing petroglyphs on the console. She touched the symbol again, and the light went back on. Other petroglyphs looked less familiar. Could this be a place of residence? A place of worship? A gathering place?

No. The dome, with its burnished shell, its humming and perfect circular design, felt more like a machine of some sort, and Celene was standing right in its center. How did she know that? Suddenly, she felt cold, as if a nefarious shadow flew over the cave. This place did something to her, something altogether frightening and compelling.

When Kin returned with the bag containing the shards, Celene brushed aside the silly foreboding. What secret so important to the future of humanity did the Anaz-voohri hide in the shards? Maybe she would discover who she really was and learn the identity of her biological parents. Hopefully she would accomplish the work her stepfather didn't get a chance to finish. And if humanity was in real danger, she must help save it.

Kin set the bag on the steps but did not join Celene on the central platform. "This place gives me the creeps. It reminds me of a cursed cave in China, where it was said evil spirits resided."

Celene found the thought of Kin being afraid rather humorous. "Do you fear evil spirits?"

Kin shrugged. "I fear only what I cannot kill."

Not an easy thing to admit for a ninja. Celene, too, felt the subtly disturbing atmosphere, as if humans were not welcome in this place. But her professional curiosity overruled the uneasy feeling.

As she unwrapped one shard, a long red one with irregular facets and sharp broken angles, Celene let her instinct guide her and placed the crystal on a geometrical depression that almost seemed to fit but not quite. When she let go of the shard, the console surface changed shape to accommodate the irregular crystal in a tight fit. "Would you look at that?"

The lights flickered and died. Kin remained quiet. In the dimness of the dome, thousands of luminous symbols appeared, like a firmament. A three-dimensional book surrounded them, with hundreds of pages filled with information.

"Cool! Now that's a book."

Looking uneasy, Kin stared at the writing filling the cave.

Celene stepped down the high steps then ambled among the pages of characters and pointed at a few basic signs.

Kin surprised her by enumerating them. "Fire, water, air, rock, smoke," then he stopped.

"Forest, sustenance," she volunteered. As she went on, Celene felt a trance take hold of her. "Ship, humans, exploration." Suddenly she wanted to be alone in the cave. "I think I can translate these, but I need to focus."

Kin took the hint. "I'll be out on the ledge, keeping an eye out for unwanted visitors. Call if you need anything."

Relieved, Celene also felt guilty for asking Kin to leave. She didn't want him to know how easy the language seemed to her. It felt as if she had known it all her life. She turned on her epad and started recording the translation in voice mode. "File one: Ecological study reveals breathable atmosphere with high levels of carbon monoxide and a depleted ozone layer. Few forests are left, and the animal population is scarce, except for a few tamed species bred for food consumption and unable to survive on their own in the wild..."

* * * * *

Anaz-voohri swarm

Deep within the bowels of the ship traveling with the swarm at top speed between the stars in the black emptiness of space, Wasaw awoke to a strident alarm. He'd never heard it before, but excitement filled him as he recognized what it meant. Light-years away on planet Earth, where the legends of his childhood took place, someone had entered the secret Sipapuni cave, and that someone had to be sister Celene.

Wasaw had seen pictures of old Earth. He remembered his grandfather's description of the secret cave among the deep canyons. How he longed to return to the celebrated promised land. He took a deep breath. "The planet of our ancestors awaits!" he exhaled in religious fervor.

Draping the shimmering cape over the natural armor of his muscled body, Wasaw mentally turned off his sensitive ear implants to protect them from the high-pitched whine. The alarm hadn't activated in eight hundred years, not since the ancient masters chose his Anasazi ancestors. That included his legendary grandfather, Masaw, the original guardian of the cave, the one with whom Wasaw shared genetic material, and function.

No distraction troubled his thoughts along the empty corridors of the vast ship, covered in purple and teal synthetic skin. Among the ridges and arches, decorated with Kokopelli figures, Wasaw felt at home. He'd lived on this ship all his life.

Wasaw remembered the legends his grandfather told about the ancestors. How they must have felt used. No longer human, implanted with electronic parts from birth, exploited and abused by their abductors, the genetically altered descendants of the chosen Anasazi had evolved into the fierce Anaz-voohri warriors.

As he levitated up the vertical shaft on his way to the top deck, Wasaw remembered his grandfather, who always smiled mysteriously when he explained the notion of freewill. Already programmed into the human genes, freewill proved more difficult to neutralize than their abductors suspected. The new gene binding their loyalty to the masters gradually lost its hold, but the Anaz-voohri kept pretending that it worked. After centuries of military service, they secretly prepared a full-blown rebellion. One day, as planned, the masters found their entire military force composed of fierce Anaz-voohri.

A blue flash told Wasaw he had reached the top deck. Exiting the vertical shaft, he hovered toward the command center at the prow. What a glorious morning

that must have been, when the former slaves destroyed
their masters' key installations and defenses.   By
nightfall, the so-called gods who'd survived the
massacre mourned their destroyed civilization.

With a fleet of fast ships stolen from their former
masters, the Anaz-voohri had fled *en masse* before their
abductors received any help from neighboring allies.
The free Anaz-voohri, drunk with a new feeling of
independence, took only survival supplies along with
the deadliest weapons.

For a while, they wandered through the void in
search of an identity, prowling, preying on convoys and
cargo ships.   They used stealth technology, killing to
survive, to eat, to erase any trace of their passage.
Early on, a few groups separated from the swarm to
seek fortune as independent space pirates.

Unfortunately, the Anaz-voohri's querulous nature,
even against each other, soon depleted their numbers.
When they lost their ability to reproduce, the cloning
labs in the fleet proved insufficient, and the race started
to degenerate.   If his people didn't find a planet with
adequate cloning facilities, they would soon be extinct.

How Wasaw wished for company on his vessel.
The prospect of a child to share his knowledge filled
him with joy.   What an honor to be considered worthy
of reproduction.   Captain Kavak was right.   There were
many ways to serve one's race.   Wasaw exhaled a deep
sigh.

The Anaz-voohri barely formed the nucleus of a
viable society.   With only a few of them on each ship,
their great fleet manned by a few thousands couldn't
conquer any inhabited planet in a war fought on the

ground.

Under military intimidation, the worlds they encountered reluctantly traded supplies but refused them shelter. This invoked their arrogance, aggressive behavior and lack of ethics, the very traits the Anaz-voohri cherished and cultivated to become better warriors.

In desperation, twenty years ago, Wasaw's dying people remembered their roots and turned toward Earth in hopes of finding a solution to their dwindling numbers. But the first contacts with Earth people didn't bring the desired results. Human governments didn't recognize the Anaz-voohri's superior thinking. Out of some ridiculous fear of slavery, they stubbornly refused to serve their betters. After a few warning strikes from space, one powerful human government even declared war upon Wasaw's race. The ants had refused their fate and declared war on the technological giant. Wasaw had never seen an ant and felt eager to meet one.

It would have been easy for the Anaz-voohri to use cataclysmic weapons to level the planet from space, but as the exalted leader pointed out, so much destruction would ruin the fragile ecological balance of the blue orb and destroy the precious cloning facilities. So his people opted to bide their time and use their superior minds to control and destroy the parasitic human population without irreversible destruction.

As he reached the command center, Wasaw stopped hovering and walked up to the pedestal on the central platform of the circular room. Standing over the luminous panel, he turned off the alarm and mentally restarted his hearing implant. He felt eager to meet sister Celene. He'd waited for that moment for the past twenty Earth years. In other words, all his life.

After implementing the automated response mechanism, Wasaw had to wait for the delay. The signal transmitted through light-years would take a few minutes to reach Earth and come back. He hoped the recording devices in the cave would still function.

Wasaw prayed his inexperience would not jeopardize the most daring planet takeover ever conceived. It had started with seemingly random abductions, genetic experiments, the spread of filoviruses and hemorrhagic plagues. The Anaz-voohri had cloned a few human hybrids and provided them with genetic material to clone more of them. These hybrids infiltrated key human facilities and conducted covert genetic experiments. Use of the cloning facilities in the future would allow the creation of a whole new wave of Anaz-voohri children to repopulate the blue planet.

Then, of course, the crowning of their success would come with Operation: Pleiades. In the final stage, the seven sisters abducted twenty years ago would fulfill their mission. And this was 2023 on Earth, the holy year when his people returned to the planet of their ancestors. The lovely blue orb toward which Wasaw's vessel now flew at warp speed with the whole Anaz-voohri swarm.

"The planet of our ancestors awaits!" he uttered respectfully. Wasaw believed the sacred phrase had the power to bring the Anaz-voohri home.

His people had wandered long enough. The time had come to populate a planet, time for Wasaw to share his genetic treasures. Soon, when his people thrived on the planet of their ancestors, a new civilization of warriors would flourish, and from there they would spread and conquer the whole universe, as was their destiny, at least according to his leaders.

To curb his impatience and calm his nerves while he waited, Wasaw hummed an old Kokopelli tune. His grandfather used to sing it to get him to sleep as a child, when Wasaw's prostheses ached as his flesh and bone still grew around them. Even through the growing pains of childhood, Kokopelli had kept him cheerful, and to this day, the music eased his loneliness.

At the chime of an incoming communication, Wasaw switched on the three-dimensional viewer. The dome of the command center filled with the holographic image of another dome, that of the sacred Sipapuni cave the ancient masters had built long ago on Earth. The three-dimensional image of the secret cave superposed itself on Wasaw's own space, and the Earth woman in the cave appeared as a holographic image in the middle of Wasaw's dome. He could see, hear, and almost touch her as he walked toward her.

What would the ancient masters who had built the cave think of a substandard human female in their sacrosanct cave? And O sacrilege, sister Celene had activated the reading device. Wasaw walked around the hologram of the Earth woman with intense curiosity. Although he'd seen pictures of her as a child during her DNA programming, Wasaw marveled at the changes that had occurred in twenty years.

The sister didn't look at all like Anaz-voohri females. She was shorter, like all heavy-worlders.

Gravity prevented them from growing longer leg bones. She looked very much like a hybrid, with no sign of implanted electronic devices on her face or body, as her alterations were at the DNA level. The dark reddish hair on her skull had grown to great length. She wore scant clothing that showed soft tan skin, unprotected by any kind of natural armor. Most interesting.

Sister Celene spoke in a language Wasaw had to research on his panel. After a few tries, he identified the Earth language as English from the database in his ship's crystal shards. He switched the command to translate her words and realized with surprise that the Earth woman was dictating an accurate translation of the database of an Anaz-voohri ship. Impressive.

Caressing a few indented petroglyphs on his console, Wasaw identified the shards as belonging to the unfortunate prowler that had malfunctioned and crashed on Earth three years ago. The accident had leveled several Earth nations in the electro-magnetic storm that ensued.

A chime called him back to the console.

The face of the exalted leader of the Anaz-voohri appeared on a flat screen. Captain Kavak looked serene, but her smooth skull glowed with the excitement he also detected in her voice. "We heard the signal. Do you have a visual on the Sipapuni cave?"

"Yes, exalted leader. The Earth woman is deciphering one of our databases. Should she be stopped?"

"Not at all, Commander Wasaw. She is on the verge of accomplishing a great deed for the Anaz-voohri race. Keep watching her closely and report her every move."

"I will, exalted leader, I will."

The flat screen went blank. Thrilled with the excitement of this new development in his boring life, and boosted by the trust of his exalted leader, Wasaw returned to watching the holographic human female who had invaded his space. She walked and talked, unaware of his presence. He reached to touch the skin of her arm and could almost feel her. The sister stopped translating and turned toward Wasaw as if she could see him. Was she aware that the guardian of the cave watched her every move and listened to her every word? No. Wasaw knew she couldn't. She shrugged then returned to her translation.

* * * * *

Hidden in the tunnel near the cave entrance, Kin listened to Celene dictating into her epad. She seemed to know what she was doing, and she certainly had a good grasp of the alien language. Maybe he should remain to keep an eye on her, but he felt uncomfortable. The very technology in that dome brought up memories of the CEM in China. He couldn't stand the vibration of all those alien machines. He identified that technology with the torture he underwent in the name of science, the DNA manipulation that made him a killer.

Could he trust Celene to do the job on her own? Yes, the unusual challenge and her professional ethics would compel her to do her best. Besides, where could she possibly go if she wanted to escape? His keen hearing would let him know the moment she stepped out of the cave. Quietly, he left her to her work.

Out on the ledge in front of the Anasazi cave dwelling, Kin sat and dangled his legs over the cliff. Night had fallen, and he watched Venus rise in a cloudless sky. Celene had seen through his most intimate fears. He felt spooked by the alien environment and she'd picked up on it. Damn the Anaz-voohri for what they did to the human race.

Why did Kin accept this assignment? He did it for the survival of humanity. And for that same humanity, he must kill the only person who shared his passion and wasn't scared of him. He had to execute the only woman who could possibly ever understand him and make him complete. No woman ever related to him as an equal before, without fear of his physical abilities. Celene knew what he could do and she still made him feel good about himself.

Even in the face of his obvious disdain, she hadn't shunned him, until just now. But he understood she couldn't bear any distraction during this important task. Too much was at stake. The fact that she still wanted him, knowing what kind of man he was, made Kin want her at his side.

He still marveled at the fact that Celene didn't try to hurt him when he withheld his affection. She hadn't turned against him. She knew he had killed before, and she didn't look at him in disgust, like the last woman he'd dated.

Only one other girl had made Kin feel good about himself before, Shani, the teenager with whom he had escaped the Center for Evolutionary Medicine in China. She, too, understood him. They had suffered the same violations.

The faraway yowl of a lone coyote reached his keen ears. Visitors? All senses alert, Kin checked his phase-gun and scrutinized the riverbed down below. Even he couldn't see the Land Rover, camouflaged under a tent and desert netting, but anyone on the ground at close range would notice it. Kin didn't expect anyone from Mythos. Actually, they had agreed to keep radio silence to avoid detection. Did the Beechcraft pilot squeal? Kin could have killed him to make sure he didn't, but it seemed unnecessary at the time and might have attracted attention. Was Kin getting soft? No. He just couldn't kill the innocent, only the scum and the rotten apples.

Kin jumped when he heard Celene walk out of the shallow cave behind him. Damn, he'd been distracted again.

"Something the matter? You look somber." She sounded excited. Probably the discovery.

"Just a coyote. Any progress?"

"I translated one shard. Nineteen to go."

"That's fantastic. It's only been two hours. You look like you need some rest, though." He rejoiced that she'd done so well.

"I'm bushed." She rubbed her forearms. "Early March and still no rainfall in the canyons this year. Makes for warm days but chilly nights."

"That could mean forest fires in early spring, too." Kin ladled a mug of hot tea from the pot and handed it to her with a health bar. "Find out anything important?"

"Not yet. Just an interesting study of our planet."
She warmed her hands around the cup and blew on the
steam. "The Anaz-voohri don't like us much for
destroying our natural resources."

"Can't blame them for that." Kin fetched a blanket
and covered her shoulders. "Anything else?"

"Thanks." Celene adjusted the blanket around her
shoulders. "I found out the meaning of the carving at
the cave entrance."

"In the shards?" Kin wondered about the
connection.

"It's part of their history." She bit into the health
bar and licked her lips as she chewed.

"What happened?"

Celene took her time to swallow and take a sip of
tea, as if enjoying her secret knowledge. "Apparently,
the aliens who abducted the Anasazi long ago didn't
abduct them all. They chose the strongest, the smartest,
the wisest of the tribes, only the most promising
specimens. About five hundred of them."

"What about the others?" Kin poured himself a
mug of black tea from the pan. The strong aroma
reminded him of China. "Our history says they all
disappeared."

Celene nodded. "Those considered sub-standard
had to be eliminated."

"Killed? Why? Sounds a little harsh." Kin blew
on the hot tea.

"Hum." Celene finished chewing. "According to
their history, these aliens had no tolerance for flaws."

"That's no reason to commit genocide." Kin

recoiled at the thought. "How were they killed?"

"In the foulest manner." Celene paused and took a breath as if what she had to say required an effort. "Before leaving in their spacecraft, the aliens released a spore into the surrounding forest. Then upon takeoff, they ignited a blaze, and the forest burned with green smoke."

"Green?"

Celene seemed to search for words. "The smoke from the burning spores genetically altered the remaining population and transformed them into hideous demons and bloodthirsty cannibals."

Kin fed a fire log to the campfire. "Cannibals? Like on the pictograph?"

"It's a side effect of the green smoke, the uncontrollable need to eat raw flesh. Within days, the mutation melted their flesh and disintegrated their bones. They must have died in excruciating pain."

"Vanished without a trace." Kin shook his head. "No wonder Archeologists found no human remains, while the corn still lay stored in sealed stone sheds."

"Yes. Those who weren't abducted didn't die of starvation, or drought, or some slow disease. They killed each other and their bodies simply dissolved."

Kin noticed the campfire light made Celene's dark jade eyes dance, and when she laid a gentle hand on his thigh, he felt his resolve melt away. How could he refuse her? And if they only had a few days left together, why not make her happy... Hell, why not enjoy her loving ministrations? After all, Kin had to live up to his reckless reputation for taking risks. He'd face the consequences when the time came.

Kin reached for her hand and brought it to his lips.

Celene seemed to glow in the firelight. "I've never felt like this before. Have you ever been in love?"

Her soft expression called to him and he didn't try to resist. "Her name was Shani. We were very young."

"Shani? It means wonderful in ancient Egyptian."

"And wonderful she was. We met at the CEM in China, where ORION conducted experiments." Kin felt silent at the painful memory.

"Genetic experiments? On you?"

"On me, on her, on many people." He scoffed. "To them we were just lab rats."

"What happened?"

"ORION's men killed her during our escape." Kin looked away to hide his emotions. Shani had died in his arms before her life had a chance to fully blossom. Some day, Carrick would pay for her life, too.

Tears welled in Celene's eye as she smiled. "And you loved each other?"

Kin nodded. Dare he love someone marked for death and suffer the same torture as before? No, worse. This time he would be the executioner and would have to bear all the guilt as well. He started to doubt he could carry out the order when it came to it.

But Kin didn't want to think about that now. He just wanted to drown in the deep ocean of Celene's eyes and capture a little corner of paradise before his life went glum, Hopelessness settled in again. For he couldn't see any possible chance for him of ever finding peace much less happiness.

When Celene parted her lips so close to his, he took them with the desperation of a man on sitting on

Death Row. He savored the moment, knowing there could be no future for them. To his surprise, Celene responded to his wantonness in kind, and he wondered whether she knew she would soon die.

* * * * *

The next morning, after freshening up, Celene donned a clean sweatshirt and a pair of shorts then met Kin on the ledge. She found him smiling and playful and thanked the powers that be for his radical change of attitude. Wearing black jeans and a sweater, as usual, he looked rather fierce with the phase-gun on one hip and a hunting knife on the other, like an old-fashioned cowboy. He stirred a mixture in the pan that smelled like heaven.

"Breakfast?" Celene felt hungry.

"Boiled cereals with dry fruits and nuts." He handed her a cup of coffee.

Celene accepted the warm cup and tasted the brew. Perfect. Cream no sugar. She sat on the warm sandstone close to the fire. She felt the morning sun bathe her face as it started to heat up the rock ledge, announcing another gorgeous day. With Kin at her side, she felt happier than she'd ever been.

They both ate the healthy fare from the pan. Sipping the rest of her coffee, Celene stretched her bare legs and yawned. The dry sage clinging to the sandstone rustled in the faint breeze.

Kin froze, staring at a spot to her left. "Don't move," he whispered urgently.

Still as a stone relic, Celene held her breath and

glanced sideways. Her heart jumped in her chest. Two feet away, a rattlesnake flashed its tongue to smell her. She'd mistaken his rattle for the wind in the dry sage. Kin pulled out his phase-gun and pointed it in her direction. Her blood gelled and her heart fell in the pit of her stomach. Whom was he targeting?

When the rattlesnake bared it fangs and sprung, phase fire flashed by, sizzling through the air, barely missing Celene. The shot decapitated the snake. Celene released her tension in one long breath, trying to calm the wild beat of her heart. She crawled away when the severed head of the rattlesnake and the few inches of body still attached to it advanced on her, slithering on the ground, intent on inflicting the poisonous bite.

Another round of phase fire exploded the snake's head in a bloody mess. The head segment stopped moving. On the ground, the length of the snake's body still twitched, oozing blood onto the sandy rock. The smell of seared flesh made Celene want to heave. She jumped when Kin laid a hand on her shoulder.

"Are you all right?" He looked pale and shaken. "The snake hardly rattled. I'm glad for my good hearing."

"I'm okay now. Thanks." Celene brushed rock dust from her shorts. "Never met such an aggressive rattlesnake before. They usually avoid people in the wild." She hoped her fright didn't show too much.

Kin scanned the ground around them in a circular motion. "Maybe it's the feel of this place. It creeps me out, too. I hope there aren't too many like him this close."

Although she loved most animals and actively defended their rights, Celene didn't feel comfortable around poisonous snakes. She motioned toward the snake body still moving on the ground. "Is it dead?"

"Not quite." Kin grabbed the length of the snake. The writhing body coiled tightly around his arm. He showed the severed end to Celene. "See? The heart is still beating." Kin pulled out the knife from his belt and stabbed the heart neat and clean. Only then did the snake go limp.

Relieved, Celene laughed nervously.

Kin grinned. He held his kill at arm's length and shook it to make it rattle. "Guess what we're having for dinner tonight?"

* * * * *

As Celene strolled back to the alien dome to resume her translation, she wondered whether Kin might actually have feelings for her, and the thought warmed her inside. She caught herself humming a strange tune. She wanted his love. Did it mean she loved him, too? She certainly never felt that way before about anyone. Since the first time she saw him at the British Museum, she felt a strong connection. It couldn't be just lust, although that played a part in how she felt about Kin.

Once inside the dome, the amount of material to translate overwhelmed her, but she decided to proceed methodically. As soon as she started, however, the translation came along quickly, but she had to slow down when the words failed her. Not the alien words, but the English words, to accurately relate all the horror of the history recorded in the crystal shards.

These aliens had requested human sacrifices as a disciplinary measure, drinking fresh blood as a delicacy. The rituals reminded Celene of Aztec, Mayan and Incan ceremonies she had studied in Central and South America. Did the same aliens pass themselves as gods among these various tribes? Though the theory seemed scientifically farfetched twenty years ago, it now made perfect sense and could explain the similarities in all those cultures.

The tone of the narration indicated that the Anaz-voohri, the mutated descendants of the chosen Anasazi, approved of such methods and shared the opinion that sub-standard humans didn't deserve to live. Celene felt appalled by the concept. What would happen if they decided to invade earth? Slavery? Human sacrifices? They'd decimate the human population, or worse, kill everyone. They had to be stopped.

Still, Celene hadn't found anything relating to an Anaz-voohri invasion plan. She went through the shards one by one on the decoding device and translated as fast as she could. She even found information about the filovirus diseases that caused the epidemic of hemorrhagic fevers. She didn't quite understand all the scientific implications, but someone else might make sense of her literal translation.

By the end of the day, she had only a few shards left to decipher but she was exhausted and decided to leave them for the next day. She suspected they must contain important information, and she didn't want to make a mistake. Besides, she felt eager to join Kin who must feel lonely by the campfire.

When she emerged from the cave dwellings onto the ledge, Kin had prepared some food from the nitrogen-pacs. Beans and tomatoes with bread and cheese, and of course, the length of the rattlesnake roasted on a spit.

"Sorry, we don't have wine to go with this gourmet meal. I'm afraid we'll have to make do with tea."

"Tea will be fine. I can use the warmth." Celene shivered. "What did you do all day? I hardly saw you when you brought me lunch."

"Kill a snake, skin a snake, work out, nap, make sandwiches, cook a snake, like a perfect cave-woman." He grinned. "How is the translation going? Anything interesting?"

"Medical information I'm sure we can use. Want to hear some of the recordings?"

"Not now. Did you make a backup?"

"You can keep that one." She tossed him a memory chip. "Just plug it into your epad to listen to it. It's going faster than I thought. I'll finish within a day or two."

Kin's expression grew serious. "That doesn't give us much time left together."

Celene laughed. "What can possibly prevent us from seeing each other after we finish here?"

"Work." Sadness darkened his eyes.

Although she didn't quite understand this sudden change of mood, Celene remained optimistic. "How about having some of that delicious-smelling food?".

Kin's infectious grin returned as he served the rattlesnake with obvious pride. "Ever ate snake before?"

"In India, with my stepfather." Celene cherished the memory. "It really does taste like chicken."

They ate watching the stars. When the Pleiades star cluster came into view, Celene paid close attention to the star that bore her name, Celaeno.

When the Orion system waxed in the east, Kin said, "Let's sleep inside the cave tonight. I feel exposed under all these stars."

Celene chuckled and helped him drag the blankets, mats and sleeping bags further inside the shallow cave.

Kin spread the mats. "You never know who's watching from above."

Celene sobered at the thought. If earth's satellites could pick up a grain of sand from orbit, there was no telling what an advanced race could observe from space. She felt herself flush. "They might have learned a trick or two if they were watching last night."

Kin smiled and dropped onto the makeshift bed. He patted the space next to him. "I don't want them to become too adept at seducing earth women."

"Seducing, hey!" She threw the blankets on him and joined him on the mats. "May be I could contribute and teach them a thing or two on how to seduce earth men."

Laughing, Kin took her into his strong arms, and Celene felt that life could never get better than that. An amazing dig and an amazing man to share her sleeping bag.

* * * * *

Kin awoke in the middle of the night and sat up, hand on his phase-gun. What had awakened him? A coyote? A rattlesnake? A mountain cat? An unwanted visitor? Next to him in the sleeping bag, Celene stirred in her sleep. God, she was beautiful! And how she trusted him. She looked totally relaxed, like a child safe in her bed, unsuspecting of the wolf who watched her sleep.

Kin hadn't slept that soundly since his parents' murders. His dreams crawled with acts of hatred, revenge, and the guilt he felt at all the lives he had taken during his murderous spree against ORION to avenge his parents, and later as a paid assassin. Now that he'd relinquished the responsibility to Mythos, he still took responsibility for the lives he had to take.

Now, even the guilt at the killing he must yet perform woke him up at night. Although Kin understood why Celene must die, he couldn't accept it. She was so good, and loving, and beautiful, and what he felt for her, that strange attraction, that unexplainable need to remain close to her, threatened his very sanity. Could his desire possibly overcome his genetic programming and years of intense training?

He heard that faint purring again, like a faraway plane circling low above the canyons. That's what had awakened him. A dangerous thing, flying a helo in the canyons at night. Mythos? No. They would have contacted him first through his communicator. ORION? How could they possibly know to look for them, here...unless someone had squealed? Then again, they had spies everywhere. It could even be some hybrids shadowing Celene to report her activities to the Anaz-voohri.

Good thing the cave overhang hid their heat signature. With the car electronically shielded and camouflaged below, Kin felt certain their campsite couldn't be detected from the sky. But if Carrick suspected their presence in the canyons, ORION would soon deploy a full scale search.

Kin spent the remaining hours until dawn watching for signs of possible visitors but heard nothing more. He heated water for coffee on the propane camping stove, careful to shield the glare of the flame. One could never be too cautious. As soon as the eastern sky turned pink, Kin gently shook Celene's shoulder. "Get up! I think you should get an early start."

"Hey!" Celene blinked and rubbed her eyes. "Good morning to you, too."

"Sorry to rush you." He regretted his brusque tone. "I just want to make sure we can finish and get out of here before ORION picks up our trail."

Celene sat up in her sleeping bag and looked around. "I have to go find a bush. I'll be right back."

Kin watched her rise and disappear, literally, behind a sage bush growing on the ledge. Some use of invisibility.

Celene reappeared next to him, startling him. "How could Carrick possibly find us here?"

"ORION has ways of finding out." He handed her a cup of steaming instant coffee. "Cream, no sugar."

"Thanks." She smiled so trustingly. "Jake, my martial arts teacher in Montreal, always says, never underestimate your enemy." She sipped the hot brew.

"Wise advice." Kin poured himself another cup

and sat on the rocky ground.

Celene scooted next to him and laid a casual hand on his thigh. "Kin, I like your company, your lovemaking, and your conversation. But sometimes you seem so faraway. I hope we are not strangers, are we?"

As much as her touch had sent Kin into searing heat, her comment stabbed him deep, and he moved away from her. No, they were anything but strangers. "Let's focus on getting the job done for now."

"For now?" She smiled again. "Then when the relics are translated and safe at GSS, can we think about a real relationship?" The hope in her face made him flinch.

Kin cleared his voice. He found it difficult to speak as a knot formed in his throat. "We'll see…"

"Then I better get to work." She rose and brushed her shorts. "I'll take rations to the dome, so I won't have to stop for lunch. It's better if I am not disturbed. I don't have much left to translate. I should be done tonight or tomorrow morning."

So soon? But Kin only nodded, trying to cover his distress. Once she was finished with the translation, Celene would have to be eliminated without delay. He just couldn't stand the thought. So he took a slow breath and waved back as Celene started toward the back of the shallow cave. He felt gloom invade his thoughts as he watched her climb through the ruined city on her way to the tunnel that led to the dome.

* * * * *

Upon resuming the translation of the last relics, Celene finally came upon the information she expected to find. Operation Pleiades might give her a clue as to who or what she was. Long reports told of covert operations on earth, secret interventions, a hybrid program, where half-humans, half-Anaz-voohri, made to look like regular humans, infiltrated human society to serve the alien purpose. Thousands of them, engineered in special labs right here on Earth.

The list went on for pages, about two thousand names. Celene dictated all the names in her epad, looking for anyone she'd recognize. To her horror, she found Armand and Dionne Dupres, her own adoptive parents. But if her adoptive parents were hybrids working for the Anaz-voohri, why did her father want to save the human race?

Then something dawned on Celene. If humans rated below Anaz-voohri standards, so did the hybrids. Her adoptive parents might have realized their lives would be in jeopardy once they outlived their usefulness. She looked for Kin Raidon among the names and found his parents. But Kin did not show on the list of hybrids. She breathed a sigh of relief. Although he may not be totally human, at least, he didn't work for the Anaz-voohri.

Celene shuddered when she read about the abduction of seven little girls twenty years ago. Her childhood nightmare came back to life when she saw the irrefutable proof. It was all there, seven reports on seven abductions performed in one summer night. The Anaz-voohri had renamed the girls Maya, Celene, Tori, Ally, Electra, Tierney, and Maeve. Wasn't Maya the name of the girl accused of creating the blackout on the east coast last December? Maya Rembrandt.

Reading the shards further, Celene translated reports on the original families of the abducted girls. She stared at the words and pictures and stopped translating. For the very first time, she saw the portraits of her biological mother and father, Palani and Hawika Harrington...

Celene now remembered her childhood bedroom in a simple house on the beach. Through the open window, she could hear the surf. Her mother smiled with large green eyes and read her stories of the islands, while Celene listened, hugging her teddy bear Punu. She remembered the feel of the sand under her bare feet, the gentle breath of the trade winds in the palm trees, and the trill of the exotic birds. Did Celene's parents still live? Suddenly she wanted to meet them.

As Celene translated the seven girls' progress over two years of DNA manipulation in the Pleiades system, flashbacks of probes and scary surgical devices brought tears to her eyes and constricted her throat. Celene remembered pain so excruciating that she had blocked the memories in her subconscious. Now, as she read, these memories slowly started to flow, and she had to stop several times during her translation, overwhelmed by the intensity of her hatred for the Anaz-voohri.

The records indicated that the Anaz-voohri had suppressed the seven girls' memories, but Celene had the advantage. These records could help her remember. Feverishly, she kept translating, wondering what dark secrets the Anaz-voohri had buried in the deepest recess of her mind...

CHAPTER TEN

Although he couldn't help but admire Celene's dedication to her work, Kin felt as if she had discarded him. She had insisted he leave her alone, and he understood her need for concentration. Considering their renewed interest in each other and the passion they shared at night, his immediate presence would distract her and slow the deciphering process. He would have preferred to spend the little time they had left with her.

But the mission came first. Its success depended on Celene's ability to translate the alien language quickly. Too many unexplainable accidents had plagued the world in the last few years. The cataclysm when the ship crashed in the Carpathian Mountains and the rampaging hemorrhagic fevers had been only the beginning. The blackout that deprived thirteen eastern states of their computer capabilities in December, triggered by another Pleiades sister, along with Celene's new powers indicated imminent danger. The Anaz-voohri's plan to take over the planet had started to unfold.

Kin couldn't help but wish for another solution to his dilemma. He couldn't imagine never again holding Celene in his arms, never drinking from the fountain of her mouth or drowning in the depths of her dark jade eyes. Each time she touched him, whether by accident or on purpose, she sent lusty currents rippling through his body.

The worst part was, he suspected Celene had started to love him. Apparently he had that power over her, and the knowledge made him want her even more. But he couldn't let his personal feelings weaken his resolve. Too much depended on his ability to kill Celene.

Kin had toyed with the idea of incarcerating her instead, but her powers of invisibility would make any prison inadequate. Even taking her to a deserted island could not neutralize the threat she represented. When the time came, the Anaz-voohri could find her and transport her wherever she needed to be to carry on the destructive mission programmed in her DNA. If only he knew what that mission was...

With nothing more to do than keep an eye out for intruders, Kin decided to go for morning practice on the top of the cliff. From up there, he could survey his surroundings in every direction, and if danger came from the sky, he could see it coming and blend with the rock. The mesa on the top of the cliff would offer a large flat surface to practice his favorite weapons, those of the traditional ninja.

As he wouldn't need the phase-gun for that, he left it in his bag in the shallow cave. He picked up his throwing knives, stars and sword and secured them to his belt. Then he started the climb up the cliff, looking forward to a healthy workout to exercise his muscles and focus on his next kill. Celene.

* * * * *

In the alien dome, Celene now felt strangely detached. Why had she sent Kin away for the day? No matter. She just didn't want him near. She felt on the verge of an important discovery and didn't feel like sharing it. Instinctively, she'd kept a particular shard for last, for no other reason than a strong gut feeling.

Since deciphering the shard about the abduction of the seven girls, Celene suspected the crystal she'd kept for last might explain more of what lay hidden in her mind. Why could she read the alien language despite its radical differences from the Anasazi petroglyphs? Had she learned it during her time among the Anaz-voohri? According to the records, she had spent two years with them but only remembered flashes of medical procedures. She recalled the repulsive feel of the examining table. It felt like living skin, not unlike the material of the console that read the shards.

Carefully, she placed the last crystal on the depression of the pedestal. As with the other shards before, the depression took on the jagged shape of the crystal, then the dome filled up with Anaz-voohri glyphs. Driven by a strange force, Celene started to translate but couldn't believe the ramifications of what she read, even as she spoke into the recorder.

"And the seven sisters will awaken in 2023, with powers to defy human ability, and carry on their mission of destruction. Each sister will strike a fatal blow to one part of the planet's population or major defense systems, to prepare for our invasion. In the end, the entire human race, left helpless by our successive strikes, will perish, except for a few flawless specimens destined for reproduction and cloning experiments. Devoid of humans, the virgin planet will return to the rightful heirs of human intelligence, the only superior beings worthy of Earth, the Anaz-voohri, who will rule supreme over all other kind of life."

Horrified, Celene kept translating. "Maya will blend with computer technology to neutralize all electronic devices, severing global communications and rendering the military useless. Celene will unleash a disaster that will transform human beings into bloodthirsty demons, Tori will infect the human race with alien DNA..."

The list went on about deadly diseases for people and machine. Each sister had been implanted with a timed trigger to perform the task programmed in their brain and their DNA. Because of their various paranormal abilities, no one could stop them, even if humanity discovered the invasion plan. Celene sensed such arrogance in the tone of the records, she had to scoff. The Anaz-voohri believed their superior race would assuredly win.

Celene felt certain she would never do anything to transform people into bloodthirsty demons, or trigger any calamity to fall upon the human race, but she shivered at the memory of the pictograph on the stone blocking the cave. If this depicted something that had happened before, could it happen again?

Something Kin had alluded to a few days back still bothered her. He worked for a secret organization and knew about the Pleiades sisters. But when Celene had asked about the seven sisters, he'd remained vague, unwilling to reveal what he knew.

Now Celene understood why ORION pursued her, to eliminate the potential threat she represented for humanity. But if Carrick knew all about the threat Celene represented, so did Kin. Then why did Kin protect her? Or was he just waiting for her to finish translating the relics to do his dirty job? Kin's words rang in her ears again, "After the mission is over, we'll see..."

His moody behavior now made perfect sense. Kin already admitted he was a weapon, a trained ninja, an assassin by definition. He killed for his secret organization. Since he only had a limited knowledge of Anaz-voohri archeology, he could only be here to keep an eye on her then kill her when the time came. Celene felt physically sick at the realization. Her whole body started to shake and she wanted to heave.

* * * * *

Up on the top of the cliff, Kin had been running for over an hour. Even a perfectly engineered body needed practice to maintain its strength and accuracy. DNA only accounted for seventy percent of his skills. He had to work for the other thirty percent. Practice made perfect., and perfect he must remain.

On a flat surface, roughly the size of a football field, Kin kept running in circles for an entire marathon. Then he practiced high jumps, envisioning a virtual vaulting pole that propelled him twenty feet high. When he landed like a cat, he flexed his knees then rolled to soften the impact, something that would shatter normal bones but not his, enhanced through

DNA manipulation. And if by chance he overestimated his physical capabilities, his internal nanobots would quickly repair any injury to his bones and tissues.

Unsheathing the ninja sword, Kin focused on the blade and stilled his mind to perform impeccable *katas*. This rehearsed sprightly dance represented swordplay in synchronicity to an imaginary attacker. The graceful movements, executed in perfect rhythm, transmitted for centuries from master to pupil, remained part of the secret ninja training.

Although traditional weapons slowly disappeared to make room for phase-guns, Kin still respected the ancient ways. In his mind, alien weapons designed for unfair combat had no nobility. Kin saw no honor in them, like he saw no honor in killing Celene...only shame.

At the sound of a helicopter in the distance, Kin lay on the ground and blended with his surroundings. He saw it as an excellent opportunity to practice. Taking a deep breath, he then released it slowly while emptying his mind, and became perfectly still, like a rock, with the color of the rock, the feel of the rock, identifying with the rock itself.

The sound intensified as the chopper flew low, grazing the top of the mesas. Kin noticed no markings on the bird. Could it be Mythos? ORION? The bird was too noisy and probably carried some tourists. Still, so close to the end of a successful mission, Kin couldn't take any chances. Secrecy and stealth had always served him best, so he remained hidden and turned off his screamer implant to end the torture to his sensitive ears.

The chopper hovered in the area, dancing slowly above each cliff, descending into each canyon. After what seemed like an hour, Kin felt cramped, immobile on the ground, but for the sake of training he didn't allow himself to move. Obviously, if someone planned to spy on them, they didn't know exactly where to look. Good.

After the helicopter flew away in a westerly direction, Kin finally released the image of the rock from his mind. As he moved his extremities to reestablish circulation, he felt the tingling of oxygen returning to the muscles. Within seconds, he rose and stretched, then walked to the edge of the cliff to look down. If he couldn't see the SUV hidden under the camouflage tent, then the helicopter couldn't see it either. Reassured, he decided to eat his ration lunch then resume his training.

After he'd thrown all his stars and knives to the only target he could find, the bleached trunk of a desiccated tree, Kin noticed the sun lowering in the west and ended his practice day with a few somersaults and stretching exercises. Gathering his weapons, he lowered himself over the edge of the cliff and started the arduous descent to the cave overhang.

He assumed Celene must still be inside the dome, so he would prepare dinner. As he opened his bag to store his traditional weapon, he noticed something was missing. His phase-gun. He always remembered where he left his gun, and he knew for certain he'd left it in the bag. Had someone visited the camp while he was up top? Keeping his stars, knives, and sword on hand, Kin blended with the shadows and went in search of

Celene. He didn't dare call her. The intruder might still be lurking. He hoped she was safe.

As he emerged from the tunnel into the dome, he stopped and peeked inside. No Celene. The relics were gone, too. Only a dim light remained in the dome, but something else caught his attention, a loud humming sound that hadn't been there before. Where did it come from?

Advancing cautiously, Kin reached the center of the seemingly empty room. Was Celene there but invisible? Had an ORION operative taken her? Abducted by the Anaz-voohri? On the side of the central console, Kin noticed a new cylindrical device of the same material as the central console. The new device showed alien petroglyphs. Kin could barely decipher the few words that blinked in sequence. "Device activated!" That's what it said. What kind of device? Who activated it?

At a loss, Kin didn't know what to make of all this. Certain that any activated device could only bring bad news, he tried to figure out how to deactivate it but found his knowledge of the alien language lacking. "Celene? Are you here?"

No answer. His keen hearing revealed no human sound, not even a breath other than his own. Only the sinister humming of the alien device filled the dome and his mind with foreboding. Would the dome self-destruct? Kin had to get out of there. "Celene, if you can hear me, get out. This thing sounds bad. Save yourself!"

Running back to the ledge, Kin gathered a few survival supplies and realized some were already gone.

Some of the food and water along with Celene's bags were missing. He also couldn't find the keys to the Land Rover. Had he left them with the car? In a hurry, burning his gloveless hands on the rope, Kin lowered himself down the cliff. When he reached the ground, he realized the vehicle was gone, too. Damn!

Only one thing to do. Kin had no other choice. He tapped the medallion on his chest. "Mythos? This is Icarus. Target is missing. Repeat. Target is missing. I'm stuck here and I need help, now."

* * * * *

The ORION headquarters flotilla anchored off the coast of Nova Scotia

In his headquarters aboard the SS Clinton, Carrick, commander of the ORION task force, cleaned his glasses to curb his impatience. Through the bulkhead, he felt the reassuring drone of the powerful ship engines.

The last time he'd seen, or rather smelled, the invisible Dupres bitch, was in his bunker in London. She'd kicked him in the plexus then fled, along with his precious relics. Today his luck might turn for the better.

"Sir," Flavia, his tall and curvy assistant, with black hair pinned back in a severe bun and impeccable makeup, stepped into the small office through the open hatch. Her large firm breasts pushed against the tight blue uniform jacket as she bent over his desk to drop a data disk. "We've got the call from Arizona on the secure line. I'm transferring it." Flavia's slight Greek accent matched her olive skin. Very reserved and professional, she walked into the adjacent room and closed the hatch to give him privacy, leaving behind the faintest trail of perfume.

Carrick liked discretion in his staff, and big tits. Although he would never dream of having an affair with his assistant, he enjoyed contemplating the possibility. A good military man always kept his options open.

His personal communicator chimed. "Carrick here. Did you confirm the findings?"

At the other end of the line, the excited voice of the ORION operative in Arizona came in uneven spurts over the sound of a helicopter. "Aye, sir. We picked up Miss Dupres' trail in Montreal. She took a private jet to Arizona. We squeezed a Beechcraft pilot into telling us he took a couple of tourists over the canyons two days ago. A little early for tourist season. An oriental man and a woman who fits the description. They drove a Land Rover back to the area the pilot showed us on a map. A night search turned out negative for a campsite, but today we got lucky."

Carrick felt his net around the Dupres bitch tighten, and his heart pumped a little faster. "What happened?"

"As we were flying low over the canyons, we saw a Land Rover leaving the area, way too fast for a tourist vehicle. We followed it unobtrusively from the air. No one was driving the vehicle. Then all of a sudden, a woman appeared behind the wheel out of nowhere!"

"Good work." Carrick felt himself flush.

"High-powered lenses confirmed the description and face structure recognition of Celene Dupres. It's a hundred percent match."

"Where is she now?"

"On the road, driving south toward Phoenix."

Carrick could almost taste his victory.

"There's something else."

"What?"

"We detected alien readings from her luggage."

"The relics?"

"Possibly. Part of it anyway. It's all in one bag."

Carrick's luck had finally turned for the better. "It must be the shards." What was the bitch doing with the shards in the middle of nowhere?

"What should we do, sir?"

"Follow her and keep me posted. I'm flying to Phoenix tonight, but you can reach me on my communicator."

Carrick ended the communication. "Flavia?"

The loyal assistant poked her dark head through the hatch door. "Sir?"

"Get Blanchard on the phone."

Flavia nodded and her dark head popped away.

When his communicator chimed, Carrick pushed the button. "Blanchard?"

"Allo? Who is this?"

"Jason Carrick, you moron. How are you doing with that alien decoding device?" Carrick congratulated himself for letting the device go to America with Blanchard instead of London. Otherwise, those civilian pirates would have seized it with the rest of the relics. How he wished he could get his hands on Mythos, but he knew a higher authority that could take away his job protected them. President Grant spoke highly of them. Better to wait, for now. After Carrick gathered enough power, he would get rid of them all.

Blanchard kept talking but Carrick only caught his last sentence. "I think it would work better if we could find a larger dome. The one I'm using is too small and distorts the images so much we cannot read them."

"Don't worry about that. Right now, I need you to take the device to Phoenix Arizona. Flavia will arrange your flight. I'll meet you there."

"Right now?"

Carrick hated civilians. They always wanted to discuss their orders. "We may have the shards, and I want you to put that machine to the test."

"Great! I'll start packing."

"Be ready to leave in thirty minutes."

"But this is delicate engineering." Blanchard's French accent grew heavier. "You can't just rush it. It has to be properly protected for shipping."

"Do whatever the fuck you have to do, but do it fast and get your ass to Phoenix on the double. Understood?

"Okay." Blanchard sighed. "I will do my best."

As he severed the call, Carrick wished he didn't have to deal with lousy civilians like Blanchard. The man was a two-bit hybrid hunter with a Ph.D. who thought he served an important cause. But Carrick would not let anything tarnish his stroke of good luck. He grinned. He might finally catch one of the Pleiades sisters. And this time, the Dupres bitch didn't know he was watching her. He had the advantage of surprise.

But Carrick wanted to be there for the fray. He didn't want some dumb operative fucking up this operation. This catch would require finesse. Celene Dupres had shown she could take care of herself, and he would not let her escape. Not this time.

* * * * *

Celene kept her mind on the dashboard satellite map as she drove the Land Rover at an unreasonable speed through canyons and dry riverbeds. Avoiding the main roads, she headed southwest. If she timed it right, she would reach Phoenix before nightfall, maybe stop for a rest and change into civilized clothes.

No one would notice a lone one-nighter in a cheap motel in a big city. Kin's friends would probably watch the airport. Celene planned to head for the Mexican border before dawn, ditch the car, and slip through customs in invisible mode. Mexico still didn't extradite, even for the GSS.

Celene felt like a fool. She trusted Kin, of all people. Now she was positive his seduction of her was a ploy to win her trust. He never had any feelings for her. How he must have laughed at her naivety. But now that she knew Kin meant to kill her, she was determined to show him who he set himself up against. Celene knew she could survive in the wild. She didn't fear Kin. She'd escaped him, hadn't she? He'd fallen for her lame excuse of wanting to work alone. On second thought, that had been before she discovered he wanted to kill her. No matter. It all worked out.

Guilt at abandoning Kin in the canyons gnawed at her conscience, but she knew him to be resourceful. He'd get out of that rattlesnake trap one way or another.

And then she knew he would come after her. Celene caressed the cold barrel of the phase-gun lying next to her on the passenger seat. She'd use it if she had to, but she didn't want to have to kill anyone. Even Kin. Although she knew he was her enemy, she could not stand to see him die. It was a weakness on her part. So much for not letting personal feelings interfere with her independence.

By the time she reached the proximity of I-17 near New River, night had fallen, and Celene saw some strange activity in the distance. Several helicopters and emergency vehicles, headed north with sirens blaring. At first, she thought it was the police, then she noticed several ambulances and fire trucks following. Must have been a serious accident.

Celene stopped at a La Quinta Inn along I-17 on Greenway Avenue. She parked the car in the shadows in the back parking lot where the lights did not reach her. No one would notice it at night, and Celene would be gone before daylight. She made herself invisible and quietly entered the lobby. The night clerk was busy watching a game on his plasma screen. Celene squeezed behind the desk and checked the rows of keys. Indication of many empty rooms.

Careful not to make any noise, Celene lifted a key from the hook. It became transparent upon contact. Heart beating wildly, she discreetly pushed the glass door and walked out. She found the room easily at the end of the complex. She entered it, locked the door and closed the blinds. Then she turned on the light and made herself visible again.

The modest room felt like pure luxury after the past

days in the wild. Celene had brought food and water and wouldn't need to show her face anywhere tonight. She dropped the bags on the bed and went to the bathroom to draw a bath. Glad to shed her dusty clothes, she enjoyed the warm water and took her time. After scrubbing all the grime from her skin and hair, she wrapped herself in a large towel, dried her hair, then returned to the bedroom.

She pulled ration packs out of her bag then turned on the plasma screen, just to make sure she hadn't become a national fugitive. If Kin had pulled a few strings, he might try to use the police to find her. But the headline news talked about something else altogether.

With evident consternation, the anchorman commented on a large fire that had just broken out in northern Arizona. The forestry department suspected arson. The high country made it difficult to access the blaze. But the most disturbing feature of the fires, even from a distance, was a green halo around the flames that made them look surreal, and a thick green smoke. Celene's heart faltered in her chest. Green smoke!

CHAPTER ELEVEN

Huffing despite his perfect physical condition, Kin braced his feet against the egg-shaped boulder and pulled on the cables. He'd never move that boulder by himself. Letting out a disgusted breath, he let go of the rope and wiped the sweat off his brow. He resisted the urge to scratch an itch under his arm, where the black sweater had stiffened from perspiration. He needed a shower. Sponge baths with a gallon of water from a bottle didn't quite do the job.

It would take two or three strong men to lift that boulder, and when the Mythos helicopter arrived, it would only have one pilot aboard. The fewer people involved in this operation the better. Beside, the bird would not land, just extract him, as ordered.

Kin had taken pictures inside the alien dome for his report to Mythos, but now he had to conceal the entrance of the cave. It wouldn't do to have adventurous tourists get into the dome. Kin touched his medallion. "Mythos? Icarus here. We need to send a high-level clearance team to close the dome entrance and sanitize the site. Three men should do it."

The familiar male voice from Mythos came loud and clear through his screamer. "It's going to take a while before we can gather a team, brief it, and get it there. They'll probably get there in the morning."

"I don't expect tourists at night, but do your best. There is equipment to remove, too."

Nothing went right today. Kin felt deceived. His feelings for Celene had clouded his judgment. Had she found information about the seven sisters in the shards? She must have. Otherwise, why would she run away? Or did she figure out days ago that Kin would kill her as soon as she finished the job, and she'd waited for the perfect opportunity? He scoffed at his own gullibility. Why didn't he guess her intent? She had fled without giving him the last of the recordings, possibly the most important. Why had he trusted her?

Deep down, though, Kin felt glad he didn't have to kill her right now. He still clung to the hope that he would find a way to keep her alive, although he had no idea how he could possibly manage it. He admired her astuteness. When did she drive off? Since he didn't hear the car leave, she must have left while the helicopter hovered over the neighboring canyons. And if it was ORION lurking this morning, how did she escape their scrutiny? Or did she? She could have fallen prey to Carrick's men.

No. Although he couldn't be sure, Kin suspected Celene smart enough to escape them. Her powers of invisibility gave her the advantage. But where did she go? If she fled during the helicopter flight, she'd been gone for hours and would have a considerable head start. Kin berated himself for underestimating her.

The map on her epad showed the Mythos helicopter within range but Kin couldn't hear it. Good, they'd sent a stealth bird. He went out onto the ledge. The sinking sun in the west bathed the canyons in golden light. He pulled an emergency flare out of his bag and launched it to signal the pilot.

Within minutes, the chopper hovered quietly at his level, close to the ledge, barely emitting a purr. Kin saw the pilot motion for him to get down, then the bird turned sideways and directed its javelin in his direction. Kin dropped to the ground. Was the pilot going to shoot him? Kin heard the whiz of a cable through the air and the clang of the javelin piercing the rock. The cable joining the javelin to the helicopter tightened.

Seizing the handle hanging from the cable, Kin let himself slide all the way to the helicopter cabin and hoisted himself up inside. The pilot disengaged the cable and the bird veered away and gained altitude.

Kin dropped into the co-pilot seat. "Were you trying to shoot me with that thing?"

The pilot grinned behind his radio mike. "Where to, Boss?" Kin remembered working with him before and liked the guy. A good agent, just a little reckless, like most operatives in the field.

"I'm not familiar with Arizona." It was Kin's first mission in the area. "What's the nearest city where we have an office and a decent lab?"

"Phoenix. That's where I flew from."

"Then head home." Kin felt inside his breast pocket to make sure the memory chip containing the two days of translation was still there.

The pilot glanced at him. "We're going to have to go around a ways. There's a forest fire between here and Phoenix, a big one." He pointed ahead. "It's a no-fly zone."

"Isn't it a little early for forest fires?" Kin watched

the ominous plume of smoke in the distance. He hadn't been able to see it from the ledge. The incandescent green smoke looked like a radioactive halo in the golden sunset.

"Isn't that green smoke weird?" The pilot returned his attention to the controls.

"Weird indeed." Kin remembered the pictograph on the boulder blocking the cave and the story it told. He fished from his pants pocket the powder sample from the boulder. He'd need a complete analysis. "Let's get to the lab first."

"What about your lost target? You want to send a portrait to the local police and the FBI? With the fire taking precedence, they may not get it on the network tonight."

"No," Kin said in an intense whisper.

The pilot didn't seem to hear and went on. "We could tell them she is the suspected arsonist. That would get her face on the news. Then we could pull a few strings and get her back."

Kin raised his voice a notch. "I don't trust the local police. Too many ORION spies. Besides, she must be far away by now. We'll have to trace her ourselves." Kin wondered how much the pilot knew about his mission. Probably not much. He'd only had time for a speedy briefing.

Kin had a very bad feeling about that fire. It couldn't be a coincidence. And if it had anything to do with the drawing in the cave, did Celene trigger it? Was that the calamity she was supposed to unleash? If it was, Kin had failed his mission to prevent it, and now he must circumvent the damage.

"A good old hunt, then?" The pilot grinned. "Like the old days."

Kin couldn't help but like the man. "A dangerous hunt. The woman is armed with a phase-gun and she's smart." If Celene had realized all her potential, whatever it might be, could Kin catch her before her trail ran cold?

* * * * *

Somewhere above Maine, the ORION jet streaked west over the United States toward Phoenix, Carrick smoothed his impeccable hair and stared at the plasma screen turned to an Arizona news channel. What kind of sick fuck had started a fire in the region of his operation? Carrick hated surprises. This would create chaos in the area and crimp his local operatives. He didn't like it one bit.

Carrick turned to Flavia in the next seat. "Contact our local agent."

Flavia was already making the connection on her epad through headquarters and handed him the device. "Here, sir."

"We need to find a dome for the reading device. Preferably a large one. Know of any dome in the Phoenix area?" The silence at the other end of the line infuriated Carrick. "Well?"

"We are checking, sir. There is a planetarium in the Science Museum."

"A planetarium? I guess that's a large dome. Requisition the whole building immediately and make it secure. A man named Emile Blanchard is coming to install a device in the dome. Give him all the help he requires and have him meet me when I arrive at Luke Air Force Base.

"Where is the Dupres bitch now?" Carrick was not about to let his prey slip out of his carefully stretched net.

"In Phoenix, sir." The operative sounded proud of his success. "We followed her on the ground to a motel along I-17. We have the car under surveillance. Apparently she didn't check in, but we have spotted her in one of the rooms with spy software. She is smart for an amateur, but she doesn't know we are watching her."

"Good. And don't forget that this amateur has powers of invisibility and can give you the slip anytime. Don't fail me now." Carrick glanced at the blaze on the newscast. Was the plane's plasma screen going bad, or did his eye trick him? "What the fuck is wrong with that fire? It looks green."

"Affirmative, sir," the operative said, matter-of-fact. "The fire has a green phosphorescent halo and emits green smoke." The operative hesitated. "Looks toxic, if you ask me."

"Radioactivity? Chemical warfare? Terrorism?" Carrick had a bad feeling about that fire. The possibility of an Anaz-voohri offensive always lurked in his thoughts. "Could be a trick from our alien enemies. Maybe they are trying to protect that Dupres bitch. Check on that fire and keep me posted."

"Aye, sir. What about the prey?"

"We can't take any chance of her moving again. Assemble a team and go get her now. Use stealth and ruse rather than force, or she will disappear on you.

And I want her alive when I get there. Don't fuck this up, or else. Understand?"

"Aye, sir."

Carrick hoped the local team could carry out the task without glitches. He hated the lack of efficiency of some local offices but couldn't afford to wait. Once he had the bitch, Carrick had no idea how he would extract the important information locked up in her brain, but with the most sophisticated science at his disposal, he would find a way. He'd give anything to study her invisibility trick for military applications. He imagined an army of invisible soldiers. What an advantage he'd have! And totally invisible assassins would work better than mere ninjas.

Although exhilarated at the idea of impending victory, Carrick refused to allow emotions to blind him. The future of the planet rested on his shoulders. With earth ruled by a bunch of idiots only he could lead the fight against the alien enemy and insure a viable future for the human race.

* * * * *

Horrified by the green blaze displayed on the plasma screen of her motel room, Celene kept listening to the newscast and wondered how it happened. Who had done such a terrible thing? Could it have something to do with the alien dome? Would the green smoke actually transform people into cannibalistic demons then within a few days melt their flesh and bones? She wanted to help, although she couldn't see how.

Celene donned khaki cargo pants and adjusted the phase-gun on her belt. She covered the gun with a tan sweatshirt and checked in the mirror. Let them come and try to kill her. With such a weapon and her invisibility powers, she feared no one. Not ORION soldiers, not even Kin and his SWAT team.

But before she dropped in on the firefighters headquarters to volunteer her help, Celene had a last duty to Kin. Turning on her epad, she logged onto an untraceable internet network, loaded the last audiofile of her translation, then sent it to Kin in an anonymous email. That way, he would have the rest of the file for the GSS but would not know where to look for her.

How could Kin have faked such passion? The anguish of his betrayal went so deep, it brought tears to her eyes. But no time for that. She had to make sure the strange fire wasn't the alien weapon described in the cave. But what if it was?

When her communicator rang, she burrowed into her bag then adjusted the piece on her ear. At the sound of Kin's voice, her heart almost stopped.

"Hi, stranger. Thanks for the email file."

Should she answer? Could he trace her through the call? Her anger spoke for her. "How did you get this number?"

"I work for a powerful secret agency, remember?" He sounded calm but intense.

Celene felt violated but remained silent to mask her anger. Jake always said, never show your emotions to your enemy. Did Kin just notice her missing?

"There was a strange device activated in the cave. I think it might have triggered the fire. What do you know about it?"

Kin didn't seem to mind her stubborn silence as his melodious voice went on. "Are you still in the area? The fire emits green smoke, like on the pictograph."

"I know. What a tragedy."

She heard him clear his throat. "Did you activate the device in the cave?"

"Me? What device are you talking about?"

"Something that could have triggered the fire and the green smoke?"

Outraged, Celene would have gladly kicked him. She could no longer hold her temper. "Are you accusing me of arson? How could I possibly do such a thing?"

"Calm down. I'm just trying to figure this out. What do you remember just before you left the cave?"

Celene drew a blank. She remembered nothing of her leaving the cave or the canyon. From the time she figured out Kin was sent to kill her until the moment she found herself on the main road near I-17, she had no recollection at all. Could she have caused that disaster? No. She refused to believe it.

"Do you remember anything about a humming device?" Kin's voice grew impatient.

"Nothing." She sensed doom hovering over that memory lapse.

"Celene, we need your help. The green smoke has to be connected to the machine in the cave. I tried to turn it off, but I couldn't figure out the petroglyphs. If anyone can deactivate that thing, it's you. And if you don't help us, thousands of people are going to die a horrible death."

Celene needed to think. She had to stall. "Did the firefighters reach the fire yet?"

"Not yet. We've declared the area a biohazard and forbade low-altitude planes. For now they're only dropping fire retardant and dry water as usual, but they do it from higher altitude. As soon as they can find enough bio-suits the firefighters will go fight that monster up close. We have to stop this before it gets out of hand."

It sounded so dangerous. "Isn't the cave close to the fire?"

"Several miles away, and I managed to get some special gear. With high-tech suits and filtering masks, we can avoid smoke exposure. I need your help." The desperation in Kin's voice tore at her heart, but could she trust him to tell her the truth?

Celene had felt so fearless a few minutes ago. Would she now jump into the dragon's lair with no regard for her own life? "What tells me this is not a trick to get me within range so you can kill me? Isn't that what you're required to do?"

"How can you possibly think I would want to kill you?"

How she wanted to believe him. "But it's your mission, isn't it?" Celene's whole being revolted against giving in. Did he really want to save those people, or was this just a ploy to kill her?

Kin didn't answer right away. "I have my orders, but I doubt I could carry them out. Not after what passed between us." The sincerity in his voice touched a deep chord in Celene. Would he really ignore his orders to keep her alive?

She heard the anchorman on the plasma screen declare the area a level seven biohazard. The cameras showed the evacuation of the closest towns and villages. Thank God. "You told the truth about the bio-hazard area. Can I trust you? Do you really need my help to save these people?"

"Listen, I can't blame you for not trusting me, but there is more at stake here than both our lives."

Celene thought about the defenseless population. And what about the wild animals she loved so much? Would the alien spore affect them as well? Even if it didn't, the fire would kill them anyway and destroy their habitat. She had to help. In the back of her mind, Celene tried to remember the last thing she translated about the Pleiades sisters but couldn't. She'd have to check her recorder.

As she remained quiet, Kin kept coaxing her. "You have to believe me, you are the only one who can figure this out."

As the best expert in Anaz-voohri language, Celene knew she had to help. Even if she knew Kin would kill her afterwards, she must save these people. It was her one life against thousands. The math was easy, but her final decision took a few seconds. "All right. I'll help. What should I do?"

"Where are you? I'll come pick you up in a chopper."

"Don't you have anything less obvious?"

"It's a quiet chopper."

Celene sent her satellite coordinates then collapsed on the bed. She still had a phase-gun and her invisibility powers. Why did she have to care so much about strangers? Why couldn't she just walk away and save her own life? Tears streamed down the side of her eyes onto the pillow. She cared because she was human, that's all she needed to know. Otherwise, she might as well be a despicable Anaz-voohri. The fear of approaching death dried her throat, but she must be brave.

When she saw the chopper land silently in the parking lot, she came out and walked against the wash of the blades to climb inside. Kin's strong arms helped her in. She noticed the pilot already wore a white suit without the mask, and two more suits lay in the cargo space in the back of the bird.

The helicopter took off and she grabbed a strap until the helicopter stabilized.

Kin handed her a suit. "Need some help?"

Celene shook her head. She'd used suits before, on digs suspected of biological infection. She donned the white coveralls over her clothes, phase-gun and all, then she pulled on the white gloves. She never liked the feel of the hermetically sealed material, it made her sweat. She left the hood and breathing device off for now and sat next to Kin on the side bench. She felt for the phase-gun through the suit and wondered whether she could fire it that way if need be.

Kin's features seemed drawn tight. She couldn't help but notice that he looked good in white. Why did he always wear black? He smiled at her and she wondered if by chance his smile might be sincere.

How she wanted him to be good and wholesome, and fair, and just, but she knew his first duty was to his secret organization. How could she love a man who had an organization in lieu of a conscience? Could he possibly be as heartless as a machine? Where was the humanity in this splendid body? Then again, he was risking his life to save these people.

When the pilot caught sight of the fire, he told them to get their headgear on. Now they looked like faceless scientists in a sterile room. How would they reach the ledge in that kind of gear?

But Kin had thought of everything. As they approached the coordinates, he pulled out a double harness and clipped it to a cable. The helicopter's floodlights swept the ledge in front of the shallow cave as the bird hovered above the cliff. Celene remembered that just this morning she had coffee with Kin on that ledge, after a night of passion.

Kin adjusted her harness clumsily through the gloves then clipped his into place. For a moment, they swung in each other's arms at the end of the cable in the night breeze. The necessary embrace reminded Celene of past pleasures. They landed precariously on the ledge on the third swing. Kin unhooked both harnesses then waved to the pilot who landed the bird on the flat top of the cliff but kept the engine running.

Due to their bio-hazard suits Celene and Kin could only communicate by signs. The apparel muffled the sound of their voices too much, and there had been no time to install a two-way radio system. Armed with a glow stick, Celene followed Kin through the Anasazi ruins and down the tunnel leading to the dome.

Immediately upon entering the alien dome, Celene could feel the vibration. She couldn't hear it, but the whole aspect of the cave had changed. The colors, the light... A new pedestal had appeared near the central column, and it glowed with unfamiliar petroglyphs. Celene bent over the console to read the new signs and pictures. Dots around a circle signified fire. And there was the character for smoke, and green. Green smoke! Celene tried to touch then press the symbols in sequence, but nothing happened.

Maybe she was going about this the wrong way. If she could just relax and breathe, she might be able to focus on her task. But no one could relax or breathe in a white suit. She couldn't feel the skin texture of the console, maybe it needed her touch, skin to skin. Could she remove the gloves and still be protected from the surrounding smoke? When she signaled Kin she must remove her glove, he shook his head furiously, but Celene ignored him. She removed the glove and saw Kin's shoulders drop in the white suit. Did he really care what happened to her?

As she depressed one symbol that meant open, the sides of the column glowed with more symbols. Maybe this would work. Celene looked for a character that meant close, or end, or some picture that would give her a clue. This language seemed much more archaic than that of the shards she'd just translated. Each symbol depressed uncovered a hundred more. She'd have to try them all in various sequences and combinations, and find logic in this chaotic language.

Then she found it, the character that meant spore, the same spore described in the pictograph blocking the cave, the spore the aliens had released on the planet to kill off the rest of the Anasazi population. She pressed the symbol, and more choices opened. How did she stop the spore from feeding the burning forest with that awful green smoke? And she had better be careful and not make things worse instead of stopping the process.

After eliminating a number of symbols, Celene found herself with two choices. It reminded her of old James Bond movies. *The green wire or the red wire?* At her side, Kin observed in tense silence. When she stopped and looked up at him, he stared back. She could barely see his eyes through the tinted glass of his visor. She pointed at both symbols in turn and raised shoulders and hands in a gesture she hoped said, "I don't know which one."

Kin nodded and laid a gentle hand on her shoulder. *Relax,* he gestured, *take your time.*

Celene sweated profusely in her hermetic suit and caught herself praying. *Dear God, if I get out of this alive, I swear I'll do good and help others for years to come.*

Signaling to Kin, she counted with her fingers, one, two...on three, she pressed one of the symbols. Immediately, the vibration stopped and the lights changed in the dome as the process interrupted. Then another process started, with awful rhythmic sounds like some kind of alarm. This time, Celene could hear the frantic sounds seeping through the suit.

When Kin took her by the hand and ran back to the tunnel, Celene followed wholeheartedly. She had no idea what she had triggered now, but like Kin, she didn't want to stay to see what it was. It looked and sounded ominously urgent.

Once out on the ledge, Kin clipped them both to the harnesses and pulled the cable. Immediately, the helicopter lifted and the cable went up and away as the bird flew over the canyon. They hoisted themselves into the cabin. Kin held Celene steady while the pilot veered off, until the chopper settled. In the distance, the fire still glowed, but the green tinge had started to fade from the smoke.

As they gained altitude, Kin pointed back to the ledge they had just left, as if expecting something. The pilot veered and flashed the lights toward the shallow cave. Celene stared but could see nothing until suddenly, the very rock seemed to waver. An incredible explosion filled the sky with light and fire, showering the canyons with rocks of all sizes. The sound hurt Celene's ears even through the breathing mask. No wonder Kin wanted to get out fast. She had initiated a self-destruct sequence.

They hovered, waiting for the dust to settle on the canyon. The scenery had suddenly taken on a different look. The cliff wall had recessed farther into the rock and new caves had opened, surrounded by debris. Celene could see there was nothing left of the dome or any alien installation in the cliff.

They flew away from the canyon, and as soon as they reached safe skies, Kin removed his headgear, as did the pilot.

Celene did the same. "Sorry about blowing up the dome. I should have pushed the other symbol."

"Maybe it wouldn't have made any difference. Maybe the dome was rigged to self-destruct in case of tampering during the process." Kin slipped out of the white suit with ease.

Celene struggled out of her suit trying not to look

clumsy. "I guess the aliens who built that dome didn't want it to fall into human hands."

"Can't blame them." Kin took her suit and hung it with his on the side pegs. He took Celene's hand and examined it carefully. "We'll have to get you to a hospital. Removing your glove wasn't safe back there."

"A hospital?" Celene now felt lost and vulnerable. Was her mission finished already? Then what was she doing in a helicopter with Kin, the man who must now kill her?

Kin turned on the plasma screen in the back of the chopper. It showed a group of forest rangers driving toward the fire in their usual gear.

Celene pulled Kin's sleeve. "You have to stop them. They can't go unprotected. It's still too dangerous out there."

Kin shrugged. "I can't order the rangers to go back. They know it's dangerous. They probably got tired of waiting for the suits, and when they saw the flames turn to their regular color, they figured it must be a normal fire after all."

"Can't we warn them?"

"They have no reason to believe our story. And they certainly won't take orders from me."

Turbulence caught the helicopter sideways. Looking at the plasma screen, Celene noticed that the wind had picked up and carried the flames quickly, spreading the fire to more forested lands. She realized with horror that the edge of the newly ignited woods burned with a greenish tinge. "The alien device has spread the spore to a vast area, and as the rest of the

forest burns, it releases more green smoke." Wanting
Kin to react, Celene faced him squarely. "You've got
to stop these reckless souls. We can't take any chances
of contamination."

Kin tapped his medallion then deliberately turned
his back to Celene. He whispered something she
couldn't hear and his secret communication made her
uncomfortable. Who was he talking to?

When Kin faced Celene again, he grinned. "We're
going to throw them white suits before they get too
close."

But the plasma screen showed more alarming
pictures. Some people in the vicinity of the fire had
inhaled the green smoke. They seemed agitated,
struggling against the paramedics who restrained them
as they boarded the ambulances.

Celene shuddered. "Good God!"

Kin spoke to his medallion again but this time
didn't bother to turn away from Celene. "Mythos?
Icarus here. Did you analyze the powder I gave you
earlier?"

Celene didn't understand. "What powder?" Then
she remembered the sample she collected and felt
foolish.

Kin held out one hand to quiet her. "Any idea
about an antidote? We're going to need it fast."
Suddenly somber, Kin looked straight into her eyes
with frightening intensity. "Is there anything in your
translation notes about a possible antidote?"

"I don't remember everything. Let me check."
Celene retrieved her epad from her cargo pocket. She'd
wanted to check on her last translation segment

anyway. She set it for the last fifteen minutes of recording and plugged in her earpiece

Celene turned toward the bulkhead to avoid any distraction from the plasma screen. In that relative isolation, she focused on the words. Curiously, she did not remember translating that whole segment. Why? But it was her voice on the digital recording, and she recoiled at the kind of information she'd translated before leaving the dome.

After enumerating the various plagues and catastrophes that would befall humanity at the hands of the Pleiades sisters, a very personal message emerged, as if the shard knew who was doing the translation, as if it had waited for her to come to this particular place at that particular time.

The shard itself, or its creator, thanked her for activating the alien device meant to decimate the population of the southwestern states through inhalation of the green smoke. It said her DNA made her immune to the smoke, as a reward for helping the Anaz-voohri. Her powers of invisibility would allow her to escape but would dissipate shortly after she accomplished her mission. There would be a place for her after the invasion. She and the other sisters, along with a few selected hybrids, would be allowed to live the span of their natural life but not allowed to reproduce.

Was she really the arsonist, the criminal, the despicable being who had brought this genocide upon the southwestern states? Even against her will, how could she let anyone manipulate her into this unspeakable evil? Celene felt violated, and tears of rage rolled down her cheeks. But she felt also crushed by utter shame. If she was such an abject murderer, she did not deserve to live.

* * * * *

Anaz-Voohri swarm, speeding through space toward Earth

Wasaw regained consciousness on the floor of the deck as his ear implant echoed with the strident sounds of multiple alarms. All around the domed room, the ship's warning lights blinked furiously. Wasaw's body ached with the slightest of movement and he felt his head ready to explode. What had happened?

An urgent incoming message made him stand up and walk gingerly to the console. He brushed the response symbol with one finger and stood at attention.

The sinister face of Captain Kavak filled the wall screen. "Commander Wasaw, you have some explaining to do. Our whole fleet experienced an energy surge, and we've lost the signal from the cave. What happened?"

"I'm not sure, exalted leader."

Captain Kavak's dark stare meant trouble. "And what the hell is wrong with your ship? Can't you stop that infernal noise?"

Wasaw turned off the alarms. He checked his electronic brain, but some of his circuits did not respond. "It seems I can't quite remember."

Captain Kavak scoffed. "Then just tell me what you do remember."

"Of course, exalted leader." Wasaw examined his cranial memory bank. "I responded to the cave monitoring signal and as I watched the holographic image, two intruders in strange white garb and helmets entered the sacred dome in the Earth canyon." The recollection, fuzzy at first, became clearer as Wasaw's self-repairing brain started to function better.

"Human intruders?"

Wasaw nodded. "They wore breathing masks hiding their features, but I believe one of them was sister Celene. Her DNA registered on my screen when her bare fingers deactivated the turbines."

"By Kokopelli's flute! She was never supposed to go back there." Captain Kavak turned away from the recording transmitter and mumbled a string of curses. "What went wrong?"

"It could be the human gene that controls freewill." Wasaw remembered his grandfather's mysterious smile. "You never know when it will kick in." He refrained from sounding sarcastic. In Captain Kavak's foul mood it could cost him his life.

"How could a human, even a sister, possibly figure out the proper deactivation sequence?" As Captain Kavak paced her quarters, the recorder followed her every move. She turned to face Wasaw. "Can you restart the process from here?"

Shaking his head, Wasaw wondered whether his leader had gone completely insane. "Not only could I never activate such machinery from so far into space, exalted leader, but the turbines have been destroyed."

"Destroyed?" The dark face of Captain Kavak turned a shade of gray.

"Along with the sacred cave itself." As his leader seemed frozen, Wasaw added, "There is nothing left."

Captain Kavak's features tightened on her bony face. "Are you certain?" She enunciated each word as if her very life depended on the answer.

Wasaw swallowed hard. "I was in the cave in holographic projection, and as it sometimes happens, I started getting physical sensations, as if I was actually there in the canyon cave. Suddenly, I saw it contract and expand in a great explosion of fire, then everything collapsed. With my personal circuits and the ship's instruments so finely tuned to the cave, the conflagration somehow created a rush of energy in my ship that hurled me through the dome and fused my brain circuits. Even the instruments are damaged."

"I see." But Captain Kavak stared into nothingness, as if stunned.

"Do you have new orders for me, exalted leader?" Wasaw knew the rhetorical question to be an insult but couldn't help himself. Anaz-voohri leaders did things right the first time and believed backup plans were for the weak, the imperfect, the substandard species.

"Watch your tongue, Wasaw. I will not declare you fit for reproduction if you show lack of loyalty or discipline."

"Aye, exalted leader." Wasaw tried to sound cheerful. "We can still succeed if all the other Pleiades sisters come through."

"I certainly hope so, Wasaw, for your own sake. Because if we fail, you will be the first to die at my hands."

Wasaw shuddered but kept his brain activity from showing his agitation. "If we fail, we'll all die anyway."

"Enough!" Captain Kavak breathed deeply and said in a calmer voice, "I'm ordering the fleet to increase speed and go into stealth mode. Return to work and find a way to turn this disaster into a victory. We should reach Earth in just enough time to initiate your ingenious new plan. You have twenty-four hours." Captain Kavak glared at him before severing the communication.

Wasaw let his shoulders droop. What ingenious new plan? He'd better think of something, and fast.

CHAPTER TWELVE

Sitting on the side bench in the Mythos helicopter bound for Phoenix, Celene felt ashamed of what she might have done, although she had no memory of it. Turned toward the bulkhead, she listened to the recording. When the translation stopped, she couldn't look at Kin. How could she possibly admit to him that she had caused the toxic fire? Beyond reason, she clung to the hope that she hadn't done it, that they would find another explanation.

When Kin squeezed her shoulder, she jumped and faced him.

"Anything about an antidote?"

How could he remain so calm? Celene shook her head. "I'm afraid not."

"Let's hope the lab finds something to counteract the spore." Kin pointed to her right hand holding the epad. "How's your hand?"

"Fine." Celene fastened her belt as they hit some more turbulence.

"Are you sure?" Kin didn't look convinced. "We'll reach Phoenix in a few minutes. We'll have you checked out."

As she gazed over the dark landscape below through the gaping side door, Celene wondered why Kin cared about her health if he planned to kill her soon. On the helicopter plasma screen, she saw borate bombers drop the red flame retardant slurry on the edges of the fire.

Outfitted in white suits under their insulated gear, firemen and forest rangers now reached the blaze and fought the unholy inferno with what seemed archaic techniques. They dug trenches, felled trees, and sprayed the brush. Celene wondered how they could stand working in those suits under such conditions. Could they even breathe in there? It had to be torture.

Kin talked to his medallion. "Mythos? Icarus. Mission partly successful. Currently in the air, on our way back to Phoenix. Do we know how the fire retardant will interact with the spore?" From his expression, Celene concluded they didn't. In the dark cabin, Kin kept his gaze on Celene. "Any ideas?"

When Celene realized he'd meant the question for her, she shook her head. "I'm not a chemist or a biologist, but I can try. What did they find so far?"

Kin listened then repeated one sentence at a time. "The powder we found on the boulder blocking the cave is some kind of spore. That spore is definitely alien to this planet and could have been artificially produced. It is highly flammable. So far we know nothing of its properties except for its toxic green smoke."

"Let's brainstorm, then." Celene liked brainstorming. It would keep her mind occupied. "What's in the smoke that makes it green?"

After a short delay, Kin said, "A toxic agent unknown to our lab scientists."

Celene focused on the analytical techniques she

often used in her archeological research. "What preserves the spore? What neutralizes it? Any indication of where it was stored? At what temperature?"

"You got that?" Kin asked his invisible correspondent.

Shutting out the distractions of the helicopter cabin, Celene kept following her thoughts. "How did it spread to the area?"

Sitting next to her on the side bench, Kin pulled out his epad from his pocket and held it for her to see. "These are the satellite pictures. It seems an unusual wind blew a cloud of spores from the top of a cliff over a vast forested area."

Celene could see the cloud spreading for miles on the small screen.

Then a spark started the blaze." Kin rubbed his smooth chin. "It would have taken strong turbines and wind tunnels to blow such a large quantity in a few hours."

"The vibration in the dome! That must have been the turbines." Celene felt excited, like at the verge of a new discovery. "A huge engine and spinning turbines that created a wind strong enough to spread the spore."

Kin smiled. "So the spore was stored inside or under that cliff? Then the explosion buried it under tons of rubble and probably destroyed the machinery that created the artificial wind as well."

"Still, something is not right." Celene visualized the explosion in her mind. "There was fire but no green smoke around the explosion, so the spore remaining in the cliff reserves didn't burn then. Why not?"

"Was it all spent?"

Celene shook her head. "No, the turbines would have stopped on their own."

"Could the spore have been stored deeper underground?" Kin raked his hair away from his face. "Or in a shielded vault?"

"Shielded from what? What's under the cliff?"

"Cave rodents? Bats? Underground streams? Dripping water? Rattlesnakes? Flooding?"

"Water! Could it be that water alters, damages, or even destroys the spore? Or reduces its potency? Causes it to rot? Or simply prevents it from burning? The conditions are dry now in the canyons, and there was a drought at the time the Anasazi disappeared. Coincidence?"

Kin grinned and spoke for his medallion. "Got that? Experiment with water and call me."

"Where are we going now?" Celene feared the answer. Had the time of her execution arrived? Was he going to push her out of the bird in full flight? It didn't seem fair. She had not acted of her own volition. "In my rush to follow you back to the cave, I left everything at the motel, including the relics."

"Now that we have the translation, we don't need the shards anymore, but still, we wouldn't want them to fall into the wrong hands. We'll pick them up first, then go to the lab and see if we can help." His casual smile failed to reassure her.

Celene didn't want to see another Mythos installation. Even if Kin had changed his mind about killing her, as he stated, she feared other operatives might not have the same scruples. But if Celene could help in any way, she must.   Her life meant little compared to all the lives she had unwillingly endangered.

The stealth helicopter landed quietly in the deserted parking lot of La Quinta Inn. Despite the few outside lights, the place looked dark. Kin squeezed the pilot's shoulder. "Keep it idling, ready to take off." Kin leapt out of the bird.

The pilot nodded, half rose, and started to struggle out of his white suit in the cramped space.

Celene jumped down and walked toward her room, but Kin grabbed her sweatshirt sleeve as she fished for the key in her cargo pocket. "Wait." He pointed at her door. "That's your room?" he whispered.

Celene nodded. She followed Kin's peripheral gaze but saw nothing move anywhere close in the night. The door of her hotel room stood ajar. Cautiously, Kin approached the door from the side and Celene imitated him, clinging to the wall. Should she become invisible? Not if Kin didn't.

When Kin pushed the door open, it squeaked. Nothing moved inside or outside. In a quick motion, he pulled out a phase-gun and entered the room. Celene wondered where he'd found another gun so fast. She felt for the phase-gun still tucked under her sweatshirt and pulled it out as well. She'd never used one but could probably shoot if she could stop trembling long enough. Kin turned on the light and went toward the bathroom door.

Celene muffled a cry of outrage. The place had been ransacked. The food supplies had spilled on the floor. Her clothes lay scattered on the bed. She couldn't see the two bags containing the relics.

Was the culprit still around? Celene didn't dare speak. Kin pushed open the bathroom door with one foot. She could hear him opening the shower and closet doors. He came back to the bedroom, shaking his head.

"Nothing?"

Kin laid a finger across his lips. He pointed at the desk and felt the underside with one hand. It came out holding a tiny object. A listening device! The room was bugged. Celene felt glad for his presence and training.

Switching off the light, Kin motioned Celene to stay behind him then scanned the parking lot right and left before venturing out, but he suddenly stepped back into the room and motioned toward the bathroom. Celene obeyed his directives.

Kin closed the bathroom door behind them and opened a small window high above the bathtub. Celene hadn't even noticed it when she bathed. Kin wormed out feet first through the opening then reached one hand to Celene to help her up. She stepped on the bathtub ledge. Half way through the window, she heard noise in the adjacent room.

Grabbing her by the shoulders, Kin pulled her outside then deposited her on the tar surface of the back parking lot. "Run to the chopper," he whispered.

Celene ran around the building toward the helicopter. Behind her, she heard the zipping sound of phase fire but didn't turn to look. Kin was taking gunfire for her! God, she hoped he would be safe. She'd never forgive herself if he died protecting her.

Now would be a good time to disappear. Using the fear that tore at her gut, she reproduced the sensation that allowed her to become invisible, but failed. Could she have lost the ability so soon? Or was it too much pressure? She couldn't do it.

Crouching under the slowly rotating blades, she climbed into the helicopter but paled as she realized the pilot lay on the floor, half way out of his white suit. Blood ran down his temple and pooled around his head. She knelt and felt for a pulse but could not find any. What now?

When a black commando dropped in front of her from nowhere, Celene realized it wasn't Kin. He wrenched away her phase-gun, but Celene launched a series of punches and kicks to the hand, to the head, to the ribs, and to the crotch. The man finally dropped her gun and crumpled to the floor in pain. He hadn't expected her to resist. Outside the chopper, phase fire still raged. Retrieving the phase-gun, Celene shot her aggressor in the leg, kicked him in the head and shoved him unconscious out of the chopper. He fell hard on the ground.

Just then, Kin's blurry shadow half-stumbled, half-ran toward her. He seemed to hold his side. Was he hurt?

"The pilot is dead!" Celene screamed in panic.

"Cover me." Kin retrieved his solid appearance and took Celene's hand to bring himself up inside the helicopter. Grimacing, he pushed aside the dead body and dropped into the pilot seat.

"Shoot at any moving target, Celene."

Celene raised up her phase-gun and started

shooting at the shapes surging out of the motel and running for the helicopter. Holding on to a handlebar to keep her balance, she could hardly see what she was shooting at in the dark. Did she hit anyone? The chopper lifted with a soft whirr. Lights came on in several rooms and civilians started poking their heads outside to check out the noise. All lights out, the chopper ascended into the night sky, away from phase fire reach.

Kin tapped his medallion. "Icarus. Pilot down, agent wounded. Need coordinates to closest Mythos medical facility." He sounded short of breath.

Celene dragged the dead pilot farther back toward the cargo hold, then she sat in the copilot seat. Kin sweated profusely, or was it blood on his face? Too dark to tell. He looked so weak. "Can you do it? Where are you hurt?"

The wan smile on Kin's face only worried her further. His jaw tightened. "Get a sterile pack from the medical kit in the back."

Celene half rose, balanced herself and stepped over the dead pilot to get to the bolted trunk marked with a red cross. She found the sterile packs and took several to the front. Breaking the seal of one, she handed it to Kin. He didn't take it but pointed to his right hip. "Pack it in there, as tight as you can to staunch the blood."

As she knelt between the bucket seats, the overpowering smell of seared flesh nauseated her. It reminded her of the massacre of her father's team. "I can't see, it's too dark."

The cockpit light went on. Celene blanched at the

sight of the blood-soaked jeans and the hideous phase wound oozing blood in spurts. He had severed an artery. How could Kin possibly operate the helicopter in his condition? Overcoming her sudden urge to heave, she applied the pack, but it wouldn't stay inside.

Kin laid one hand on hers. "Keep it in place. Hold it tight with your hand, right here."

Celene pushed the bloody pad into the wound with her fist.

"We'll be there in minutes." Kin looked so pale and drawn.

"Try to breathe," she suggested, hoping it would help. As she stared at his grimacing face, his lids threatened to close. "Keep your eyes open," she yelled. "Don't pass out on me now!"

Kin didn't answer but nodded and clenched his jaw tighter. Sweat dripped from his chin. His eyes glazed over briefly.

"Can you hear me?"

As he did not respond in any way, Celene slapped his leg. He jerked and groaned. The movement let out a spurt of blood that hit her face and tasted like metal on her lips. Some spark returned to Kin's eyes and he righted the helicopter, but soon his head just dropped and the helicopter skipped. Celene shook Kin's arm to no effect. With the strength of desperation, she slapped his cheeks. Tears and blood blurred her vision. "Stay with me, damn it! We're not going to die, not here, not now."

As she tried to get his hands back on the slippery controls, awareness returned to Kin, she could feel him strain to remain awake. Blood smeared the pedals. Kin directed the helicopter toward a helipad on the top of a tall building. After a hesitant approach, he landed the bird precariously, then he collapsed, unconscious.

Paramedics and doctors in scrubs rushed under the wash of the blades. Celene helped them get Kin out of the pilot chair and onto a stretcher. A soldier turned off the engine. Refusing any help for herself, Celene followed the stretcher at a run into an elevator then to an emergency unit, but the sliding glass doors closed in front of her. Authorized personnel only, said the sign. Celene felt ready to faint. Was Kin going to die? She couldn't bear the thought.

A young man in black uniform and impeccable crew cut approached her and saluted. "Miss Dupres?"

Celene shivered at the sight of the phase-gun at his belt and realized hers was showing over her bloody sweatshirt, tucked in the belt of her cargo pants.

The young man stared at the butt of her phase-gun, a standard Mythos issue, highly illegal on a civilian, but he didn't ask her to surrender it. Instead, he said, "Could you please follow me to the bio-lab?"

In an attempt to stall, Celene forced a smile. "May I use the washrooms first? I must look a fright to meet lab guys in white coats."

The soldier answered her smile and pointed to a door. Hurrying inside, Celene felt an uncontrollable urge to heave and rushed into a stall, where she threw up her ration dinner. When she could stand and breathe again, the mirror above the sinks revealed a disheveled female commando with a big gun, pale, and bloody from head to toe. Kin's blood, the pilot's blood, so much blood. No wonder no one questioned her presence or asked for her gun. She looked like a psycho after a killing spree. Celene rinsed her mouth, washed her face and hands, then she retied her long hair into the ponytail.

Now would be a good time to escape. She tried to become invisible again without conviction. She couldn't. Now she knew for sure she had lost her gift. She looked for another exit or a window in the washroom. No such luck. She wondered whether she would ever get out of this facility alive. But if they needed her in the bio-lab, she must help. As long as Mythos needed her, they would keep her alive.

When she left the washroom, the young soldier waiting on the other side of the door led her through a maze of corridors, stairs, and elevators. Celene knew she would not know how to find her way back. Back to where? To Kin? To the top of the building? She couldn't fly a helicopter. She felt trapped.

The young soldier let Celene inside the lab, even more elaborate than the one she'd used in London for her analysis of the first shard. She counted seven technicians in lab coats, male and female. They stared at plasma screens and monitors of varied sizes and shapes. Banks of computers sat on a row of tables, and large plasma screens covered the upper part of the walls. Glass shelves of petri dishes and lengths of cold storage drawers attested to a busy facility.

The soldier led Celene into an enclosed glass office and saluted the Hispanic woman behind the desk. She had short black hair and looked in her mid thirties. The woman's eyes sparkled as she rose to meet them. "Celene Dupres?"

Celene nodded. She liked the woman's wholesome smile.

The woman extended her hand. "Doctor Bonita Gomez. You can call me Bonnie."

Celene accepted her solid handshake. "Hi, Bonnie."

Bonnie indicated the chair across her desk. "Would you like some tea? You look like you could use a cup or two." She nodded to the young soldier.

"Thanks. Tea sounds wonderful."

The soldier saluted Bonnie and smiled. "I'll bring the tea, ma'am." He went out the door.

"We like the way you think, Miss Dupres. It seems that you were right about water." Bonnie sat and turned her desk screen so Celene could see the chart it displayed. "Water considerably retards the effects of the spore. If we can get enough of it to flood the area, the spore would just disappear into the soil and decompose. The problem now is to get this much water to the forest."

Celene sat and felt suddenly very tired. "The canyons are tricky for land vehicles. Any shift of the wind could trap the rangers and firefighters in a cul-de-sac from which they could not escape."

"They're already working under those conditions, but tank trucks are not nearly enough." Bonnie sighed. "Besides, we need more water than that."

"Planes?"

Bonnie shook her head. "We have a few water bombers but not enough. We've asked for more." Her face lit up. "We could convert fuel tanker planes to drop water. It's been done before." She made a note in her epad.

One positive idea. Celene started to feel energized. "Is there a lake close enough to dip large buckets and carry them with helicopters?"

"The nearest lake is so far away, the few helicopters we have would hardly make a difference."

"So, you need more helicopters."

Bonnie's fingers flew on her epad.

"What's the weather report? Any rain in sight?"

A sad smile answered that one. "I wish." Bonnie looked up as the young soldier returned.

He deposited a loaded tray on the desk. Two cups, a teapot, sugar, creamer, lemon wedges, as well as a plate of shortcakes. Bonnie served the tea.

"Thanks." Celene poured cream in her cup and took one sip. Return to civilization never felt so wonderful. Taking a shortcake, she dunked it in the tea. "Don't you guys have a map of the underground waterways?"

"You mean underground lakes and rivers?" Bonnie's dark round eyes sparkled. "I'm sure we can find one." She punched a few keys on her keyboard. The map of northeast Arizona, on the large wall screen on the other side of the office glass wall, started to fill with underground rivers and lakes in bright blue. Then Bonnie superimposed the outlines of the advancing fire in red.

"Where's the wind coming from?"

Bonnie used a pointer to indicate the direction of the wind. "From the northwest and should remain that way for a while, but the fire generates its own microclimate and changes the wind currents in the vicinity. We never know where the fire will expand next."

Celene pointed at a blue underground lake, two miles from the edge of the raging fire. "How deep down is this one?"

"Not too deep... Wait, we may get lucky. Look here." Bonnie pointed at a discoloration on the map. "The underground lake pours into a waterfall on a cliff side and feeds a pond, then the water disappears again underground."

"A waterfall? Perfect." Celene started pacing. "How do we capture a waterfall and get the water to the fire?"

Bonnie followed her comings and goings. "We can't have helicopters fill giant buckets so close to the cliff. The wind could smash them against the rock face."

Celene stopped pacing. "Can we pump the water from the pond at the bottom of the fall and use light conduits or hoses to bring it to the forest? What about feeding a battery of sprinklers, like a wall of water on one side? Could we use industrial fans to propel the water further out?"

Bonnie rewarded Celene with a bright smile. "We won't know until we try." She tapped the end of her pointer on the desk. "What about the rest of the perimeter?"

* * * * *

Kin awoke to the clamor of monitors beeping like an army of crickets. He turned off his hearing implant and realized that his head hurt, a disturbing sensation that prevented him from thinking straight. Where was he? What had happened?

Although he did not recognize the place or remember how he ended up here, he assumed this was a medical facility. A Mythos facility as attested by the brand of the equipment. Kin tried to sit up and felt a violent stab in his right hip. Looking down, he saw the length of his body immobilized in a metallic brace, the kind usually applied after microscopic repair surgery.

He vaguely remembered getting shot in the parking lot of Celene's motel. Within minutes, his memory started to return. Did he fly the helicopter all the way? He remembered pain. Celene kept him awake. Without her, he would have died. The thought of Celene in the Mythos facility without his protection made his blood run cold. How long had he been unconscious? Where was she? What had they done to her?

He spotted his medallion on the bedside table. He reached for it and turned it on. "Icarus here. I need to speak to Miss Dupres immediately."

"Welcome back, Icarus. Miss Dupres is in the lab. We'll let her know you are awake."

Kin breathed easier. She was alive, and she would come to him shortly. To curb his impatience, he switched on the plasma screen at the foot of his bed and surfed the channels to find the latest news from the fire.

Things had gotten worse. Streams of people flocked to the hospitals, exhibiting symptoms of what they now called the Green Rage. It started with benign symptoms, a craving for raw meat, then a maniacal aggressiveness. Using the secure facilities usually reserved for convicts, they restrained the patients who had to wear facemasks to prevent them from chewing off their own limbs or attacking their caretakers. No relief in sight for the terrible disease. What would be next? Kin tried to remember the pictograph blocking the cave. Hideous facial deformity? Melting of the flesh?

* * * * *

When Celene stepped into the room, she saw Kin close his eyes briefly. She must be a sight. Did she frighten him?

Kin offered a weak smile as he muted the plasma screen. "I have to thank you for saving my life, again."

"Don't mention it." How glad she felt to see him whole and safe.

"Did you get your hand checked out?"

Just out of surgery and he worried about her. Celene shook her head as she approached the bed.

Kin took her hand. "Your hand was exposed to the smoke. What if you are infected?"

"I can't be infected. I'm immune." She enjoyed the surprise on his face.

"Immune? How can you be sure?"

"That's what the shards say. So are a few hybrids but not all of them."

"That's wonderful news." A slow smile spread on Kin's face. "If you are immune, chances are we can use your blood to manufacture some kind of antidote to inject the people already infected."

Celene suddenly felt better. In the midst of this nightmare, her own blood might bring hope. She also felt glad she had not outlived her usefulness, yet. If the antibodies in her blood could provide a vaccine or a cure for the green plague, as long as she could save all these human lives, neither Mythos nor ORION would dare kill her.

CHAPTER THIRTEEN

Celene hated needles. She had trouble relaxing in the reclining chair of the small white room. This was no time to be faint-hearted.

The male nurse tightened the tourniquet on her arm. "Are you all right?"

"I'll be fine," Celene lied.

On the other side of her chair, Bonnie held Celene's hand reassuringly. She'd taken time from the bio-lab to be with her. "We're so lucky that you happen to be immune to the Green Plague. Our lab confirmed the antibodies in your blood. And you are a universal blood donor type, too. That helps. We'll be able to manufacture enough serum to treat most of the smoke inhalation victims."

"Most of them? Why not all of them?" A partial victory would not satisfy Celene.

"You are not heavy enough to take more than one pint of your blood."

"How much do you need?" Celene felt the cold swab of alcohol on the inside of her elbow and tried to ignore the male nurse.

Bonnie didn't seem to notice. "Ideally, we'd need twice as much."

"Then take it." Celene winced at the needle prick.

Concern rounded Bonnie's brown eyes. "But you

might get weak or pass out if we take too much."

"More people may die if you don't." Celene just wanted to erase the evil effects of the smoke, even if it cost her her health. As Bonnie hesitated, Celene steeled her resolve. "This is no time for caution. Just do it."

Bonnie reluctantly nodded to the nurse, who discarded the pint-sized plastic bag he had prepared and replaced it with a larger one. Bonnie squeezed Celene's hand. "It's very brave of you, and we appreciate your sacrifice. Thank you."

Bonnie watched over Celene like a mother hen. The woman probably had no idea Celene had started the fire, or she wouldn't be so nice to her.

"Open and close your hand, please," the male nurse said in a neutral voice.

As Celene did, the blood started to flow into the transparent bag taped to her forearm. The male nurse checked the bag then slapped Celene's forearm a few times to keep the blood flowing. Apparently satisfied, he left the room.

"This is going to take a while." Bonnie reached for a white blanket from a metal shelf against the wall. She unfolded it and covered Celene from chin to toe. "You might get cold." She smiled as she would to a sick child. "I'll check up on you in a little bit. Just relax." Bonnie dimmed the lights as she exited the small room.

Celene focused her mind on the hypnotic flow of blood leaving her body beat by beat, spurt by spurt. A great fatigue invaded her body. Nice and warm under the blanket, perhaps she could nap for a few minutes. Exhausted, she didn't fight the weight of her eyelids. Images of a sunny Hawaiian beach filled her mind, as hula dancers swayed to the slow whine of a slack-key guitar.

* * * * *

Luke Air Force Base - Phoenix, Arizona

Carrick stepped down the movable steps of the Navy jet in the pink Arizona dawn. Flavia followed him out, carrying his briefcase. He liked the way she thrust her breasts forward to balance the weight. The few agents Carrick had brought with him officially saw to his safety, but in truth, he wanted his own men to handle the operation. He didn't trust the locals.

In a foul mood, Carrick resented the fact that the flight authorities had detoured his plane because of the fire. As if a high-flying jet would get in the way of their precious firefighting operations. Carrick knew he had much more important matters to attend.

A major in a navy uniform saluted Carrick on the tarmac then cleared his throat. "Welcome, sir. I am the local agent in charge of the Arizona sector. We spoke earlier. Your car is waiting, sir."

"Where is Blanchard?" Carrick felt in no mood for Blanchard's civilian attitude. "I told him I wanted to see him as soon as I got here."

"Sir, Dr. Blanchard is already at the Science Museum and insisted on installing the equipment right away." The major in charge didn't look like much of a leader. He shook in his boots in front of his superior.

Carrick enjoyed frightening his subordinates. They served him best when scared shitless. "Then take me there immediately."

"Aye, sir." The major led the way to a limousine and opened the door for Carrick and Flavia while the special agents accompanying Carrick boarded a waiting Air Force minibus.

The major gave instructions to the limo driver then stepped inside and sat across from Carrick.

As the limousine moved past the hangars, a dozen motorcycles caught up with the limo and formed a V-shaped battle formation in front of it. The motorcade rapidly left the base in the direction of the freeway and arrowed its way through the early morning traffic.

"Sir, I have some good news and some bad news." That worried look on the major's face wasn't a good omen.

Carrick growled. He hated bad news and felt of a mind to shoot the messenger. "What did you fuck up this time?"

The major swallowed hard. "We recovered the crystal shards."

"I assume that's the good news. What's the bad?"

"We could not apprehend Miss Dupres." The major's eyes shifted from Carrick to Flavia. "She had some help from the oriental man who accompanied her to the canyons. They fled in a stealth helicopter."

"To where?" Could these local operatives do anything right? But what could Carrick expect from cowboys?

"We lost track of the stealth bird, sir. It flew away without a trace."

"Where in hell did the bitch find enough credit to get a stealth bird?"

"Don't know, sir." The major paused. "We

expected the woman to do a disappearing act, as you said, but the oriental man with her was the one who used ninja tricks. Still, I think we got a good shot at him. We found lots of blood on the ground. Probably ruptured an artery."

"Ninja?" This reeked of Mythos. Carrick didn't like it a bit. Why did this rogue secret society always interfere with his operations? And why did they protect the Pleiades bitch? Mythos should be by his side fighting the Anaz-voohri. It didn't make much sense. What was Mythos really after? His job? His head?

The major kept blabbering. "We'd already killed the pilot, so the wounded ninja flew the helo himself. He can't have gone very far in his condition."

"So they are still in the vicinity. Did you check the hospitals?"

"Aye, sir. No luck there. All they have are fire victims."

"Flavia, launch a search for that Dupres bitch, would you?" Flavia already had the laptop out of Carrick's briefcase and took notes. Sometimes Carrick wondered whether she could read his mind. He wondered about other things as well. Did she wear frills under her navy uniform? He fancied her wearing red lace. He glanced out the window as the motorcade sped up in the HOV lane on the freeway. "Where are the relics now?"

"Dr. Blanchard has them and is testing the machine."

"Already?" Carrick hoped the decoder from the Anaz-voohri ship would shed light on the information contained in the shards. Blanchard seemed confident it would work. "Any problem from the local authorities about requisitioning the museum?"

"Not at all, sir. They want to do the right thing by ORION and support the fight against the alien threat." The major shrugged. "I guess the green fire spooked them. They wonder what we're doing here but dare not ask."

"Let them ask." Carrick made it a warning. "Just don't give them any answers."

The motorcade took an off ramp loop over the light rail transit and headed toward downtown Phoenix. Carrick noticed the traffic lights turning green to let them through. The military limo must be equipped with a remote sensor that switched the signals ahead of them. Efficient.

The major cleared his throat. "The local officials are asking if you are here to help with the fire. Will you talk to them?"

Downtown, the huge plasma screens lining the streets and buildings broadcast pictures of the green fire, and the accompanying commentaries remained grim. No progress in the fight, just a growing number of victims. Carrick sighed. "I'll see them later." He would have to check on that blasted fire. Something told him he might find a few answers there.

The limousine stopped in front of the Science Museum. The major opened the car door and held it while Carrick and Flavia stepped out. Carrick's bodyguards joined them on the sidewalk and followed them through the front garden that reeked of orange blossoms. The two armed guards in front of the main glass door straightened and saluted as Carrick and his retinue entered.

"This way to the planetarium." The major led them through a vast marble lobby.

They entered the planetarium through a small side door. Carrick held his breath when he saw the display of lights produced by the alien device. The dome looked full of three-dimensional pages, like a whole library, pages and pages of alien pictographs and hieroglyphics. There was so much to decipher, so much information he could probably use. Carrick's spirit soared.

At the center of the dome floor, he spotted Blanchard in a white smock, bent over the central pedestal and strode toward him. "You did it, you old dog!"

Emile Blanchard raised his pale blue gaze at Carrick's approach and smiled. "Watch your feet. Don't step on the cables."

A network of electronic cords tethered the alien console to an ominous black trunk sitting on the floor. "What kind of power are you using?"

"The best alien technology." Blanchard winked. "Special issue from Area 51. I was worried for a while, because we didn't have any power source strong enough to feed the device, but with a little help from the military, I finally rigged that thing correctly." He straightened with pride. "I used traces of alien DNA to fool the controls. It still needs fine tuning. What do you think?"

"Fan-fucking-tastic! Do you have someone to translate all that?"

"Celene Dupres would have been my first choice."

Blanchard scratched his balding gray head. "But if we can't find her, I have an old Pueblo Indian who teaches Anasazi culture at ASU and is familiar with much of the ancient language."

Carrick slapped Blanchard's shoulder. "Start the translation immediately. We'll see what we can do to get you the Dupres bitch."

"Celene is a good girl." Blanchard looked offended. "I've known her since she was twelve. Just because her father was a filthy hybrid doesn't make her a bitch. Besides, her father told me she was adopted, so she's not even a hybrid's daughter."

"You don't know shit about her." Carrick couldn't tell Blanchard about the Pleiades sisters. As a civilian hybrid hunter, Blanchard didn't have top clearance. "Don't meddle with what you know nothing about. The woman will destroy us all if we don't stop her!"

Blanchard shrugged and returned to the fine-tuning of his precious machine.

Carrick turned to the local major who waited a few feet away with Flavia. "Take me to that fire. How far is it?"

The major looked surprised. "I don't think they'll let you anywhere near the fire itself, sir. You'd stand a better chance at the fire headquarters, where the press waits."

"I want to see the man in charge, moron, not the fire."

"The fire chief would be at the fire headquarters, sir. It's only fifty miles north of town."

"All right." Carrick checked his watch. Already seven in the morning. "Let's go."

* * * * *

Celene awoke, alone in the small white room. By the dim light, she noticed the blood bag missing from her arm. The needle now dripped a clear liquid into her veins from a bag hanging beside the reclining chair. She felt much better, as if she'd slept for hours. Had she? With no windows in the room, she couldn't tell whether it was morning yet.

The epad was gone from her cargo pocket. No way to know the time or to contact anyone. Worse, her phase-gun had disappeared from her belt. Celene didn't like that at all. She needed to get out of here before she became an official prisoner. The fact that they took her weapon and her epad made her feel like one.

She winced as she pulled out the needle from her arm and closed the puncture with the tape that held it in place. As she didn't know how to straighten the reclining chair, she climbed out of it from the side. When her feet touched the floor, however, her head swam. She held on to the chair, waiting for the sensation to subside, then she walked, slowly at first then more confidently toward the door.

The same guard who'd guided her before now waited in the hallway. He saluted her, blocking the door. "Ma'am? I was told to escort you to the bio-lab as soon as you were awake."

Celene nodded but didn't care for the guard or the fact that he held his phase-gun at the ready. Why would they assign her a guard in a safe facility unless *she* constituted the dangerous element? She bit back a tart comment and followed the guard toward the narrow stairs leading down to the bio-lab.

The door of the white immaculate lab stood open. At her desk in her glass office, Bonnie stared at the screen of her electronic microscope. Celene tapped on the glass to get her attention.

Bonnie looked up and smiled then motioned Celene to come in through the open door. "We let you sleep. You looked like you needed it."

"Thanks. I guess I did. I feel much better." Celene didn't mention she still felt weak as she approached the desk. The guard remained in the hallway but did not leave.

"You should eat something." Bonnie pulled a plastic card from her breast pocket. "We took two pints of blood." She handed the card to Celene. "The cafeteria is just one floor down. Get whatever you want, just charge it to my account."

Celene took the offered card. "You're too kind."

"Bless your heart." Bonnie's dark round eyes twinkled. "The antidote will be ready soon."

"I'd like to see how Kin is doing." Celene hoped he would recover fast.

"Of course." Bonnie smiled as if she understood. "He is on the twelfth floor, healing nicely, but right now he is heavily sedated. Otherwise, he would be traipsing around against doctor's orders." She laughed. "Most men don't know what's good for them."

Celene found the idea of Kin helpless and sedated rather humorous. He didn't sound so dangerous anymore, and he hadn't given out her secret, so she felt inclined to trust him again. "If you don't need me here,

I'll just go, then."

"You do that. I'll see you later." Bonnie returned her attention to the images on her screen.

Before turning away, Celene hesitated. As Bonnie looked up at her questioningly, Celene motioned toward the guard. "Does he have to follow me everywhere? He makes me nervous."

"Sorry." Bonnie's smile didn't soften the blow. "We received orders to keep you under close guard until Kin is back on his feet in a day or two."

"Why?" So Celene was a prisoner. She tried not to show her shock.

"We weren't told exactly why, but someone at Mythos headquarters thinks you are the key to the success of Kin's mission. Whatever that may be."

"You don't know what Kin's mission is?"

Bonnie shook her head. "As lab people, we know little about what's happening in the field. Even less about special missions. Kin takes his orders directly from Archer, the big boss himself."

Celene wanted to flee, but she smiled for Bonnie's sake. At least they weren't going to kill her on the spot. As she exited the bio-lab, the guard tagged along.

"Take me to the cafeteria." Giving orders made Celene feel less of a prisoner. Still, she already entertained the thought of evading that loutish young guard. But she'd do it on a full stomach.

The modern cafeteria offered ready meals to go in clear plastic containers. Ravenous, Celene ordered a tuna sandwich, as it claimed to be albacore and dolphin friendly. She always watched out for endangered species. She grabbed a can of orange juice from the ice bin as well.

"Now to the twelfth floor." Celene took the lead, discarded the plastic container in a recycling bin and bit into the sandwich. She finished it in the elevator and gulped the juice. She now understood the layout of the facility. All the offices or rooms seemed piled on top of each other, with one elevator and many small sets of stairs connecting all the floors in a haphazard pattern.

When they reached Kin's room on the twelfth floor, the guard took position in the hallway and Celene went inside, closing the door for privacy. Kin slept like an angel. He did look harmless. Seeing him sleep reminded Celene of the few nights they'd spent in each other's arms. She'd trusted him then. How easy it would be to trust him again, love him, place her fate in his hands. She walked to the bed and deposited a kiss on his forehead. When he didn't move or open his eyes, she realized he must be heavily drugged.

Kin looked so peaceful. He could have died from the wound, and the very thought made Celene ache. She couldn't stand the thought of never seeing him again, and yet she would have to leave him now. She couldn't take the chance to stay. The fact that she saved his life might count for something, but she feared he might still have to kill her. It seemed so unfair after all they'd gone through together.

Once reassured that Kin would be fine, Celene had to think about her own situation. After eating, she felt a little stronger. Time to escape. Since she had lost her power of invisibility, she would have to muscle her way out of this facility.

Celene wanted to go help with the fire. She'd

allowed this disaster to happen and she felt compelled to help fix it. No one but Kin knew she was responsible, so she felt safe showing her face outside. The firefighters had asked for volunteers earlier, and who better than a capable immune person to help. In her good physical condition, Celene could probably work as hard as any man on the front lines.

First, she had to escape the guard's vigilance, then get out of this cramped facility without windows. The dry bloodstains on her clothes, from last night's encounter with ORION, would attract attention once outside. Looking around Kin's room, Celene opened a closet opposite the bed. Several black uniforms hung on the bar. Perfect. The fashion nowadays favored cargo pants and military styles anyway. She would blend right in.

Discarding her bloody khaki pants and sweatshirt, Celene slipped on a pair of fresh black cargo pants. They fit a little baggy but she tightened them with her belt. Then she pulled a black cotton sweater over her head.

What about the guard? Celene opened the door slightly and poked her head in the hallway. "Can you help me for a second here?"

The guard nodded and Celene opened the door wider to let him into the room. Before he could react, she kicked the phase-gun that flew off his hand to knock off a cart of medical supplies. Then Celene pivoted and hit his jaw in a wide arc kick. The guard, momentarily stunned, fell to his knees. Celene followed with a punch to the head and he collapsed to the floor. She checked his pulse at the throat.

Once satisfied the guard would survive, Celene bound his hands and feet to Kin's bed with surgical tape and taped his mouth shut, so he couldn't call for help when he came to. She retrieved his phase-gun and slipped it under her belt.

What would Kin do when he awoke and discovered what she had done? Better make sure he couldn't tell anyone right away. Celene tiptoed to the side of Kin's bed and snatched the medallion from his bedside table. Without it, he couldn't contact anyone until they checked in on him. She deposited a light kiss on his brow. "Sleep tight, my angel." She secretly hoped he was her good angel, not the angel of death.

Slipping the medallion around her neck, Celene tucked it under her sweater, then she left the room and closed the door silently. If she followed her instincts, she could find some kind of exit on the lowest floor. Not everyone flew into this place as she did. The personnel had to enter and leave the facility from somewhere on the ground floor.

Celene reached the elevator without attracting attention. No one on the floor even looked at her twice. Amazing how she suddenly blended in under the uniform. She could probably leave the building unhindered. What then? She'd have to improvise.

The ground floor didn't advertise any exit signs, only a flight of stairs going further down. Celene followed the stairs to a heavy metal door and pushed. On the other side, she found an underground parking lot. The door through which she had just exited closed behind her with a metallic clang. It bore no markings of any kind, but when Celene tried to open it from the outside, she couldn't. Apparently, Mythos tried to keep people out, not in.

Several cars lined the walls of the covered parking. Celene needed transportation, but most cars had owner DNA recognition, and she didn't want to trigger an alarm and attract attention.

As she pondered her options, a bright yellow Dial-a-Bike came rolling in. The glorified motorbike with anti-gravity capabilities had a plexiglass top. The light vehicle approached with a quiet purr. Celene pulled out her phase-gun and hid it behind her back, trying to look as if she belonged there. Casually, she walked toward the space where the bike turned to park. The driver lifted the plexiglass door and watched her as she strutted toward him.

"Nice bike." Celene smiled seductively.

The man smiled back. He didn't look like a secret agent, more like a technician, probably a computer geek or a biologist. When Celene pulled the gun on him, he immediately raised his hands.

"Get out and keep the engine running."

He hesitated.

Celene could tell the man loved his bike. "Do what I say and you'll get it back without a scratch."

The man backed away slowly.

Celene didn't know how to fly the silly thing, but she could probably drive it like a motorcycle. The experimental machines had the reputation of being highly unreliable. Only one way to find out. Celene had no other choice. She had driven a motorcycle before, and this shouldn't be much different.

Leaving the man speechless in the parking lot, she

spurred the bike on and followed the exit arrows. When she neared the exit, the gate lifted automatically to let her out. To her surprise, bright sunlight welcomed her outside. The Dial-a-Bike's plexiglass shell darkened instantly in the sun. It felt like early morning. Celene must have slept for hours.

Looking up at the building she had just exited, Celene saw a brand new tower, huge, with row upon row of wide bay office windows. People came and went in and out of the main lobby through a wide entrance. Mythos probably occupied the core of the building, like a tower inside a tower. How clever! No wonder each floor had limited space with all the offices packed on top of each other. Behind the windows, the offices of perfectly public businesses lay in full view. No one would ever suspect Mythos had a secret facility occupying the core of that tower.

For the first time in days, Celene felt free. She was free to help others in their time of need, free to make her own choices, free to gamble her life and go fight a fire. She remembered the newscast mentioning the place along I-17 where they recruited firefighters, about fifty miles north of Phoenix. With such a ride, she'd zip through the morning traffic and get there in no time.

CHAPTER FOURTEEN

Fire Headquarters, fifty miles north of Phoenix

As the limo pulled into the parking lot of Horse Thief Basin High, the school commandeered for the fire headquarters, Carrick severed his communication with the ASU bio-lab. Outside the tinted windows, the school parking lot crawled with emergency vehicles, police cruisers, newscast vans and pickup trucks. Carrick turned to Flavia, who sat across from him in the limo, next to the local major. "So tell me again what we know about this fire before we face the music."

In her Greek-accented voice, Flavia read the screen of the laptop on the pull-up table in front of her. "A gray powder around the area, first mistaken for ashes, proved to be an unknown substance of alien origin. It emits highly toxic fumes as it burns. Some private lab determined that water is more effective on this fire than the usual chemicals. The complete extent of the toxic agent on human physiology remains unknown beyond what the local authorities call the Green Rage, a debilitating disease that renders victims madly aggressive and even cannibalistic. There is no cure in sight, and the rate of degradation is so rapid that the victims will certainly start dying within a few days if we don't find a cure."

"How did that substance get there?"

"Yesterday's satellite pictures of the area demonstrate a gray plume spreading over the forest from somewhere in the canyons. That's our only clue."

"I knew it! That's what the Dupres bitch was doing in the canyons with the relics. She's been busy playing with fire. And if the toxic agent is of alien origin, that confirms it. It's an Anaz-voohri attack." Was this the extent of the destruction she could wage, or did she have many more tricks up her sleeve? Carrick berated himself for failing to eliminate her when she raided his bunker. What had gone wrong? She seemed to elude him at every turn, but he had to catch her before she destroyed his career.

The major hesitated. "Should we consider evacuating the city of Phoenix?" He looked pale, although it could have been from the gray tint of the limousine's windows. "I already told my wife to take the kid and fly to her mother in Florida."

Carrick bristled at the implications of evacuating. It would spell complete disaster and loss of face. Phoenix had grown so fast, it was not designed for escape in case of alien or terrorist threat. It had few highways and only one civilian airport. The panic would turn into riots at Sky Harbor Airport over who would leave and who would stay. "What's the weather report?"

Flavia consulted her screen. "For now the wind carries the smoke away from the city."

"Good." Carrick glared at the local major. "Is that the regular wind pattern for the season?"

"No, general. We are presently experiencing a heat wave." The major cleared his throat. "The winds could change anytime. And if or when they do, we'll only have a day or so to evacuate Phoenix… I don't think it can be done."

Carrick pondered the consequences. Could he eradicate the threat in one day? Should he take the chance of not evacuating? Anything was better than chaos. If Phoenix fell prey to the alien disease, it would just have to be quarantined then leveled. Such a drastic event would make the world realize the importance of Carrick's mission. He could blame the disaster on his lack of authority and request more power to do his job efficiently in the future.

The major seemed to be waiting. Upon a nod from Carrick, he exited the limo and held the door open. Carrick brushed his pants before stepping into the bright sunshine. Flavia, who had already stored the laptop in the briefcase, carried it as she followed him out.

Carrick looked up at the pure blue sky. Where were the Anaz-voohri sons of bitches? Watching from space? Earth Watch didn't mention any alien vessel in Earth's vicinity, but the enemy had been known to slip through the satellite network on so many occasions, he felt Earth Watch was worthless.

An Air-Evac helicopter crossed Carrick's field of vision and landed at the closest end of the nearby football field. More helicopters took off and landed in a tight aerial ballet. The whirr of chopper blades filled the air.

Although the signs indicated the headquarters office was inside the gymnasium, Carrick ambled toward the improvised airfield, unconcerned about

Flavia and the major scrambling behind him to keep up with his quick strides.

Rows of ambulances lined both long sides of the football field, with white tents erected at one end. The journalists, at bay behind yellow tapes, filmed the activities. Carrick ducked under the tape and entered the field. The grass was so dry, the helicopters lifted clouds of dust and dry grass under the wash of the blades. "Can't they hose down the field?"

"They save the water for the fire, general." The major sounded apologetic. "We live in the desert."

A medical team in civilian clothes with a Red Cross armband rushed toward the Air-Evac bird that just landed. Volunteers, in other words, amateurs... They wore surgical masks and goggles against the flying dust and carried stretchers and medical boxes. Carrick stopped at the edge of the group of white tents and watched the medical team on the field unload two firefighters and strap them on stretchers. "What happened?" he asked the medical aid checking the men's names on his epad.

The medic glanced at Carrick's uniform and medals. "One removed his mask and is contaminated. He attacked and wounded the other fireman."

"Is the disease contagious? Can it be transmitted by direct contact?"

"Not as far as we can tell. It seems only smoke inhalation can provoke it."

"Good." As Carrick watched the team bring the victims to the tent, one of the wounded became agitated and broke his restraints. He fell off the stretcher then leapt on his feet and attacked one of the medics. The rictus on the madman's face didn't look human. His pulled up lips made his teeth look sharper, and he exhibited exceptional strength as he shoved away the other medics rushing to restrain him.

Carrick pulled out his side phase-gun. He calmly aimed into the fray, waited for a clear target and shot once. The zing of phase fire went unheard over the helicopter noise, but Carrick saw the sizzling hole in the madman's forehead just before the man collapsed.

Carrick returned the phase-gun to his holster and smiled at the petrified medic next to him. "One less to take care of. I don't know why you bother trying to save these freaks. They'll probably all die anyway. Casualty of war."

When he glanced at Flavia, she remained cool and collected, but the major seemed ready to have a heart attack. As the Air-Evac chopper took off again, a large helicopter landed and the noise made conversation impossible. A ragged team of firemen stepped out of the large bird, helmet and gas mask in hand, dragging their boots as they left the field. A fresh team of firefighters in full gear except for their headgear, rushed into the big bird, which took off immediately.

Carrick walked around, inspecting the white tents. A temporary triage assigned the victims to appropriate hospitals, and loaded them in the various ambulances waiting along the football field. In one large closed tent with plastic windows, a medical team performed an emergency surgery. Another tent served as a morgue, judging by the dozen body bags already lined up on the ground. Two medics just carried in another body bag and laid it at the end of the row. They avoided

Carrick's gaze. Must be the freak he'd just killed.

He deemed it a well organized operation for a bunch of cowboys. Of course, Arizona had grown over the past twenty years and had seen its share of fires. Still. He turned to the major. "Let's go see the fire chief."

The major, still pale, nodded and led them toward the school gymnasium. Inside, the thick walls muffled the sound of the choppers, but the place echoed with messages issued over the PA system. One half of the building handled the new recruits, distributed equipment, and assigned the teams. On the other side, the buzz of the journalists, crammed behind a yellow-taped section labeled press room, made Carrick's head ache. They had enough electronic equipment in there to fill a dozen television studios.

The large plasma screens lining the high walls of the gymnasium didn't feature a home game or local advertising but continuous coverage of the fire on all fronts. One screen featured sky views from a helicopter's high-resolution lenses, monitoring the progress of the fire line as well as the struggle of the firemen below. On another screen, a handheld camera in the field relayed shaky pictures of the men working on the front lines.

The live sounds of the inferno conveyed the dangerous conditions. The men moved slowly and looked short of breath, probably crushed by the heat, lack of air, and exhaustion, as if they struggled simply to remain on their feet and conscious. A third screen showed images of the ongoing evacuation. Panic filled the faces of the civilians running away from the green smoke on bottlenecked country roads.

As Carrick crossed the gymnasium, one anchorwoman stared at his uniform, assessed Flavia's official bearing, then her face lit up with recognition. She signaled her cameraman and, microphone in hand, she rushed toward Carrick, who hurried in the direction of the fire chief's temporary office.

"General Carrick, what is ORION's involvement in this fire? Is there reason to believe that aliens are involved? Is this is an Anaz-voohri terrorist act?" The hive behind the taped area stirred, and a horde of news-hungry anchor people rushed up to join the fray.

Bad Timing. Carrick kept walking and gave the journalists his grimmest facial expression. "No comments yet. Press conference in a few minutes." He'd better have a strategy before addressing the press. The media required careful handling.

As he elbowed his way through a forest of microphones, Carrick considered this opportunity to demonstrate Orion's efficiency in extraordinary circumstances. Scare them shitless first, then save the day and take the glory. Already, his presence at the scene would stir rumors and generate a national alien panic as it spread in the next few minutes. Nothing like a good alien scare to consolidate his power...

Carrick squeezed through the door held ajar by the major and popped into the fire chief's small office, Flavia close behind him. The major joined them inside then pushed the door shut, muffling the questions of the press.

The fire chief, surrounded by a few assistants, looked up from a map on the table. He seemed stressed, unshaven, and red-eyed. He'd probably spent a sleepless night. At the sight of Carrick's uniform, the fire chief wrapped up his session and sent his men out with their orders. As they exited, the journalists behind the door pushed to get a shot of Carrick, but the major muscled the door shut.

"Thank you for coming, General." The fire chief offered a firm handshake. "I'd have preferred better circumstances. We are a little over our heads here, as you can see. Our men are not trained for this. When the suit rips or melt, or when they remove their masks because they can't breathe, they are infected by the Green Rage. We know how to fight regular fires, chemical fires, even nuclear fires, but this goes beyond our field of expertise."

"Of course it does. And I now have confirmation that this toxic abomination was engineered by the Anaz-voohri. Knowing them, its purpose can only be to decimate the population of the whole southwestern United States. If this fire is not stopped immediately, millions of people will die from inhaling the green smoke."

The fire chief paled as he raked slim fingers through unkempt hair. "We've never asked for that kind of help before, and normally we wouldn't, but if that much is at stake, we need the National Guard, the military, any Special Forces and heavy equipment available in order to stop this thing. Hell, we'll even accept help from the Global Government if they'll give it."

"That's why I'm here." Carrick congratulated himself for coming after the Dupres bitch himself.

Now he could take the credit for stopping the fire. He turned to Flavia. "Authorize the release of GSS forces and funds for this task force."

Flavia, already seated at one end of the small desk, had opened the computer briefcase, and her fingers made clicking sounds as they flew across the keyboard. "Got it, sir."

"Number one priority." Carrick turned a sympathetic gaze to the fire chief. "You'll have our full support. This is a matter of international security."

"We appreciate your help, general. Is there any kind of bio-suit insulated to resist high temperatures? Our men cannot work efficiently in the ones we have."

Flavia answered mechanically as her eyes remained glued to the computer screen as she kept typing. "We can have them manufactured within a few hours. I also found a number of thermosuits from an abandoned space program. Those will be here within the hour."

"Bio-hazard vehicles to shuttle the men back and forth would help, too. I heard the military had those." The fire chief smiled at Carrick's answers as he went through his wish list.

Carrick enjoyed showing the extent of his power. "You've got them, as well as the special forces trained to use them."

More requests came from the fire chief, punctuated by suggestions from Carrick and Flavia. It now included the latest military and space equipment and enough water bombers to drain all the surrounding lakes, as well as surface teams to cleanup after extinguishing the fire. Amazing what kind of forces could be set in motion when money was no object.

After Flavia made all the necessary requests and received approval, she rose to her feet and approached Carrick to straighten his tie. He caught a whiff of her scented soap.

She smiled as she stepped back. "You're good for the cameras, sir."

Flavia always looked out for him in front of the media. Any public appearance nowadays meant global broadcast, and today, because of what he had to say, the whole world would be watching.

Carrick walked out of the office with confidence, followed by Flavia and the fire chief. Bracing himself for the assault of the press, he held up his hands in entreaty and walked up to the small podium, already set up with several microphones. Carrick looked over the crowd of reporters. To the side, the new recruits suiting up to go fight the fire stopped and hushed as well.

The fire chief spoke first and Carrick could see the spark of relief in his tired face. "Dear friends, we are not alone anymore in this gruesome fight. I give you General Jason Carrick, head of the Operation Readiness Intelligence on Nations, better known as ORION."

A few claps from the crowd forced Carrick to smile and bow in thanks, but he quickly regained his austere composure. "Dear citizens of Earth, we officially are under alien attack. We've confirmed this green toxic fire to be part of a covert Anaz-voohri operation. What's worse, we've been betrayed by one of our own. I give you the human traitor who inflicted this calamity upon her own race. This woman, Celene Dupres, is in league with the Anaz-voohri and we need your help to find and apprehend her."

The crowd murmured when Celene Dupres' face filled the three plasma screens of the gymnasium and all the camera lenses focused on her portrait.

Carrick paused for emphasis, congratulating himself for Flavia's timing on getting the bitch's face on the screen. "With the authority given to me by ORION, I have authorized national and international measures to circumvent this shameful blaze, and you will see major changes within the hour as new contingents and the most sophisticated heavy equipment come into action in the fire zone. Your fire chief will keep you apprised of further developments."

* * * * *

Celene parked the Dial-a-Bike at the far end of the Horse Thief Basin High parking lot, in the shade of tall oleander bushes. She might be gone for a long time and didn't want the expensive machine to get in the way of the constant traffic in and out of the fire headquarters. Before opening the tinted plexiglass door, she removed the gun from her belt and stashed it on the back seat. She wouldn't need it, and it would only attract suspicion. She stepped out and walked toward the school buildings.

On the street curb, a team of firemen in full gear, oxygen masks tucked under one arm, ate energy bars as they boarded a fire truck pulling a water tank the size of a jet refueler. The word on fighting this particular fire with old-fashioned water rather than the usual chemicals had apparently gone out.

Helicopters flew overhead and she could see white tents and ambulances around the football field. Firemen returning from their shift exited a helicopter while another team took off. White Red Cross tents and ambulances waited for casualties. Celene looked up when a large military transport, like the one at the dig site in the Carpathian Mountains, landed at the far end of the field. Its size made the other choppers seem like fireflies.

At the sight of the full contingent of men in blue uniforms spilling on the dry grass and forming ranks, Celene shuddered. They reminded her of ORION soldiers. The fire chief must have called the military to help.

A sign on a classroom wall said Volunteers' Office and pointed its arrow toward the gymnasium a hundred yards away. Someone had parked a limo in the reserved handicapped parking space. The government plates indicated a local official of some sort. How callous.

A group of bedraggled firemen back from their shift could barely walk straight as a volunteer led them into one of the classrooms. When she passed the open door, Celene saw exhausted men collapsing on cots and covering themselves with blankets. A temporary dorm. Other men inside removed their protective gear and threw it on a rolling cart. Celene could be wearing that same gear in a few minutes after she registered. Other fresh recruits like her followed the path to the gymnasium. She smiled her thanks as one held the door for her to enter the building.

Inside, Celene spotted the volunteers' section on

one side. On the other side, reporters surrounded some big wig, probably the politician who came in the limo. While waiting in line, Celene thought about Kin. Would he worry about her when he discovered her escape? Would he miss her? At least, he hadn't told anyone she was responsible for the fire. It gave her a chance to help. And if it meant risking her life, she would gladly do it to help save the people she had endangered.

Her turn finally came and she approached the registration desk.

"Name?" the man asked without looking up.

To avoid being traced by Mythos, Celene lied. "Ashley Miller."

The man looked up and stared at her for a few seconds, a puzzled expression on his face. His jaw went slack, then he yelled, "Here she is! It's Celene Dupres!"

How did they know her name? Had Kin betrayed her after all? Celene looked around frantically as all activity ceased and the journalists turned their cameras in her direction. They looked like they knew what she had done, but who had told them?

Now would be a good time to disappear. Too bad she'd lost the ability. Only one thing to do, fight her way out. She didn't want to injure any innocent people. The menacing faces of the volunteers advancing upon her, however, quickly changed her mind.

Her martial arts training taking over, Celene adopted a loose fighting stance and raised her fists. The throng around her thickened, and none of the angry men and women staring at her seemed intimidated.

"Let's get her!" someone yelled.

The circle of volunteers tightened, then they rushed her all at the same time. Before Celene could say or do anything, hands grabbed her arms and shoulders. She struggled to get free but too many people held on to her. She felt pulled, pushed, and finally lifted off her feet. The mob half carried her toward someone of obvious importance she couldn't see.

The journalists, braver now that she had been subdued, held microphones and cameras above the heads of her captors to get to her. Celene's ears rang with the beat of her blood rushing through her veins. She vaguely heard insults mixed with questions from the journalists, but she was too upset to hear what they said.

She needed to remain calm and made an effort to overcome her fright to face the situation. When the crowd parted and she recognized in front of her the square face the gold-rimmed glasses and the steely fixed stare of Jason Carrick, Celene shuddered. She had walked right into the hands of her worst enemy. The smug expression on his face did nothing to reassure her. She could tell this fanatic wanted her dead.

Carrick's crooked smile congealed. "Miss Dupres, how nice to see you again. I'm afraid I must hold you for interrogation. We have reason to believe you are responsible for this disaster."

All the cameras pointed at Celene and she felt herself flush. "I never wanted this to happen," she protested, trying to break loose, but in her heart she did feel responsible nevertheless.

The crowd roared at her near admission and

enraged faces yelled obscenities. Spit flew into her face. Rough hands dug into her arms and shoulders. Someone kicked her shin.

Furious, Celene kicked back and almost broke free, but four ORION soldiers surged from behind Carrick and grabbed Celene from the hands of the mob. "I came here to help," she yelled to the crowd, as the soldiers cuffed her wrists. She fought and struggled in vain.

The journalists, now brave enough to venture closer, fired questions right up to her face. "What do you have to say?"

"Why did you light the fire?"

"Did you act alone?"

"Are you an alien lover?"

"Did you manufacture the Green Rage virus?"

"What do you have to say to the families of the firefighters who died from the blaze?"

Suddenly the truth hit Celene. People had died. She hadn't known until now. "How many people died?" she asked, but no response came forth.

The soldiers dragged her out of the gymnasium in the midst of the jibes and insults from the volunteers and even a few journalists. Celene didn't have the heart to look at these people anymore. She was responsible for the deaths of several firemen, and she felt crushed by the weight of the shame she felt about it. Her hand, with her alien DNA, had started this ignominious fire.

At her side, Carrick posed for the cameras and waved at the crowd along the path. When they reached the limousine, the soldiers shoved Celene inside, secured her handcuffs to a metal bar and sat on each side of her to keep guard.

Carrick, his tall female assistant, and another military man climbed aboard and sat facing Celene. The door clapped shut, and the limousine pulled out of Horse Thief Basin High parking lot.

Carrick smiled coldly. "Now, Miss Dupres, you are going to tell me everything I want to know, whether you want to or not."

Celene's hands sweated heavily inside the cuffs. Icy tendrils of fear chilled her spine. What would happen to her now?

CHAPTER FIFTEEN

Anaz-voohri swarm, cloaked and hiding on the dark side of the moon

Kavak's brain circuits flared in a futile attempt to master her rage. "What is happening to our forest fire? This small amount of green smoke will not contaminate the whole population of that area as we planned." She made an effort to loosen the grip of her deformed hand on her glass flute as it made the blue cordial inside tremble. She didn't want to appear anxious in front of the subalterns manning their stations on the bridge of her flagship. Through the clear bay window, Kavak could see the dark side of the moon.

Young Wasaw stood at attention in front of the captain's chair. "I suspect that the canyon turbines did not spread enough of the spore before they were shut down."

"The fire must work for our invasion to succeed. The rest of our plan depends on it. We cannot take any chances."

"The humans seemed to be fighting the fire more efficiently than we expected, exalted leader."

Once again, Kavak admired Wasaw's perfect body but she didn't let it distract her. "Lowly humans do not have the technology to defend themselves against our biological weapons. How is that possible?"

"At this distance, I cannot tell." Wasaw cleared his throat. "But they must be using water."

"Water in the desert? I though our ancestors made sure there was no water around the cave, at least none that could be easily tapped."

"These humans proved resourceful in the past."

"Don't remind me!" Kavak fumed at being patronized by such a greenhorn and barely controlled her anger. She drained her glass and set it on her side table none too gently.

Wasaw flinched. "We could go down to the planet to rekindle the fire."

"Aren't we close enough?" Kavak indicated a large screen showing the blue orb. "We can see the fire from here." She needed more cordial to get through this difficult time but refrained from pouring another glass. She didn't want Wasaw to suspect her inclination for the human drink. "We've lost too many ships to these humans already. Every single time we show up, even in the middle of nowhere, they manage to destroy one of our ships. How is getting closer going to fix the problem?"

Wasaw took a deep breath. "We have enough of the spore in my ship's tanks to spray a new cloud on the whole forest, but we must get really close in order to be accurate. Then we will only have to ignite the spores. We can only do that at close range."

"How close?" Kavak shuddered. The last time she'd visited the planet, she'd lost her favorite ship, most of her crew, and almost her life. She would not repeat the same mistake. Humans had become more than a nuisance. Although their primitive weapons couldn't pierce the shields of a ship, they'd showed unexpected cunning.

"We must get just above the forest, hover at low altitude, about three hundred meters."

"I don't like it." Kavak rose and paced in a circle around Wasaw. "I'm sure they have lots of people working on that fire. Showing our vessels to so many would be suicidal. These pesky humans never give up, even when they know they cannot win."

Wasaw's cranium flared brightly. "It's morning now in the canyons. Why don't we wait and do it under cover of night?"

"No. That might be too late." Kavak looked at her empty glass wistfully. "By then they might be organized and find ways to counteract the fire. Timing, remember? Timing is everything."

"Then why not light another fire in a deserted area, far enough to divide their forces. Or we could light several fires. So many they can't possibly fight them all."

Kavak's brain circuits hummed with delight. "Wasaw, you are a genius! I knew you would come up with a plan." Kavak congratulated herself. Handsome and smart. The best specimen for reproduction. "Let's do it now, while all their attention is focused on the canyons."

The young male's excitement lit up his face. "Our vessels are faster and stronger than any of their miserable flying machines, and our multiphasic shields can withstand their attacks. We'll have to use my ship to spray the spore, of course, since the reserves are in my cargo hold."

"But your science vessel was damaged by the cave blast." Why was there always a problem? Kavak hated last minute changes of plans. "And your ship doesn't have adequate weaponry for combat."

"But we have no choice but use my ship. Besides, we shouldn't endanger another ship, and I am willing to sacrifice my humble vessel and my life for the cause."

"No." Kavak wished she could share the youth's enthusiasm. It reminded her of her early years. "I need you alive for other things." Perfect specimens were vital to the Anaz-voohri, the future of the race depended on their survival.

"What do you propose, then?"

Kavak hesitated. She should have a warship accompany Wasaw for protection, but the young male was right. They had lost enough ships. Overcoming her distaste for such tactics, Kavak decided to improvise. "Since your vessel is underarmed, I will lead this mission aboard your ship and bring my own weapons and gunners. They are the best in the fleet."

"But, exalted leader, this could be a dangerous mission, as you pointed out."

"A very important mission that cannot be botched, and a glorious one when it succeeds." Kavak contemplated the added fame it would bring to her reputation as a warrior. "Also, there is no room for error and I trust my gunners."

"It will be a great honor to have you aboard my humble vessel, exalted leader." Wasaw bowed deeply.

"We'll remain cloaked until we get just above the forest and need to spray the spore. If we are swift about it, we can do the job and leave undetected and unscathed." Kavak feared the many satellites around Earth might pick up their cloaked presence and trigger an alarm, but she didn't share her fears with Wasaw.

"What are your orders, exalted leader?"

"The fleet will remain hidden behind the moon. You and I depart as soon as your ship is properly armed."

* * * * *

Temporary ORION headquarters at the Phoenix Science Museum

Carrick and his assistant stepped out of the limo. One of Celene's guards exited, the other pushed Celene out of the car at gunpoint. She couldn't do much handcuffed behind her back, but Celene kicked his shin on her way out, swiftly rewarded by a jab of the barrel in her ribs. It hurt and probably bruised her bones, but she wouldn't give any of these ORION goons the satisfaction of hearing her cry out.

Carrick led the small party at a fast clip through a garden, his shiny boots echoing on the concrete path leading to the recessed entrance of a building. Recognizing downtown Phoenix, Celene glanced back and spotted the Mythos tower merely two blocks away. As she caught her breath in the heavenly scent of orange blossoms, she thought of Kin, so close, yet out of reach. How she wished he were here now.

The four ORION men guarding the building entrance remained immobile as Celene and her escort pushed through the glass doors. Brass letters on the white marble wall read Phoenix Science Museum.

Once inside, the building did look like a legitimate museum with a marble lobby, a ticket counter, and posters of a King Tut exhibit on the wall. In front of the box office, a maze of blue-taped empty lines seemed ready to dam a flow of suspiciously absent visitors. Armed soldiers lounged around on benches or leaned along the walls. Celene counted about twenty. Why did Carrick bring her to a museum?

Carrick instructed his female assistant. She opened her briefcase and set up her computer behind the ticket counter. Signaling for the guards to bring Celene, Carrick crossed the lobby and went through a small door marked Planetarium. The more aggressive of the two soldiers framing Celene shoved her through that same door.

Celene found herself on the ground floor of a vast darkened room. A soldier flipped a switch and floodlights revealed many circular rows of blue bucket seats arranged in stadium sitting under a smooth half-sphere. Several black plastic crates sat haphazardly on the floor, connected with a network of electronic wires.

"Handcuff her to a chair," Carrick barked.

When a soldier pushed Celene down, she sat and noticed the bolts holding the seat to the concrete floor.

"Get your hands behind the backrest." The soldier looked young, too young to be doing Carrick's dirty work.

Celene had to think fast. She offered the man a timid smile. "He didn't say how you should cuff me. You don't need both my hands, you know?" She sneezed on purpose, eliciting a flinch from her guard. "Why don't you tie only one to the side of the chair, that way I can still do a few things for myself and you won't have to hand feed me later. At least I could blow my nose."

The soldier seemed to see the logic of her thinking. He motioned to his friend. "Hold her and keep your eyes on her."

Celene didn't resist or try to escape while they freed her right hand and cuffed the left to the steel frame of the seat. Any untoward move would have been suicide with so many armed soldiers around.

After rattling the cuffs to make sure she couldn't escape, the soldiers finally moved away to take positions at the door. Sitting there, Celene now had a clear view of the circular floor. In the middle, she recognized Emile Blanchard. Celene's blood rushed to her ears at the sight of her father's betrayer. The low life talked to Carrick in whispers. Those two deserved each other.

The small console next to the two men looked like the alien reading device in the cave. Now it all made sense. Celene knew exactly why Carrick had brought her here, to decipher the relics. "I won't do it," she shouted at the two men.

Emile Blanchard squared his tall frame, turned his grizzled head toward Celene and smiled warmly. How could he smile after what happened? Carrick's expression revealed nothing. How she hated both of them; Blanchard for betraying her stepfather and Carrick for hunting her like a rabid dog and wounding Kin in the process.

Carrick flashed one of his cold smiles. The gray fix of his stare through the gold-rimmed glasses only added to the threat exuding from his clean-shaven features. "Oh, but you will, Miss Dupres, you will tell us exactly what we want to know." He remained at a safe distance, probably for fear to soil his perfectly pressed uniform if she tried to kick him.

"Or what? You'll kill me? I don't care." Celene really believed she'd rather die than help these government-appointed terrorists.

"There are ways to make you talk, Miss Dupres, alive, or dead. We could even clone you and reprogram your DNA to tell us all you know. Or we could keep you alive and connect your brain to an alien computer to read your thoughts. So, you see, you will cooperate."

Celene wondered how much of his threat Carrick could actually carry out but didn't care to find out right this minute. "You don't scare me." Brave last words. Celene could hardly control her shaking.

"When I return in a few hours, I want to see some progress on this translation, Miss Dupres, or else, people will start to die, innocent people, women, children, animals, your favorite kind."

Celene shuddered. Would Carrick resort to killing innocents for leverage? He probably would. Maybe if she accepted, she could make the progress so slow that it would not help him at all. She had to delay him, but giving up too easily would raise suspicion. "I hate you, and I don't want to help you, but I can't let innocent people die for me, so I'll do it, but on one condition."

"I am listening."

"No soldiers in the room. Just me and Blanchard."

Blanchard, who sat on a crate a few feet away, listened with obvious interest, the small tool in his hand all but forgotten.

"Agreed." Carrick smiled diabolically and waved the two guards away. After they left the room, he added, "These soldiers don't have clearance anyway, but they'll be right behind that door, and there are more guards at each door on the upper levels as well."

"And you'll leave, too?"

"Believe me, I have better things to do with my time than babysit you."

Celene shook her shackles. "And I will need both my hands free. I can't translate without walking around to read each page."

Carrick burst into loud laughter, making the metal decorations on his chest tremble. "Do you think I was born from the last rain? Although this facility is heavily guarded, I am no fool, Miss Dupres. Blanchard can be your eyes. You are staying cuffed to your seat, and you are going to help us one way or another, alive or dead. Your choice." Carrick turned to Blanchard. "Keep an eye on her and yell at any suspicious move. Understood?"

Blanchard rose from the crate and nodded. Carrick left the planetarium and closed the door.

All alone with Blanchard in the dome, Celene felt the anger she'd bottled up tighten her chest. "You are the most despicable person I know!" All the bile that had built up since Armand Dupres' murder spewed out. "I considered you a beloved uncle, our closest friend. How could you?"

Blanchard's bushy eyebrows rose in surprise. "I never did anything to you, child. Why do you hate me so?"

"You betrayed us." The words seemed too weak for what Celene felt right now. Tears threatened to choke her, but she struggled to keep her calm.

Blanchard shook his balding gray head. The white smock emphasized his pale blue gaze. "I never betrayed you, child. Armand was a filthy hybrid. I may have considered him a friend for a short while, but after I discovered he was a hybrid, I only pretended. My true friends are human like you and me."

"I know my father was a hybrid, but I don't believe he worked for the Anaz-voohri." She wished she could strangle the appalling man.

Blanchard returned to adjusting the controls of the reading device. "It doesn't matter whether he was working for them or not. Armand constituted a danger to the purity of our race." He smiled at her with understanding, as he used to, years ago. "There are many ways to win a war, kiddo, and the Anaz-voohri may just want to breed humanity out of us and make us part of them. Did you ever think about that?"

Celene snorted.

"You are lucky you were not Armand's true daughter, otherwise, ORION would have killed you long ago." He stepped back from the decoder, hands on his hips, a satisfied expression on his face.

"Lucky?" Suddenly, Celene realized Blanchard didn't know she was one of the Pleiades sisters. Could it be he knew nothing about ORION's secret projects? If Carrick hadn't told him, Blanchard had no idea how dangerous or valuable Celene was to ORION. Perhaps she could turn this to her advantage.

"Now, we have a job to do." Blanchard cocked his

head as if talking to a child. "Are you going to help me decipher these shards or not?"

Playing for time, Celene wanted to keep him talking. "Not until you tell me how you found out my father was a hybrid. I certainly didn't know it. And I never heard anything or saw anything that could implicate him as a hybrid in my whole life with him." She'd say anything to delay the translation.

A fleeting smile animated Blanchard's pale blue eyes. "It was your mother."

Celene felt the blood drain out of her face. She hadn't thought about her adoptive mother and her mysterious death in a long time. "What about her?" She felt her rage flare anew. "What about that sweet woman?"

"I found out she was a hybrid during a dig in the Pyrenees." Blanchard nodded with pride.

It was in the Pyrenees that her mother had died. Obviously, Blanchard had no idea how his words affected Celene. She wanted to cry, but she had to remain strong, let him think she shared his loathing for hybrids. Celene wanted to know what had happened to the dear woman, if only for her father's sake. "Go on."

Blanchard smiled as if about to tell a favorite epic story. "Marianne was pretty, and at one time I envied Armand for his beautiful wife."

Celene tried not to wince at her mother's first name used familiarly by such a despicable man.

"But one night, as I came to her tent in hopes of seducing her, I saw her use a strange device to communicate with an alien vessel hovering above our camp. I listened to her for a while, then I saw the spaceship move away through the clouds."

Was Marianne really plotting with the Anaz-voohri? Could it be that Armand Dupres had sheltered Celene from that knowledge all her life? "You are lying."

"Hear me out." Blanchard sat back on the crate, at a safe distance. "The next morning, I knew what I must do. I offered to work with her on an isolated site of the dig behind a hillock. The area was riddled with caves, and I knew of a particular shaft that went deep underground."

Celene caught her breath but did not interrupt.

"We were out of sight behind the slope. When I grabbed the shovel, Marianne saw me, and she knew right away I'd found her out. She tried to run but I grabbed her. The hybrid bitch screamed. As the wind carried her voice away, the waterfall and the mountain side muffled any kind of sound from those digging on the other side." He shook his head derisively. "She knew I was going to kill her, but all she talked about was her husband. When she begged me to spare his life, I figured out he must be a hybrid, too."

"So you killed her?"

"I sure did." A slow smile touched Blanchard's lips. "I shattered her skull and threw her into that hole. Then I cleaned the blood from the shovel, erased all traces of struggle and went running for help, saying she'd fallen into the deep cave. No one ever suspected anything."

Although she felt devastated, Celene didn't want Blanchard to see her dismay. "My father suspected foul play, but never from his very best friend."

"That's the beauty of it! After some research, I found out Armand was a hybrid, too. But when I contacted ORION, they asked me to stick with him and report his every move."

Celene felt trapped with this abominable Blanchard she had once cherished as a friend. She had to think. She wore Kin's medallion under her sweater and knew it was a communicating device, but she had no idea how the thing worked. She raked her brains for more questions to keep Blanchard talking. "Any other hybrid hunters like you I should be aware of among our old friends?"

"Quite a few, actually."

"Go on." Celene casually pulled out the medallion from under her sweater with her free hand and played with it. She could feel no specific button, knob, or anything as to how to make it work. Was it DNA activated?

"Your sweetheart in Moscow, the handsome conservator of the Archeological Museum, Sergei Ivanovitch, helped us spot hybrids and was keeping tabs on Armand while we were in Russia."

"Sergei?" Celene couldn't help the surprise and the betrayal in her voice. *The bastard!* So that's why the crates bore his museum's seal. "And all this time, he pretended to be helping me? He can go to hell!"

"Be content, sweet girl." Blanchard laughed. "He's in hell right now."

"What do you mean?"

"Helping you cost him his life, courtesy of General Carrick." Blanchard drew a line across his neck with the small electronic tool he still held.

"Sergei is dead?" This was too much to take at one time. Celene needed to center herself, or she would lose her mind.

"The General doesn't like loose ends."

"So I noticed." Celene remembered the translation. They'd better start. Carrick did not make empty threats.

"Interesting piece, your medallion."

Celene laid her hand over it protectively. "It was my mother's," she lied. "A souvenir from China. Ming dynasty."

Blanchard rose and stepped closer. "May I see it?"

Apprehensive, Celene let him come close. She couldn't show her revulsion for him, or she would lose his support. She might need him to escape.

Now so close she could feel his breath, Blanchard took the medallion in his hand. "An exquisite piece." He tapped the jade dragon lightly with his electronic tool. "It's ancient jade all right. Definitely Ming design." He raised one brow. "I never saw it before, and Marianne never mentioned it."

"I guess she didn't tell you everything." Celene couldn't prevent the smugness in her voice.

Blanchard let go of the medallion and sighed. "Marianne had too many secrets." He flashed Celene a sudden smile. "Shall we start the translation? I'm glad Carrick could find you. You are the best I can think of."

Celene nodded reluctantly, and when Blanchard turned off the light and activated the device, she was not surprised to see the planetarium dome fill up with pages and pages of luminous three-dimensional pictographs. But she couldn't concentrate on the alien writing. All she could think was, how would she ever get out of this mess?

CHAPTER SIXTEEN

Kin awoke from a drugged sleep in the white sterile room of the Mythos installation. The hospital smell made him want to throw up. His head swam, and his bed moved and rattled as if in an earthquake. The room steadied around him, but the bed kept rattling. "By the great wall of China!"

His vision focused on the foot of the bed, where the red face of a young soldier emerged, black and blue where his eye was swollen shut. The young man's taped mouth made muffled sounds. He obviously struggled and strained, but Kin couldn't see against what. Then he realized the young man was shaking the heavy hospital bed.

In an effort to sit up, Kin fell right back on the pillow. The metal brace immobilizing his right side from chest to thigh restrained his movements. The pain he'd experienced right after the surgery, however, had subsided. He waved to the struggling soldier. "Hold on, buddy."

Tossing blanket and sheet aside, Kin pulled out the IV feeding his hand and examined the brace fitted on top of his blue pajamas. It looked simple enough. A few large bolts held it in place. He had to strain to loosen the first bolt with his fingers to unscrew the chest plates, then the hip plates. Kin struggled to reach the bolts over his lower thigh. The tightness in his hip did not interfere with the sense of freedom he experienced when the brace fell away.

Kin took a deep breath and smiled. He probed the tenderness of his hip wound with careful fingers through the bandages. It still hurt, but he had to get up. Kin sat up slowly, fighting the urge to heave. He dangled his legs above the floor, eased his weight on the right foot then gingerly tested the right. He could stand without too much pain.

In two careful steps, Kin reached the foot of the bed. The soldier struggled on the floor, hog-tied, hands and feet bound together behind his back with surgical tape. Tethered to the bed frame, he looked more pissed and humiliated than hurt.

Kin chuckled but sobered immediately as it made his hip hurt. "Who trussed you up like a pig for the market?" He reached for the tape on the soldier's mouth and pulled.

The soldier flinched as the tape came off then he rubbed his jaw against his shoulder. "The feisty little bitch gave me the slip."

"Celene?" Who else could overcome this big boy of a soldier? Relieved at the idea that she had fled, Kin wondered where she went. If she made it to the outside, how safe would she be without his protection? He had to find her.

The soldier arched and motioned to his side blade. "Can you get to my knife?"

Kin nodded. He winced as pain flared in his hip when he bent over to reach for the soldier's blade. Kin cut the tape binding the man's feet and hands. "She did a nice job."

"Yeah, a real pro. Thanks, man." The soldier rose on unsteady legs and shook his wrists. "You okay? You shouldn't be on your feet, man. Better get back to bed."

Kin handed back the soldier's knife. "That's what the doctor might say." He moved his hip tentatively. Some mobility returned, and he decided to stay out of bed. "I think I'd better exercise these muscles before they forget how to work." Besides, he needed to find Celene and wanted to know if the fire had stopped burning. Did the antidote work? Probably. Celene wouldn't have escaped otherwise.

The soldier offered a handshake. "Thanks for your help, man. I'd better go report. I'm in big trouble. You take care of that injury."

Kin shook the offered hand. "No sweat. I'll be fine."

After the soldier left, Kin limped to the open closet displaying several sets of black clothes in various sizes. He recognized his boots on the floor. He selected a pair of jeans and a sweater. The pants fit tight over the bulky hip bandage. Good. It would act as a hip brace of sorts.

Had the microsurgery healed enough? He hoped moving around would not cause internal bleeding. Surgery had come a long way since the turn of the millennium, and recovery times had shortened considerably. Besides, Kin's nanobots would speed up the healing process.

During his stay at the CEM in China, when ORION had manipulated his DNA to make him a killing machine, they added fast healing to his genetic code. They'd increased his pain threshold, too. Still, Kin had to sit on the chair to pull on his boots. His head swam a little as he stood up again.

Kin intended to stop by the armory for weapons. When he went to get his medallion from the bedside table, he realized it was gone. Who had dared? Only Celene came to mind. But why would she do such a thing?

More confident by the minute in his ability to walk, Kin left the room but stopped in the hallway. He didn't know the layout of the facility. It was his first time here, and he'd been unconscious when he came in. He walked the length of the corridor and only found three empty hospital rooms. Entering the elevator, he hoped to find some direction there but nothing identified the floors, so he pressed the buttons in succession on the way down. Each time the elevator stopped, he peeked into the hallway.

After several floors of sterile medical offices, he glimpsed an operative rushing along the corridor. From the seriousness of the armed man's face, he must be answering an important call. Kin recognized the distinctive smell of sweat and weapon common to all Mythos offices. This must be his department. He exited and followed the man.

If the operative answered an urgent call, Kin wanted to know what had happened. The man entered an office and Kin stopped in the doorway. The bank of plasma screens on the wall displayed images transmitted by various operatives in the field. The men and women at the computer tables talked into their headsets to relay instructions and information. Kin smiled at the familiar buzz of efficient activity. He'd found the monitoring room.

Looking for someone in charge, Kin walked to the young woman with short blond hair and serious gray eyes talking to the operative who'd just rushed into the room. "What's happening?" Kin asked, now quite in his element.

The girl faced him and glanced at his black uniform. "We have a feed from the field that has been going on for hours, but we don't know why we are receiving these images or what they represent. We are recording them as a precaution. It's coming from Icarus, but he doesn't respond to our hails. He could be in trouble."

Snapping up at his code name, Kin turned on his screamer implant and focused on the monitor. The display of alien pictographs confirmed that Celene must have his medallion, but he couldn't see her. She had to be wearing it. "The problem is Icarus is not in the field. I'm Icarus, and I'm right here."

The girl studied his face then quickly punched a few keys. Kin's official portrait in black silk robes, with longer hair in a pigtail, appeared on her computer screen. "Right you are. Sorry. I had to check."

Kin waved away the apology. "Where is the feed coming from?"

"Hard to tell. We cannot track the device by satellite. It's shielded."

"I know." Kin stared at the screen displaying luminous three-dimensional pictographs floating in a dark dome, and an old man in a white smock. "Do we have sound as well?"

"Yes. I'll send it to the speakers and feed the images to the main screen."

As soon as the speakers went online, all eyes focused on the largest wall monitor showing the pictographs. The workers in the room quieted and listened.

The feminine voice in the speakers complained. "I could translate faster if I wasn't cuffed to this stupid chair. I wouldn't have to explain every subtle nuance to you. This could take forever. Why don't you tell them to untie me?"

Kin recognized the voice immediately. "It's Celene Dupres, my target. She is translating alien relics.

The old man on the screen shrugged. "Sorry, kid, what the boss says goes. Let's get back to work."

Kin didn't recognize the man. "Can we ID the old wizard?"

The blond woman started a search on a laptop. On a split screen she pasted the old man's face on one side. On the other side, various ID portraits from a government data bank scrolled at great speed, comparing facial structures.

A young man turned to Kin. "Celene Dupres? She was caught by ORION at the fire headquarters early this morning. She's accused of starting the green fire. Check this."

On another screen, Kin now saw Celene struggling between bodyguards while Carrick paused for the journalists.

"Damn!" Kin had left Celene unprotected and now

ORION had her. Pulling up a chair as his hip pulsed painfully, Kin sat down. "Can we figure out where she is from the pictures we are receiving? It couldn't be very far from here and has to be some kind of dome." The canyon cave came to Kin's mind, but he'd seen it destroyed. Besides, the dome on the monitor looked smaller. "Any half-spherical buildings, geodesic domes, cupolas, or architecture of this kind in the area?

The blond woman and the young man seemed excited by the challenge and punched more keys on their keyboards.

"Does anyone recognize the room on the main screen?" Kin asked the whole team.

Most of the workers shook their heads without taking their eyes off the screen. Others searched on their computers.

The girl shook her head as well. "Maybe I can enhance the picture, it's so dark."

"Can you widen the angle, too?" Kin hoped it would reveal new details.

The girl nodded. The monitor now brightened and a wider angle showed row upon row of blue bucket seats from the circular floor, all the way to the domed ceiling.

The laptop on the desk beeped. The file faces had stopped scrolling and the computer flashed in big red letters MATCH FOUND. A younger picture of the old man appeared on the other side of the split screen.

The girl opened the file. "The man is Emile Blanchard, a Canadian archeologist."

Kin had heard the name before. "Who is he associated with?"

The blond girl scrolled down the file. "He recently worked with Armand Dupres on several digs. Last seen ten days ago on his way to the Ukraine."

"That's it!" Kin remembered now. Celene said her father's team had been butchered in Ukraine. This had to be the man who betrayed her father. "He works for Jason Carrick." Kin shuddered. Celene needed help, and fast.

A male worker interrupted. "I found several domed rooms listed in the Phoenix area. There is a church with a cupola in Sedona, The observatory south of Phoenix, the planetarium at the Phoenix Science Museum. There are also a few geodesic domes in the surrounding countryside. Most of them private homes built in the sixties."

"This doesn't look like a private home. Too many seats..." Kin had to think fast. They don't look like church seats either. Can you find out from the images which structure this is most likely to be?"

"I have a hunch." The blond woman went online and clicked on the city website. "Here is a picture of the inside of the planetarium at the Science Museum. See the design of the blue bucket seats? They tilt backwards so people can look at the ceiling without twisting their necks. They were custom-made for the Phoenix Science Museum."

"Great job!" Kin struggled to keep the excitement from his voice. "Can we hack into the Museum's security cameras?"

The blond girl smiled devilishly. "You bet we can." She accessed the city security grid from the website.

After a few strokes and several pass codes, images from the museum security cameras appeared on several screens. One showed the planetarium, and this time, Kin could see Celene cuffed to one of the seats of the bottom row. She looked tired and disheveled, and she wore his medallion. The building entrance and the lobby looked heavily guarded.

Kin's blood rushed to his head. "How far is the Science Museum from here?" He knew ORION would kill her as soon as she finished the translation. Kin wouldn't rest until Celene was safe.

"Only two blocks."

Suddenly the main screen lit up, and the medallion's camera focused on the stocky figure of Jason Carrick with his gold-rimmed glasses, a somber expression on his face. The workers in the room gasped. They all recognized Carrick.

Kin's heart pounced in his chest. "I need the blueprints of the Science Museum and an assault team right away."

* * * * *

Phoenix Science Museum

Celene didn't like the cruel glint in Carrick's eye as he stormed into the planetarium and leered at her. Exhausted from hours of translation, she was in no mood for his harassment.

"Thank you for your cooperation, Miss Dupres. With the basic knowledge you imparted to us, we will be able to continue the translation with our own staff."

Blanchard nodded, a proud expression on his face.

Celene castigated herself for giving Blanchard too much information. Unable to leave her chair, she had to explain to him how the decoding of the language worked. Obviously, he'd picked up on it faster than she expected.

Carrick paced in front of Celene, each of his steps fueling her hatred. "There are other important things I would like you to do for me." He stopped pacing and faced her. "I know you can disappear at will. Could you explain to me how this is achieved?"

"Do you think that if I could disappear, as you say, I would be here shackled to this chair?" Her short temper made her words snap. Careful, she reminded herself. This man was dangerous.

"Your theatrics do not fool me." Carrick straightened and locked his hands behind this back. "I know the ability lies in your DNA, probably a gift from your Anaz-voohri friends."

Stepping in front of Celene, Blanchard faced Carrick. "Leave her alone. She has nothing to do with the Anaz-voohri."

"Oh, yeah?" Carrick grimaced. "You are a scientist, Blanchard. Think logically. How do you explain the fact that she understands their language so well?"

Emile Blanchard scratched his balding gray head. "She's just very bright with languages, always was, even as a kid."

Celene couldn't help but smile inwardly at the naivety of the old man's reasoning. How simple his world must be, all black and white, humans against hybrids and aliens, and nothing in between. In his eyes, she was human and consequently innocent.

Carrick motioned Blanchard to step aside. "You have no idea what we are dealing with, here, so fuck off."

Reluctantly, Blanchard moved away, but he remained close. Carrick approached Celene and his quicksilver glass eye made her shiver. Too bad he remained out of her kicking range. She would have loved to drive her booted foot where it hurt most.

As if he'd guessed her thwarted intent, Carrick smiled. "I know how to get the information from your DNA if you don't want to tell me. It's all written in your bone marrow. Unfortunately for you, my scientists tell me it doesn't matter whether you are dead or alive." The man visibly enjoyed making his macabre threat.

"I can't tell you anything because I don't know anything." And that was the plain truth. Celene really didn't know anything about the process, how she'd gained the ability, or how she'd lost it. It had only happened a few times under certain conditions. "I can't become invisible and that's the end of it." She didn't even have to lie.

"I dared hope you would cooperate, but I was wrong." Carrick reached for the gun at his hip, not a phase-gun but an old-fashioned side arm.

Celene felt suddenly cold, as if all the blood had drained from her body.

Aiming at Celene, Carrick grinned. "*Au revoir*, Miss Dupres. You will not be a threat to the human race anymore, and you will give us in death the secrets you refused to divulge in life."

"Don't shoot!" Blanchard yelled.

Celene closed her eyes and prayed. *Dear God, please help me.* The shot echoed in the high vault of the planetarium. Celene's heart did a summersault, but she didn't feel a thing. She opened her eyes to see Blanchard collapsing in front of her, holding his chest.

Stunned, Celene stared at the man who'd stepped in front of her to take the bullet. The depth of human foolishness never ceased to amaze her. Blanchard crumpled at her feet. The crimson stain on his white smock spread rapidly and pulsated with spurting blood. Celene stared into his pale blue eyes. "Why did you do that?"

Blanchard only smiled and his gaze went out of focus.

"Stupid fuck!" Carrick exclaimed. "Why did you have to interfere?" He aimed for Celene again.

Several doors at various levels of the planetarium slammed open and armed commandos stormed into the place. Carrick kept his aim on Celene and yelled to the intruders, "I said whatever happens, do not interfere." Then he looked around and the anger on his face grew into puzzlement. "Who the fuck?"

But the men in black had already reached him and knocked the weapon out of his hand. That's when Celene realized they were not ORION soldiers but a Mythos SWAT team.

Celene almost fainted from the relief she felt at the sight of Kin standing before her.

"Are you all right?" Kin knelt to her level and touched her face.

Shaking uncontrollably, Celene started to sob as all

Vijaya Schartz 267

the pent up tension left her. She let her tears flow freely and leaned her face into his hand. With her free hand, she pulled his face closer for a kiss and through her tears she saw him wince.

Suddenly Celene remembered his wound. "What are you doing here? You should be in bed," she sobbed.

"Thanks for the welcome." He kissed her cheek lightly. "I had hoped you'd be pleased to see me."

Her nervous laugh sounded hysterical, even to her ears. "I am happy to see you, believe me."

Beyond Kin, Carrick struggled against two strong commandos who overpowered him. "You can't touch me! Mythos will pay for this. I'll have you all in front of a firing squad for assaulting a GSS General."

Unimpressed by Carrick's ravings the commandos handcuffed him to one of the heavy crates. One commando remained to stand guard over him while the other threw Kin a small object. "The key."

Kin caught the key and nodded his thanks then knelt before Celene to unlock her restraints.

She saw the imperceptible flinch in his face as he bent over. "Still hurts, hey?"

Kin's grin only confirmed her suspicions. He'd rescued her against doctor orders. Somehow that pleased her. Kin pushed the remote button and the cuffs came off.

Celene rubbed her left wrist. By God, she was glad to see him. She rose and threw her arms around him, hoping her wet smile conveyed her gratitude. "You saved my life. Again." She chuckled. "Seems like a habit of yours."

His grin widened as he stepped back from her embrace. "I don't let anyone take away what's mine."

"Yours?" Celene mocked, as if offended to be considered property, but inside she felt warm and safe knowing that he valued their relationship. How she'd missed him.

He lifted the jade medallion off her chest, untangled it from her long hair at the back of her neck then slipped the chain around his neck. "Yes, mine. Didn't you steal my family crest?"

Confused, Celene frowned. "Oh, you mean that thing?"

"Of course. It's a priceless heirloom. What else did you think I meant?"

"Nothing." She hated to give him the advantage. He knew what she'd concluded and seemed to enjoy her embarrassment way too much.

A commando entered the planetarium from the lobby and rushed toward Kin. "Sir, we have a bigger problem." He motioned to the tall Mediterranean woman behind him to come forward. Celene recognized Flavia, Carrick's assistant.

"What?" Kin asked, some impatience in his voice.

Flavia hesitated then straightened her curvaceous figure. "Luke Air Force Base spotted on their radar an alien ship above northern Arizona," she enunciated with a slight accent. "They are awaiting orders from General Carrick as to what action to take."

"Is this a trick? Can we confirm this?" Kin tapped his medallion. "Mythos? This is Icarus. Can you confirm the sighting of an alien vessel above northern Arizona?"

As Kin remained silent for a while, Celene guessed he listened to the voice of Mythos. "Thanks," he finally said then nodded to the small group. "According to our satellite pictures, the spaceship is right now in north central Arizona, and it seems a new fire emanating green smoke just started in that vicinity."

"Dear God!" Celene couldn't fathom the destruction a new green fire would bring.

Carrick laughed derisively. "What are you bunch of clowns going to do about it now? While you are playing little soldiers and preventing me from doing my job, they merrily light more green fires. Perfect!"

"Shut up." The commando guarding him hit his shoulder with the butt of his gun.

Carrick grunted but did not relent. "You don't have any other choice but to let me go, now. I have a job to do. This is my department. Or are you going to let the alien scum eradicate the human race while you idly stand by?"

The commandos murmured in protest at his insult.

"He's right!" Kin shouted.

The men fell silent.

"Only he can stop them." Kin signaled two of his men. "Take the shards and the decoding device."

"This is high treason in war times," Carrick yelled.

"Don't worry," Kin controlled his voice to keep it calm. "We already have the translation. We'll get you a copy." He motioned to his men. "Let's move out. Give the keys to the assistant and she can free him and the rest of his soldiers after we are gone."

Grabbing Celene by the arm, Kin pulled her toward the exit. "You come with me. We have another job to do."

CHAPTER SEVENTEEN

"Fucking amateurs," Carrick muttered as Flavia unlocked his handcuffs. Rubbing his wrists, he watched her full breasts stretching the blue uniform as she stood up.

"I have to free the men, sir. I'll be right back." Flavia walked out of the planetarium at a military jaunt.

Carrick couldn't believe the audacity of the Mythos operatives, but filing an official complaint would only be a waste of time. President Grant would refute his accusations. Lawson Archer, the man behind Mythos, had powerful connections and a bottomless bank account. Carrick hated these civilians with more money than brains. They had way too much time on their hands to mess with matters of global security.

"Are you all right, sir?" Flavia's dark doe eyes looked concerned as she returned, carrying her briefcase. She'd kept a cool head during the ordeal. Not a hair out of place on her perfectly tight bun. He might give her a raise.

"Get me the general in charge of Luke Air Force Base on his private line."

Flavia set her briefcase on the heavy trunk where Carrick had been cuffed and raised her eyebrows. "Not the flotilla, sir?"

"The flotilla is too far for their jets to make here in

time. Luke is closer."

Flavia opened the laptop and handed him the pencil-microphone as the Luke A.F.B. seal appeared on her computer, then the tired face of a stressed out general filled the screen. These local hot shots knew nothing about real stress. The slightest incident bent them out of shape.

Carrick pulled down his uniform jacket, as he knew the laptop relayed his image in return. "I want air to air missiles, squadrons of fighter planes, and our latest hardware targeting this alien ship immediately. Hit it with everything you've got. Just be fast about it, before they disappear. And remember, they will shoot back. They want war? They'll have war. Send your best."

The general's face grew somber. He fidgeted in his chair. "I see... Did the President approve this decision?"

"I don't give a fuck about the President. I'm in charge of this war, General. You have your orders. Or would you prefer to face a firing squad for treason?"

The general sighed. "I'll send our top guns."

"That's all I ask." Carrick severed the communication from the pencil mike and turned to Flavia. "Now give me the ORION flotilla. These cowboys will need back up if they survive the first attack."

* * * * *

Kin looked winded from running with Celene the two blocks to the Mythos tower, and she wondered how his wound fared. He showed signs of fatigue and pressed is hand against his still tender hip. She followed him inside the elevator at the foot of the Mythos tower. "Where are we going now?"

Kin pushed the button marked roof. "To the helicopter. It has a full battery of the latest missiles. Let's give these Anaz-voohri a taste of what's waiting for them if they want to fight us up close."

"But you are in no condition to fly, even less to fight." Celene didn't want to think of what would happen to her if she lost him. He almost died once and she didn't want to take that chance.

"Never stopped me before." He grinned. "It's easier to sit in the pilot's chair than run two blocks, and I just did that. Besides, I'm counting on you to keep me from passing out. You did a good job of it last time."

Celene wanted to protest but she knew nothing would stop Kin when he had an idea in mind. Besides, if they did not stop the Anaz-voohri, there would be no civilization left in this part of the world. Celene hated herself for creating this disaster.

The elevator opened onto the roof level. Celene shuddered as she recognized the stealth helicopter in which they'd barely escaped with their lives after the scuffle with ORION. But she also felt a thrill about going up against the Anaz-voohri. They'd messed with her life, and now she would get a chance to get back at them. The idea of shooting down the bastards made her feel powerful, in charge of her own destiny.

Kin addressed one of the armed sentinels guarding the rooftop. "Is the bird ready?"

The man saluted. "Aye, sir." The guard motioned his men to clear the helipad and relayed orders in his helmet communicator. The sentinels surrounding the chopper retreated to the edges of the roof.

Celene had palpitations as she boarded the helicopter. Blood still stained the cargo floor and the pilot seat. Was she out of her mind going into combat with a simple helo against a spaceship? But the intensity in Kin's face made her equally determined. She knew she'd follow him anywhere.

Kin checked the controls and started the engine in silent mode. He smiled reassuringly and she answered in kind as the bird lifted above the tower and veered north above the city.

When had she started to trust him again? He'd just saved her life for the fourth time but never mentioned what would become of her. Was he still under orders to kill her? She couldn't think of that now. An alien ship had started new green fires, and Celene knew she must do whatever it took to stop it. If they failed, nothing would matter anymore.

* * * * *

Anaz-voohri ship over northern Arizona

Kavak actually enjoyed her trip to the planet, even in Wasaw's clumsy ship. On the bridge Wasaw and the pilot navigated the vessel without incident. Kavak's previous fears seemed now irrelevant. How could she ever think substandard humans had the power to impede her plans? Within half an hour, Wasaw had successfully ignited two new green fires and no earth people had even tried to interfere. Obviously, their rudimentary technology had not detected the spaceship.

As Kavak approached Wasaw from behind, he turned to face her, looking startled.

Kavak smiled inwardly. She liked to test her subalterns. A true warrior would never let anyone sneak up on him. "I want you to start a new fire near the city, where the wind will quickly blow the smoke over the populated areas."

Wasaw cleared his throat. "The wind blows in the wrong direction, exalted leader."

"Can't we change that?" Kavak had no patience for scientists. They tended to let details get in the way.

Sheepishly, Wasaw nodded. "We can create a vortex centering on the city. It will attract the winds from all over. But we run the risk of bringing rain clouds from the oceans over the fires. The clouds may not burst, of course, but then again, they might extinguish the fires."

Kavak sighed. "How long before the rain falls?" She barely contained her impatience.

"A day or two."

"So what? That's ample time for the smoke to infect the whole population in this part of the continent. And since they have no antidote. "Images of destruction and violence filled Kavak's mind with delight. She had waited long enough to conquer the blasted planet. The Anaz-voohri needed it more than these unworthy humans.

"What if they bring reinforcements to fight the fires?" Would Wasaw ever cease his negative comments?

"Good! They'll all get contaminated." The thought brought a smile to Kavak's lips. "Let's do it."

As Wasaw prepared to drop the load of spores over a new stretch of woods, Kavak saw him hesitate and asked, "What's wrong?"

Wasaw turned around abruptly and yelled at the pilot. "Shields up! We have company."

On the screen, several dots appeared around the spacecraft and launched their crude projectiles. Several explosive shots bounced off the vessel's shield.

Kavak held on to a secure seat as the craft lurched. "By Kokopelli's flute!" Did these puny humans think they could thwart her plan? Rage flushed her body and face. Humans had defeated her before, but usually through ruse, never through sheer force. Their weapons couldn't pierce the multiphasic shields enveloping the hull like a sheer impenetrable net. "They can't hurt us! Just ignore them and finish the job!"

"But I can't drop the spore with the shields up." Wasaw shrank under her stare. "Besides, we moved out of range. We are now above the city."

"Go on with the vortex, then. We'll light the fire later." Kavak switched the deck screen to the gunners' turrets. "Battle stations! Retaliate! Fire at will!"

On the screen, her best shooters came into action.

A beacon pulsed red and beeped on the wall panel. Kavak motioned with her chin. "What's that?"

Wasaw glanced up at the panel then focused on his console. "That's sister Celene's marker, exalted leader. She must be near, very near."

"Really?" Finally some good news! A slow smile touched Kavak's lips. "I have an idea."

* * * * *

Celene let out a cry when the alien ship above them fired back and hit one of the fighting jets. She held on to the armrest as Kin banked the helicopter, avoiding the crossfire. As one of the small planes burst into flames, Celene saw the pilot eject and a parachute deploy.

A dozen military jets now harassed the big alien ship, dodging and shooting like bees stinging a rhinoceros. The black, unreflective surface of the craft would probably go unseen in the dark vastness of space. The large Anaz-voohri vessel looked bulky, clumsier than the sleek golden spaceship Celene had seen buried in the Carpathian Mountains. Of oblong design, this vessel showed irregular bumps and a few sharp angles, as if extra storage tanks and accessories had been added as an afterthought.

Celene's mind reeled as she took in the size of the ominous ship. "Why don't you shoot?"

Kin's jaw stiffened as he stared at his targeting screen. "Look at the jets. Their missiles are ineffective and ours would be, too. This is a waste of ammunition. I want to make every strike count," he said between clenched teeth. "There is some kind of electromagnetic shielding around the hull."

"I'm surprised they don't shoot at us. I'm sure they can see us." How such a large heavy structure could remain immobile in mid-air above them baffled the mind.

"Maybe they think we are no threat to them." Kin gave Celene a flicker of a smile. "I guess we look like harmless onlookers as long as we don't shoot."

The jets had moved further back and now fired from a distance, but the alien shooters exploded the missiles in mid air before they reached their target. Another jet went down. A large missile, more like a small rocket, whistled toward the ship, but it, too disintegrated under the alien artillery fire before even touching its target.

"That was a ground to air missile." Kin looked discouraged.

Celene wanted to do something, anything. "Can we get closer?"

Kin scoffed. "And I thought I was the reckless one."

At the moment, Celene could think of nothing to fight the behemoth but refused to give in to helplessness. "We cannot afford to lose this fight. What about a nuclear bomb?"

Kin shook his head. "That would endanger the city below. And even that might not damage the craft."

"So we do nothing?" Celene saw a flicker just below and pointed down. "What's happening? Look!"

Around the underbelly of the alien vessel, a shimmering crown had formed, a strong magnetic field of some kind. It started spinning like the eye of a hurricane, attracting dust and debris into its vortex.

"This can't be good." Kin veered the helicopter away from under the alien vessel. "I don't want to get caught in that gusty wind." He circled the vessel to position the helicopter above it.

"I wonder what they are doing." As she finished the sentence, Celene felt a tingling in her arms and legs, a sensation she previously associated with becoming invisible. But she could still see her body. A white flash enveloped her, she felt herself flying into a beam of bright light, then she lost all sense of time and place.

* * * * *

Kin blinked at the blinding light. When his eyes readjusted, he realized he must have blacked out for a few seconds. The helicopter was on a collision course with the ship. He redressed the chopper at the last second, barely avoiding impact. Celene wasn't in the copilot seat anymore. "Celene?"

No answer.

Had she just vanished like she used to? "Celene, are you there? Talk to me. What happened? Tell me you are okay."

No response. Kin reached to touch the invisible Celene, but his hand went right through the space she had just occupied and his fingers brushed the vinyl seat, still warm from her body heat. "Celene!"

Kin realized with cold dread that Celene wasn't here at all. As he stared at the black alien vessel, he felt in his gut that she had to be inside. Was that why the aliens had not fired at the helicopter? They wanted her alive? Why? A chill ran up his spine and he could feel his heartbeat throbbing in his hip wound.

Would he ever get her back? How? He had to find a way, for after knowing her the way he did, life without her was too grim to contemplate.

* * * * *

Celene awoke in the middle of her worst childhood nightmare. She lay helpless on a table that felt like skin under her back. Was she naked under the shimmering sheet? A dark alien female with large black eyes gazed at her. Dressed in the same shimmering fabric as the sheet, she snarled as her cranium glowed with sinister shades of hellish fire. When she reached out with a four-fingered hand, Celene wanted to scream but she discovered she couldn't utter a sound. She felt no ties binding her to the table. She only felt sheer panic, paralyzed in the hands of an alien demon.

The strange female pushed back a strand of Celene's hair then turned to a young male behind her. "Can you fix her for me? And no mistake like last time."

The young male clucked his assent. "This improved sequence should correct the problem."

Celene recognized the ancient language of the relics, but hearing it spoken raised the small hairs at her nape. It sounded beautiful despite the fierce appearance of the alien beings. She knew she'd spoken it in her youth. It carried memories of purple domes and Kokopelli dolls, along with gruesome fears, like being paralyzed on a table that felt like skin.

When the young male approached her holding a long needle, Celene struggled, but she could only scream in her head. No muscle even stirred as she wailed inside. She felt the cold metal prick on the side of her neck, then the needle pierced deep into her spine.

Although paralyzed, Celene felt herself relax. All fear vanished. She floated in a euphoric trance. Around her, she registered shapes and voices, but they drifted on the surface of her awareness, as if they had no relevance, no real meaning.

The female nodded. "If we are finished here, let's go light another fire at the edge of the city."

The young male shifted from foot to foot, a worried look on his face. "We'll need to lower the multiphasic shield to drop the spore."

"That'll only take a few seconds." The female sounded irritated. "By then they'll have given up shooting at us when they realize their weapons are ineffective against your precious ship."

"But we can't cloak while the shields are up."

"Even your clumsy ship is far superior to their tiny stingers. We'll be fine." The fierce female watched the young male leave then sat on the side of the table and gazed into Celene's eyes. "We'll return you to your glass flying machine, now. From now on, dear child, you are back fighting on our side, and whenever you hear my voice in your head, you will do exactly as I say."

* * * * *

Without a word of warning, Celene found herself floating down a bright beam of light, then back in the helicopter's copilot seat next to Kin. Naked against the cold vinyl, she shivered and flinched at the loud sounds of battle. The fight still raged around them, and one plane dove straight for the spacecraft. It shattered on impact with the shields in a thunderous explosion, but the ship remained unscathed.

Kin blinked a few times, did a doubletake and gave

her a confused look. "Where have you been? I was worried sick. Are you okay? What happened to your clothes?"

Suddenly self-conscious, Celene felt a tingling in her arms and legs and promptly became invisible. Invisible? When had she regained that ability? She moved to the back of the helicopter, holding on to the handlebars for balance with a new appreciation for Kin's skillful maneuvering.

"Hey! Are you there?" Kin glanced around the cabin.

"I'm here. I'm fine. I just need clothes." Celene found a jumpsuit in the parachute locker.

Keeping his gaze on the ominous ship, Kin maintained a good distance from the fight to give the fighters room. "I thought you couldn't make yourself invisible anymore."

"So did I." Celene zipped up the baggy gray jumpsuit and made herself visible again. She was still barefoot.

"I'm relieved you're back." Kin gave her a sidelong glance as she regained her seat. "For a few minutes I thought you were inside that ship and I would have to go and get you."

"I was inside the ship." Tears of silent rage ran down her face. "I never felt so helpless, so violated. They want to use me again."

"For what? What did they do to you?" The look of concern on Kin's face melted Celene's heart. He really seemed to care.

"I'm not sure what they injected me with." She felt for the needle prick at her nape and her finger came back with a drop of blood. Her humiliation slowly turned to anger. She would make them pay for the desecration of her human body.

"That's why they are not shooting the helo. They are protecting you."

More squadrons joined the fight against the spaceship and fired shot after shot with no effect. The guns under the belly of the spacecraft retaliated with terrifying accuracy and although more fighters arrived on the scene, their numbers quickly diminished. A huge bomber made a pass above the alien vessel and dropped a large device. Kin moved the chopper even farther from the impact zone. The bomb detonated, unsettling the helicopter. The explosion, however, didn't harm the black ship. It was as if bomb was absorbed by an invisible net.

"I wish I knew how to disable their shield." Kin barely avoided a fighter plane. "I've gone over their entire hull. I found no obvious weakness."

Celene refused to help the Anaz-voohri in any way. Still, she hesitated. Finally she willed herself to say, "They are going to drop their shields to start a new fire at the edge of the city."

Glancing at her, Kin frowned. "How do you know?"

"I heard them talking." Fading memories of the ship floated at the edge of Celene's mind like a dream after the first cup of coffee. Had she really heard it? She didn't feel so sure, but it seemed their best chance.

"Great job. Are they monitoring our communications?"

"I don't think so...too primitive for them."

Kin tapped his medallion. "Mythos? Icarus here. Order all the fighting squadrons to standby and be ready to shoot down the alien vessel on my signal." Kin didn't seem to like the answer and shook his head impatiently. "I know it's not standard procedure. Let me worry about that. Just do it, okay?"

The alien ship lifted suddenly and flew north in a horizontal trajectory, leaving the ominous vortex growing on its own above the City of Phoenix. Now the size of a large dust cloud, the vortex attracted low altitude winds from all directions. Above it, however, no wind or dust troubled the azure sky.

The fighting planes followed the ominous black craft, which seemed in no hurry. So did Kin. When the alien vessel stopped above a stretch of woods, the planes surrounded the alien ship but did not fire.

Kin switched on the radio. "Ready to shoot on my signal?"

"Roger," came the voices through the speakers.

When Kin faced Celene, he looked pale. "How will we know when the shields are down?"

A feeling of doom crept into Celene's mind. "I have no idea."

"This is our only chance. We'll just have to wing it." Kin brought the helicopter closer to the vessel, where they could see its underbelly. "Tell me as soon as you see anything, a spark, a slight change in color, a trap door opening, anything happening at all."

On the black surface of the hull, Celene detected a slight wavering, a shimmer. Optical illusion? "Now!" she yelled in her excitement.

"Shoot at will!" Kin shouted in the radio as he fired

the first strike.

Celene protected her ears but kept her eyes open as she watched with amazement. Dozens of projectiles hit and penetrated the black hull. The ship shook. Fire and smoke spurted from several gaps in the dull surface. The ship's guns fired back but missed their targets as the damaged behemoth now rocked from side to side. Finally, the great hulk of the alien craft rose slowly under heavy fire. Then the ship vanished from view.

A loud cheer rose through the helicopter radio speaker as the jet fighters hooted and made crazy loops in the sky to celebrate their victory.

"Where did it go?" Kin scrutinized his instruments. "I get nothing on the radar either."

A trail of smoke betrayed the ship's trajectory, but Celene suspected it was now long gone. "It cloaked," she said matter-of-factly.

Kin seemed to relax. "It escaped, but we did hurt it bad. They won't bother us for a while." He switched on the radio. "Great job, boys!" Kin laughed, as if to release all the tension of the past hour.

So did Celene, but she had a bad feeling about the ship's ease in getting away.

* * * * *

Anaz-voohri ship in distress

Kavak tried to make sense of the chaos on Wasaw's ship. All the sensors beeped and alarm sirens wailed. Choking smoke obscured the command deck. At least they were cloaked and the planes had stopped shooting their exploding missiles. Without their shields operational, the crude weapons could prove deadly.

She bumped into the pilot in his seat. "Make for the hidden side of the moon and tell the swarm to be ready to leave."

The pilot clucked his assent.

Wasaw emerged from the smoke with an angry frown. "How did they know we lowered our shields?" He looked in no mood for evasive answers. Apparently he cared a great deal about his clumsy ship.

Kavak tried to control her own rage. "I suspect our little mole betrayed us." Her voice trembled. "It's all your fault. I thought she was supposed to be on our side. Didn't you fix that freaky freewill gene?"

Wasaw sighed dejectedly. "She cannot refuse a direct command from you, but freewill is more than just a gene. This human female shows exceptional resistance to our technology."

"Very well. If it takes a direct order, I will give it to her." Kavak mentally connected her brain waves to the circuitry injected into Celene's spine. "Celene dear, kill whoever gave the order to fire on our ship, and destroy the despicable little planes responsible for the damage."

An automated response system from Celene's bloodstream confirmed that she had received the command.

CHAPTER EIGHTEEN

The commanding presence in Celene's head would suffer no refusal or delay. Making herself invisible, she left the co-pilot seat and snatched Kin's phase-gun. The weapon became transparent as she pointed it back at him from behind his seat.

Kin glanced at his empty holster. "What are you doing?" He sounded more surprised than alarmed. Hands on the helicopter controls, he hovered in the spot the Anaz-voohri vessel had occupied a minute ago. Around him, the fighter jets still drew wild victory loops.

"I want you to shoot every single one of these planes." Celene's words came unbidden, surprising her for speaking them. Like a guest in her own skin, she watched herself move, as if someone else controlled her hands and feet and spoke through her.

"Have you lost your mind?" Kin laughed. "You chose an odd time for a joke."

"This is not a joke." Even to Celene her words made no sense. "You will shoot them down!"

"What's the matter with you?" Was it a trace of impatience in Kin's voice? "They are not the ones who want to kill you. Today they are on our side. Even if I wanted to shoot these guys, they'd blast me before the first strike hit them."

Celene's hand pushed the phase-gun against the back of his head. The force that controlled her body didn't prevent her heart from beating wildly. She wished Kin would fight back and defeat her, but he couldn't pilot and battle an invisible enemy at the same time, not without his being fresh out of surgery. "Shoot them now!"

"I don't think so." Kin glanced back at the spot where she stood and smiled devilishly. Did he believe this was a game? "Hang on!" he shouted.

Kin banked the helicopter in a daredevil maneuver that unsettled the bird and threw Celene against a bulkhead. Her shoulder hit a metal handlebar. She fell and almost dropped the phase-gun. Her head pounded as she struggled to rise and grabbed onto a ceiling strap for balance. For an instant she had control of her body again, but the commanding presence returned. "Shoot those planes or die!"

"If you kill me, you die, too." Kin redressed the helicopter. The sudden descent had brought them into the low altitude whirlwinds rushing toward the vortex. "I know you can do many things, but you can't pilot this bird."

"My death is irrelevant." Celene shuddered at the implications of her involuntary words. Would she kill them both? She braced herself as the helo went into another dive then sideways.

The chopper flew in haphazard patterns like an autumn leaf, keeping Celene off-balance. She couldn't tell whether it was Kin's way of protecting himself, or the effect of the gusty winds from the Anaz-voohri vortex.

"I don't know what they did to you in that ship, but you are not yourself."   Kin's hands gripped the controls, whitening his knuckles. "Don't let them get to you, Celene. Fight it!"

As Celene struggled against the force that made her point the phase-gun in Kin's direction, panic filled her mind. She didn't want to kill him. She would never forgive herself if she did. But the presence in her head demanded she comply. "I must obey. I must." Her hand trembled with her resisting efforts.

"No, you don't. No matter what those Anaz-voohri did to you, you fought it before. Fight it again, damn it!" Kin started an erratic descent.

Trapped in a body that did not obey her, Celene despaired. Her battle against the alien control didn't go well. Only the fact that she couldn't aim the weapon and keep her balance at the same time prevented her from shooting him. The helicopter banked. Through the gaping door, she glanced at a hazy football field below, marked with white landing circles, like a bunch of helipads. "What are you doing?"

"Trying to land." Kin's clenched jaws betrayed his struggle to steady the helo. "Safer here than to get into that maelstrom in the city. The winds would smash us against the buildings."

Amid the swirling dust below, Celene could see several grounded birds, the Air Evac and Red Cross rescue choppers used to shuttle the firefighters, and several TV News birds. Red letters on the field said Horse Thief Basin High. She recognized the fire headquarters. The ambulances had gone. The wind now tore at the empty Red Cross tents, abandoned to the raging dust storm.

A sudden gust blew the chopper toward a copse of trees beyond the end of the football field, but Kin's skilled maneuvers avoided disaster. After several tentative approaches, he managed a difficult landing. Shaken, Celene untangled her wrist from the ceiling strap. When she looked up, Kin had shut down the engine, unbuckled his harness, and now rose from the pilot seat. Head bent, he walked slowly toward the back of the cargo hold, hands up. Celene moved aside to avoid a collision and noted that she still had some freedom of movement when it came to automatic reflexes.

"I'm at your mercy, girl. Just kill me now if you must, and be done with it." Kin's serious tone held a trace of sarcasm.

For a second, Celene thought he could see her. Her struggle against the urge to aim the phase-gun at his head only slowed the movement of her arm. Why wasn't Kin fighting her? How could he be so reckless with his life?

Kin deliberately turned his back to her and sat at the edge of the gaping door. Legs dangling above the grass, he faced the open field partially swallowed by the dust cloud. "Hurry up, I'm waiting," he taunted. "I bet my very life that you can overcome those bastards again."

Celene felt as if she'd swallowed a rock. Did he want to die? She didn't want to do it, but her finger started to press the trigger. *Please, God, don't let me do this.* Tears rolled down her invisible cheeks. What could she do to help him? Become visible and give him a fighting chance? Could she?

In an ultimate effort to break the spell, Celene threw herself out of the helicopter and flinched as pain shot up her right ankle. Bracing herself against the strong wind, she hopped on one foot, the spiky dry grass poking her bare sole. Dust swirled and stung her eyes as she now faced Kin, but her phase-gun remained aimed at him. Attempting to make herself visible, she saw her arm waver in front of her then vanish again.

Kin slid down from the helicopter floor and stared at her with surprise. "Hey, you look awful." The wind muffled his words and whipped his hair in front of his face. "Are you all right? You need help." He advanced upon her.

"Don't come any closer or I'll kill you!" Celene heard herself yell. She struggled to become visible, but again her image only wavered.

Kin kicked the phase-gun and sent it flying out of her hand into the dusty grass. He seized her wrist then pulled her close and held her to him in a tight embrace.

Celene felt her body struggle in his grip, but he didn't let go. Her strength was no match for his. The contact of his body made Celene want to surrender, but it took the alien presence a few seconds to realize that Celene had been neutralized. As suddenly as it had come, the alien control left. Spent but free, Celene regained her shape and gratefully collapsed against Kin's chest. "I'm sorry. It wasn't me. I couldn't help it."

"Are they gone?"

She nodded.

"They didn't get the best of you, did they?" She

could feel him grin against her cheek.

How could he be so strong and unshakable when she'd almost killed him? Thank God she hadn't. Celene managed a weak smile. "It was close."

"But they didn't win." He caressed her hair. "Don't worry. It's over."

How she wanted to believe him, but Celene felt tired. Tired of fighting, tired of trying to save the world. All she wanted now was sleep. Sleep forever and never have to worry about the Anaz-voohri using her for destructive purposes. As her legs gave under her weight, she felt Kin catching her and picking her up, then all went black.

* * * * *

Kin winced as he deposited Celene on the only empty cot in the school library transformed into a temporary Red Cross hospital. His hip wound pulled painfully. Nurses, doctors and medics ministered to rows of patients, who lay on folding cots and tables. He guessed they'd had to evacuate the tents when the windstorm started.

His gaze searching for help, Kin noticed more beds between the rows of bookshelves. Some patients exhibited bloody bandages, most looked heavily sedated. The hushed voices and the sterile smell of medicine pervaded the place.

A medic in white coat and blue surgical mask approached with a small electronic blood pressure cuff. He pushed up the sleeve of Celene's jumpsuit and affixed the device on her wrist. It started humming.

"Has she been exposed?" The medic's voice sounded muted behind the mask.

"No, just passed out from shock and exhaustion." Kin hoped no one would recognize Celene from the morning broadcast. But how could anyone compare this dusty ashen face and this matted hair in disarray with Celene's pretty picture? She looked as if she'd just been pulled out of a collapsed building. Only Kin could see her beauty and strength beneath the layers of grime. He knew she was good and wholesome, and he loved her.

The medic read the digital dial then removed the small device from Celene's wrist. He checked under her eyelids and tapped the smudgy skin of her face, eliciting a moan. "She looks dehydrated but she'll be all right. I'll start an IV."

Kin thought of asking the medic to give her a sedative, in case Celene fell under the murderous alien influence again, but a sedative might not work, and the request could raise suspicions. Instead, he said, "She was distressed before she passed out and she might get agitated again when she wakes up. I'll check up on her in a little while."

The medic's eyes twinkled as he smiled under the mask. "We'll keep an eye on her for you. Don't worry. This is the easiest case we've had all day."

"I'll be at the fire headquarters." Kin started for the door and stopped. "Where is it?"

"In the gymnasium. Just make a left outside the door."

Nodding his thanks, Kin left the library and braced himself against the dust-laden winds on his way to the gymnasium.

When he entered the headquarters, the frantic activity suggested pandemonium. Firefighters in full gear and medics rushed in every direction, yelling orders above the din of TV News channels. A number of civilian families that looked like refugees from the storm camped with small children on the central parquet floor. On the bleachers, fire volunteers sat dejectedly.

A few pale journalists recorded their grim reports in the cordoned off press area. Others complained about their station going off the air when some transmitter tower fell. A group of reporters watched the overhead screens, stunned expressions on their faces.

Following their gazes, Kin caught the live satellite images of the vortex above the city. It quickly gained in strength, and intensity. Three large fires, now fueled by strong winds, spread at an alarming pace. Green smoke and dust advanced toward the populated areas, followed at a distance by heavy clouds from the Pacific and the Gulf of Mexico. The young meteorologist on the screen looked baffled as he estimated the green smoke would reach the outskirts of the doomed city within three hours.

Three hours? No wonder everyone panicked.

Kin checked another plasma screen that showed downtown Phoenix now under martial law. Only military and emergency vehicles drove along the city streets. Soldiers patrolled the neighborhoods, handing out white gas masks door to door.

At the main bus terminal, the army evacuated civilians in vehicles equipped with special systems to filter out the poisoned green smoke. According to the reports, several riots had already been stopped. Kin feared more would start when it became obvious there weren't enough of these busses to evacuate everyone. He knew the prototype vehicles to be in short supply.

At the airport, shut down by the deadly winds, irate passengers, grounded with no hope of escape, protested with virulence in front of the cameras. Airline personnel distributed water bottles, as if they hoped it would solve the problem. The local government officials remained suspiciously silent, hiding behind closed office doors. Kin suspected most of them had already fled the area. Few politicians had enough courage to stare death in the face.

Scrolling communiqués at the bottom of the screens advised inhabitants from the northern outskirts to drive toward Nevada or central California. The Eastern communities were told to migrate south, deep into Mexico.

For the unfortunate trapped in the city, local television networks issued reassurance and tips on how to wear the gas masks. News clips showed how to insulate offices and homes from the deadly smoke coming their way. The media also broadcast emergency numbers isolated citizens could call to get specific help, or to find out about their loved ones.

The reports confirmed that the vaccine had been distributed to all the medical facilities, and the latest equipment now battled the fires. On the fire front, a large tanker plane had just crashed, felled by the heavy winds. Although the water-bombers would soon be recalled, a few *kamikaze* pilots insisted on continuing the fight.

Kin tapped his medallion and whispered, "Icarus here. Have you any idea on how to stop the vortex?"

"Not short of a nuclear explosion," said the male voice in his screamer implant.

"Don't we have any type of bomb we could explode above the city that would not produce fallout? Maybe several at the same time to get more power?" Kin realized the futility of his suggestions but they had to try something, anything.

"I'll find out more about the bombs and call you back." Mythos broke the connection.

Kin could see there was no use in working with the fire headquarters. They were in way over their heads. No rescue or firefighting efforts would work properly as long as the vortex thwarted their operations.

Kin braved the dust storm and returned to the library makeshift hospital to check on Celenel. She lay awake, one ankle heavily bandaged.

Kin motioned to the bandage with his chin. "You're hurt?"

Celene gazed at him with wonder in her dark jade eyes. "Just a sprain."

He must look terrible and chuckled at the thought as he took her thin hand in his. "How are you feeling?"

Celene offered a tentative smile. "What's happening out there?"

No sooner had Kin explained the situation than his medallion vibrated. He tapped it twice. "I'm listening."

"We have three experimental bombs that could be exploded simultaneously above the city." The usually calm voice from Mythos betrayed obvious excitement.

Kin allowed himself to hope. "Enough power to do the job?"

"It won't be as strong as a nuclear mushroom." The voice paused. "But there could be a problem."

"What's the catch?"

"It could have the reverse effect from what we expect."

"You mean it could speed up the process? Accelerate the winds? What's the worst scenario?"

"It could bring about the deluge of the century."

"A deluge?"

Celene must have been hanging on Kin's every word. She grabbed his wrist with surprising strength. "That's it!"

"Hold on, Mythos." Kin stared at Celene who sat up on the cot. "What?"

"If you can't stop it, join it. If we increase the vortex instead of stopping it, stronger winds could snuff out the fires and precipitate a huge rainstorm. That's exactly what we need."

"Copy that, Mythos? If this works, all we have to do is protect the remaining population with gas masks for a short time until the smoke blows over, then clean up after the flood."

The Mythos voice hesitated. "Sounds radical, but it might work. We'll look into it."

Severing the communication, Kin tried to smile for Celene's sake. "It could work."

Celene's head fell back on the cot and tears filled her eyes. "Tell me we are going to save these people."

Kin nodded. "The material damage might be high,

but we are doing everything humanely possible to save the population."

"Will it be enough?" The hope in her gaze broke his heart.

"We'll see." Kin wished he had the right answers to give her.

* * * * *

For the next hour, the media networks broadcast warning after warning. When it was safe to assume that all the remaining population knew to remain indoors and wear their gas masks until further official notice, the crucial moment finally came. All activity ceased in the gymnasium.

Celene had insisted on watching the event. She stood on one leg, favoring her right ankle. When everyone pulled on their white gas masks, she pretended to have received the vaccine. No point in explaining her suspicious immunity or taking a mask that could save someone else's life. She squeezed Kin's hand as they stared at the satellite pictures on the largest screen of the gymnasium. Around them, officials, volunteers, journalists, medics, and firefighters recalled from the three fires, looked like kids playing astronauts behind their white plexiglass visors.

Silence filled the gymnasium, broken only by the sound of the dust storm outside and the occasional cough muffled by a mask filter. Even the children behaved in the family shelter area. Seeing a woman join her hands in prayer, Celene sent one of her own.

Dear God, please make this work.

A countdown appeared at the top of the giant plasma screen. The seconds passed slowly. On zero, a split screen showed three missiles launched from three military bases, one from California, one from Nevada and one from Texas. The satellite view showed the white trail of each missile rushing toward Phoenix. More long seconds ticked. Celene could hardly breathe.

When the three white trails met in a blinding flash. Celene felt the reverberation of the explosion in the very ground. She heard a collective gasp. Kin's arm reached to support her waist.

The whole building rumbled overhead. Small children shrieked through their mask filters and mothers gathered them protectively. The structure shook like in an earthquake. In the press area, a reporter ran for the shelter of a doorway while another tried to crouch under a desk despite the bulky gas mask.

When calm returned to the gymnasium and the satellite pictures cleared, Celene focused on the screen. She watched a great mushroom rise above Phoenix. The vortex pulled the winds faster and Celene saw clouds moving rapidly over the land. The mushroom opened up. Green smoke and dust, sucked by the explosion, started rising toward the stratosphere where it seemed to dissipate.

Celene couldn't see the hot spots of the three fires on the satellite images anymore. Had they been blown out like a match by the hurricane? Did they still blaze under the thick cloud cover?

A muffled cheer rose in the gymnasium. Celene

rejoiced at this success, but she wondered what would happen to the poisoned smoke up in the stratosphere. Would it remain as a constant threat to strike unexpectedly? Would the gas lose its potency? No matter how she looked at it, Celene couldn't rejoice in the face of all the destruction.

The warning at the bottom of the screen asked the population to keep the gas masks on. Celene wondered about pockets of green smoke trapped in the recesses of poorly aerated rooms. Would isolated cases of contamination pop up for months to come? She hoped children wouldn't fall victim while exploring nooks and crannies.

Within minutes, stronger winds whipped the building and rattled the skylights. Families huddled together and frightened children cried out. Branches and solid objects hurled by the tempest against the walls told Celene that the force of the storm intensified. Would the rain fall next?

Thick dust over the skylights dimmed the daylight in the gymnasium, then the sky darkened as black clouds rolled overhead. Lightning flashed ghostly shadows in the semi darkness, and thunder clapped. Someone switched on the battery of floodlights in the gymnasium. Somehow the reassuring brightness made Celene feel safer, but she shivered as the temperature seemed to drop suddenly.

"What do we do now?" she asked Kin, although she knew the answer. She needed his reassurance.

"We wait out the storm." Kin's voice sounded like that of a robot through the mask filter. He sat cross-legged on the floor and motioned for Celene to join him.

Celene sat next to him. Many who had been standing now imitated them. When the first heavy drops drummed on the roof, another cheer went up. Soon, heavy sheets of rain battered the skylights.

Celene couldn't help smiling. "I hope no one's left outdoors. Sounds like a killer hurricane out there."

Kin nodded and grinned behind the plexiglass. "Five hours of storm, they said."

Luckily, Celene had Kin with her, but many of the volunteers around her had no idea whether or not their loved ones were safe. The gas masks prevented the use of communicators, and the few computers and epads, mainly from members of the press, were made available for personal text messages. Celene looked for her epad to hand it to a woman sitting next to her, then she realized she didn't have it. She'd returned naked from the spaceship and only wore the jumpsuit from the helicopter. Was her epad in the alien ship? Was it back at Mythos? She couldn't remember.

There seemed to be no end to the torrential rain. After nightfall, the smoke warning changed to tell the population to open their windows and air the rooms despite the foul weather, before removing their masks. When the doors were propped open at each end of the gymnasium, the tempest rushed inside, and it grew cold and wet.

After the closing of the doors, Kin pulled up his mask over his head and Celene felt glad to see his face. One by one, others dared to remove their masks. Celene could hear their sighs of relief with their first breath of fresh air. Most of them smiled.

The Red Cross called for a few soup kitchen volunteers through the PA system. Celene wanted to help, but her ankle throbbed and she had no shoes.

Kin rose and kissed her forehead. "I'll go for both of us."

While Kin distributed food rations and drinks to the stranded families and fire workers, Celene accepted a blanket and a pair of hospital slippers from a medic.

In the middle of the meal, all the lights went out, generating a cry of anguish. Then the emergency lights kicked in, bathing the gymnasium in black and white shadows. Soon, the rumble of a generator brought back the plasma screens online, and some dim general lighting returned.

With nothing to do but watch the screens and wait out the monster storm, the fire headquarters looked more and more like a shelter where everyone was a refugee. People stretched out haphazardly on the floor to sleep.

Returning from kitchen duty, Kin took Celene by the waist. "Want to catch some sleep, too? There'll be a hell of a lot to do tomorrow. We'll both need our strength."

He was right, of course. Celene smiled and lay down next to Kin on the parquet, cuddling against his chest. She felt safe there. His arm held her possessively, and she enjoyed his spicy scent and the warmth of his body. Despite her exhaustion, she felt a wave of desire engulf her. But that would have to wait.

As if guessing her thoughts, Kin pulled her tighter against him. "Good night." His light kiss lingered on her lips.

Returning the kiss, Celene smiled then abandoned herself to the delights of his protective strength. She adjusted herself against his frame and closed her eyes. Within seconds, she fell asleep to the familiar vision of a sunny sand beach with swaying palm trees and hula dancers. The howls of the raging storm faded into the ocean surf breaking on a Hawaiian beach.

CHAPTER NINETEEN

Celene awoke on the hard floor to the sound of excited voices. The first rays of the rising sun touched the skylights of the Horse Thief Basin High gymnasium with pink amber light. The storm had abated, and the rain had stopped. Celene sat up and looked at the satellite pictures on the large plasma screen. They showed clear skies over Arizona and no trace of smoke or forest fires. The storm had worn itself out, and the torrential rain had extinguished the fires. Celene gave a silent prayer of thanks.

As she searched for Kin, she saw him walking toward her, carrying a tray with two large cups of coffee and four muffins.

Depositing the tray on the parquet floor, Kin sat next to her. "Cream, no sugar, right?"

"Where did you find such a treasure?" Celene inhaled the strong aroma and let it tease her nostrils.

"There's enough food and drink in the cafeteria for a siege." He grinned. "Thought you'd need your strength." Biting into a muffin, he pointed to one of the three plasma screens. "It's a mess outside."

Hands wrapped around the warm styrofoam cup, Celene looked up to watch the newscast while sipping the steaming brew. Cottonwood trees had fallen across country roads. Canals and washes ran red with desert mud. She dunked her muffin in the coffee and wolfed it down then took another. She felt so much better with food in her stomach.

The screens now displayed wrecked houses and flooded farmlands. The torrential flow of the Salt River had brought down several bridges and compromised the purity of the water supply. Come winter, there would be no orange crop in Arizona. The storm had plucked all the blooms and even uprooted entire orange groves. Fortunately, it was only material damage. President Grant had declared Arizona a disaster area and allocated federal funds.

Kin sipped his coffee. "I'm afraid the helo won't fly for a while. We'll have to find our own way back to civilization. Problem is, most of the roads are blocked or flooded. We could be stuck here for a while."

"Not necessarily." Celene gulped the rest of her coffee then rose and dumped the cup and tray in a recycle trashcan. "I may have something."

"What? A ride?" Kin followed her example.

"Come. Let's go see if it survived." Celene started running then slowed as her right ankle protested. Once outside, she took a deep breath. The place looked oddly calm. The air was crisp, clean of dust and deliciously humid. The neighboring mountains looked much closer than the day before. Her hospital slippers didn't allow stepping in deep mud, so she kept to the dirty concrete walkway on her way to the parking lot.

Walking at her side, Kin frowned. "Will you tell me?"

Celene's heart beat faster at the sight of the bright yellow Dial-a-Bike, tangled in a mess of oleander bushes hedging the parking lot. "Here it is!"

Kin whistled. "That's an expensive toy."

Pulling at the back end of the light vehicle, Celene struggled. "Help me free it. I hope it's not damaged. I promised I would take care of it."

Kin untangled the front wheel from the edge. He winced as he lifted it and had to shake it free from the oleanders. Finally, the Dial-a-Bike came out of the hedge to rest on the ground. Kin walked around the vehicle. "It looks okay. Where did you get it?"

"Don't ask." Celene opened the dark plexiglass door.

Taking the phase-gun from the back seat, Kin raised one eyebrow. "That's a Mythos issue." He chuckled. "I know…don't ask."

"Sorry, I needed it more than that sweet bodyguard." Celene snatched the weapon from his hand and slipped it in the cargo pocket of her jumpsuit. As she wondered where she had left the key, she suddenly remembered there wasn't any. "I don't know how to start this thing. It's DNA activated."

"How did you fly it here?" The look of disbelief on Kin's face was almost comical.

"I didn't fly, I just drove it. The engine was still running when I borrowed it."

"Maybe I should drive, then," Kin teased. He straddled the front seat and fumbled with the contact button, then he reached behind the dashboard and pulled out a few wires, eliciting a spark. The electric engine hesitated then started reluctantly. Kin revved it a few times. "Hop in!" he said over the purr of the machine.

Once Celene climbed in behind him and closed the door, the bike rolled out of the parking lot then rose smoothly and hovered a few feet above the muddy road. Soon they soared over the desert. Uncomfortable about trusting her life to such a flimsy machine, Celene focused on the devastation below.

A sea of mud had erased the usual landmarks. Tree branches and other debris, strewn everywhere, painted a desolate landscape. As the bike skimmed over the treetops, Celene noticed wide rivers that washed over paved roads, carrying dead birds and floating satellite dishes. Tumbled trailers lay on their side, their contents spilled in the mud.

A few residents who had not left their homes now stood bewildered in their flooded front yards. A hardy soul wielded a chainsaw, cutting the limbs of a fallen tree. There, a palm tree had fallen on a house, caving the roof inside. Farther, a tall cactus had flattened a car. Ducks swam on a flooded golf course.

Celene saw entire neighborhoods flooded to the windowsills, houses with gaping roofs and carports bent beyond recognition. Solar cells lay scattered like a deck of cards. A corrugated roof had wrapped itself around a metal lamppost. A whole row of wooden electric poles lay broken like so many toothpicks, as the severed cables lay in deep pools of water.

When they neared Sky Harbor Airport, rugged military transports landed vertically, but no commercial flights seemed to be landing or taking off. It would take time to clear the runways. Except for a few emergency vehicles, Celene noticed little traffic on the muddy roads littered with debris.

Kin flew the Dial-a-Bike closer to the heart of the city where traffic signals lay in the middle of many intersections. City maintenance vans and their repair crews picked their way through the rubble.

Downtown, bulldozers and Bobcats pushed upturned cars, fallen trees and rubble to the side. Huge dump trucks picked up debris along the main arteries. Vacuum engines pumped the water out of basements and parking lots.

Unhindered by blocked or flooded streets, the Dial-a-Bike landed smoothly near the Mythos tower and rolled into the underground parking lot which was still under a few inches of water. Kin parked the bike and waded to the massive metal door. Celene lost her slippers in the water as she followed but she let them go. She watched Kin press his hand on the door, which opened for them.

"DNA activated," Kin explained on the way to the elevator. As they went up, water dripped from their pant legs, forming puddles around their feet. They exited on a floor Celene had not yet seen. She followed Kin into a room where a dozen Mythos employees, busy at their respective stations, spoke with various government agencies, apparently to offer their help and services.

Instead of relief at finding herself in civilized surroundings, Celene felt a heavy weight in her chest. On the wall screens of the monitoring room, tuned to police, military and other emergency and news channels, more images of chaos reminded her that these people had lost everything, their homes, their precious mementos. Many would leave the area forever. It would take months, if not years to rebuild and repair all that damage.

Updates on the hospitals indicated many more cases of green smoke inhalation among the population. Not everyone had received a gas mask, and not all who did had followed instructions properly. Celene blanched as she saw the poor devils strapped to their hospital beds, struggling against the medics trying to administer the antidote. The commentaries said the cure proved effective, and those injected recovered, but hospitals all over the state were running low on the medicine and expected more casualties to come in as the day progressed.

Celene pulled on Kin's sleeve. "The lab will need more blood."

Kin nodded. "But not before you take a bath, find clean clothes, some decent shoes, and eat a hot meal."

Of course. Celene felt gritty and probably smelled rank. "If I remember, there are showers and clean uniforms in those hospital rooms on the twelfth floor."

"Go." He brushed her cheek with one finger. "I'll meet you up there in a little while."

* * * * *

One hour later, after she'd scrubbed the grime from her hair and body, Celene reclined in her own hospital bed and relaxed. Her blood almost filled the plastic bag on the oscillator to the side of the bed.

The same male nurse in white lab coat who had taken her blood two days earlier came to check on her. He looked at the bag and smiled. "That's plenty." He unhooked the bag from her arm. "Now you need some rest." He adjusted her IV then left the room.

Despite her fatigue, Celene could not sleep. The destruction and suffering she had caused filled her mind. She switched on the plasma screen on the wall opposite the bed. More channels had started broadcasting again.

The burned forest area would be off limits for tourists until further notice. Animal rights volunteers had come in from other states and would retrieve and relocate wild animals whose habitats had been destroyed.

The early estimates for material damages were staggering, but when the update on the human cost came, Celene braced herself. The storm must have claimed its victims and she had caused it all. The weight of the responsibility crushed her.

Entire families had disappeared and no one knew for sure whether they had fled or died. Between the fires and the storm, over three thousand wounded or contaminated lay in hospital beds. The death toll had reached two hundred and was expected to escalate as critically wounded died and more bodies were found amidst the rubble.

The plasma screen blurred in front of her eyes as the voice of the anchorman announced, "This is only the beginning. The rescue efforts have barely started."

Salty tears wet Celene's lips. Wracked by grief for the families of those who died, she sobbed uncontrollably.

When Kin entered Celene's room, his smile turned into a frown. "What's wrong?"

"I killed all these people, that's what's wrong." Hearing herself say it made it even more real. She was a mass murderer. A criminal of the worst kind.

"But you are not responsible for all this." Kin sat on the side of the bed and took her hand in his. He'd since cleaned up and now smelled of aftershave. "You were used by superior forces. You had no choice. You never planned or wanted this to happen."

Celene sniffed. "I'm sure that's what most Nazi generals argued during their trial."

"These generals didn't get their DNA altered by aliens. Don't do this to yourself, Celene." The gold flecks in Kin's dark brown eyes burned with intensity. "Yet you fought it. And managed to reverse the process. You even defeated those who meant to destroy us."

"If not for me, this would never have happened. No one would have died or suffered." It was the hard truth. She considered herself responsible, period.

Kin shook his head. "The Anaz-voohri would have found another way."

"And what happens when they return?" She didn't wait for his answer. "If they take control of me again, I could be responsible for the next genocide to hit the planet. Besides, how can I possibly live with all these deaths on my conscience?"

"Calm down." He patted her hand. "None of this is your fault."

"All of it is." She breathed deeply and sighed. "Are you still under orders to kill me?"

Kin's eyes narrowed as he focused on her. He said nothing.

"Well, are you?" Her cutting tone demanded an answer.

Kin looked down at her hand. "The mission has not been rescinded yet." He lifted his dark gaze to meet her eyes. "But I'm sure it will be as soon as I report what you did in the past two days."

"Forget what I did to make up for my mistake." Celene couldn't stop the flow of words. "Consider the threat I still represent to you and to society. I should deliver myself to ORION to make sure I don't ever harm anyone else. I refuse to be a liability to the human race."

"This is ridiculous." Kin rose and paced at the foot of the bed. "Carrick would kill you. I won't let you do such a thing."

"No? Then obey your orders and kill me right here and now. It's the only way to make sure I don't become an instrument of destruction again."

Kin stopped pacing and pierced her with an intense gaze. "I didn't save your life to take it away."

"You must. Besides, I'm sure you can do it swiftly. I wouldn't feel a thing. I could even die in your arms. Please, on all I hold sacred, I want you to do it. I'm not sure I'd have the courage to do it myself." She struggled not to sob. "No one will miss me much, except Jake, and Isis, maybe."

His expression softened as he approached the bed. "What about your real parents? If they are still alive, don't you think they'd want to know you?"

Celene had no answer for that. In the confusion of the latest events, she had not given much thought to her biological parents.

"And what about me?" The miserable expression on Kin's face gave her pause.

"Why would you miss me?" She hadn't meant the challenge in her tone and wished she could take it back. "We've only known each other for a week." It seemed a lot longer.

Kin lifted her shoulders from the raised pillows and took her in his arms. "I'd miss you because I love you. What about you? Don't you love me a little bit?"

The question hit Celene like a falling boulder. Her throat constricted as she gave him her answer. "I do love you." Tears fell down her face. "That's one more reason I want to die. I couldn't stand to wake up one morning and discover that I killed you in my sleep."

"That's a risk I'm willing to take." Holding her at arm's length, he stared into her eyes with fierce intensity. "You are stronger than you think. You won against their control when you returned to the cave to shut off the turbines, then again when you didn't kill me. Each time you overcome their will you become stronger. You know it's true. You must feel it."

"I do, but I can't live like this." The thought of that nightmare reoccurring seemed too much for Celene to bear.

"Yes, you can." He brought her close against his chest. "After all you went through in the past few days you feel exhausted and guilty. When you get better, you'll realize that this planet needs you. You owe it to humanity to fight on their side."

Hope flickered in Celene's mind as she looked up at him. She remembered in her darkest hour, when she turned off the device in the cave, she'd promised God that if she came out alive, she would dedicate her life to helping others. "Go on."

"Your invisibility skills and your knowledge of the Anaz-voohri and their language would give us the advantage in our fight against them. Do not turn your back on those who need you."

"I'm so scared." She trembled against him.

"I know." He brushed away a strand of her hair. "But you are strong and you won't have to face it alone. I'll be right there with you."

Although frightened, Celene wanted to believe Kin was right, that she had a place in this world. And with him at her side, she could face their enemies.

When he bent to kiss her lips, Celene embraced him and held on to him with the desperation of a drowning child. She abandoned herself to his reassuring strength, willing herself to forget the trials of the past two weeks. His male proximity, the hard muscles of his chest and the male scent of his spicy aftershave scrambled her painful memories. Her sadness seemed to fade as she drank from the fountain of his mouth.

His kiss left her breathless. She couldn't help wanting more of him as he reclined on the bed beside her. She felt some strength return and kissed him back with renewed fervor. At the contact of his erection through the blanket, she reached out and fumbled with his belt buckle.

"What if someone comes in?" He looked concerned for her even as he kicked off his shoes and pulled at the sheet.

"Let them come. I need you now." Celene scooted

over to give him room. She pulled out the IV, then froze. "Could you get fired for this?"

Kin laughed. "Don't worry. Mythos isn't led by bureaucrats." He pulled off his sweater, revealing a well-muscled chest, then unzipped his pants and let them fall to the floor.

Celene gasped at the fresh pink scar of his phase-gun wound. "Isn't it too soon for you?"

"Let me worry about that." He grinned as he stretched beside her.

As soon as Celene felt his skin against hers, her previous fears receded, and she surrendered to his loving touch. Her mind whirled when he explored her ear with his tongue. He kissed the hollow of her throat while pulling at the strings of her hospital gown. How she'd missed his body! The flimsy garment slid away under his insistent pull, the fabric brushing her breasts as it came off. Her nipples stiffened, and he took one in his mouth, tormenting it between his teeth.

Celene arched her back, but his strong hands pinned her down. He laved every inch of her with his tongue, exploring her most secret recesses. How could she have wanted to die? How could she give up something as wonderful as the taste of his skin, the feel of his silky hair, or the insistent probing of his tongue?

Overwhelmed by his skillful ministrations, Celene let her mind fly free, away from the problems of this world. Feeling in tune with Kin's body, she responded to his caresses with kisses and exploring of her own, guessing what would give him pleasure and reveling in his soft answering moans. Then she realized his swollen erection needed release.

Taking the initiative to spare his injured hip, Celene straddled him and gasped when he filled her. She could feel him vibrate under her like a finely tuned musical instrument on which she played a pleasurable tune. In slow gyrating strokes, she milked his passion. Never had she made love with such abandon, as if it was the last and only time. She must enjoy every precious moment. Happiness was a fleeting thing, and tomorrow might never come.

Celene reached her climax first, then Kin pulled her down and pinned her hips under his to ram her in deep powerful strokes that made her shudder and moan like a beast in heat. Her whole body flushed with fire. She felt him grow even more and explode inside her, still moving through tremors, as if he never wanted to stop pleasuring her.

When he fell back on the pillow next to her, Celene felt rejuvenated, as if love had freed her from a heavy burden. Even as she closed her eyes, she couldn't wipe the grin off her face.

CHAPTER TWENTY

The island of Kauai, two weeks later
Palm fronds swayed in the lazy trade winds in front of the Hawaiian shack on the beach, not a grass shack, but a modest homestead house, blessed by the *Kahuna* to exude love, harmony, and serenity.

In the bedroom, in front of a full-length mirror, Celene adjusted the crown of flowers upon her head and stepped back to admire the flowing veils of her white Hawaiian wedding dress. On the wall a frame displayed her baby pictures.

From her backpack on the bed, she took a framed portrait of her adoptive father in which she had tucked the edelweiss flower she'd picked up near the dig site in Ukraine. She kissed her finger and applied it on the glass then hung the portrait near her baby pictures.

Through the open window, Celene spotted the visitor walking up from the beach and tensed at the thought of ORION still hunting her. She quickly relaxed when she recognized her dear friend and martial arts teacher from Montreal. In a bright blue Aloha shirt and shorts, Jake walked resolutely, carrying a plastic cage.

Celene ran to the open door and chuckled. "I see you've gone local, hey?"

Smiling, Jake looked around as if looking for

someone else. "I need to see a certain Miss Leilani Harrington about a cat."

"Well, you found her." Celene bowed formally. "Leilani Harrington, soon to be Leilani Raidon, at your service."

"You look fantastic dressed like that. Just like a native."

"Jake, I am a native! Get used to the idea." Celene hugged her dear friend. "Thanks for coming on such short notice, and for bringing Isis. It means a lot to have you here. Where is Kin?"

"Left me around the corner. Didn't want to see the bride before the ceremony. Guess it's bad luck in China, too." Jake winked. "Looks like a good guy. A little quiet, maybe, but a good guy. I like him."

"I'm glad you do." Celene took Isis out of the cage. She kissed the cat's head and felt Isis purr when she scratched her ears. "I missed you, kitty girl." She motioned to Jake. "Come inside."

Jake glanced at the slippers lined up in front of the door.

Celene laughed at his hesitation. "Island style. No shoes allowed inside."

"Just like in a dojo." Jake removed his tennis shoes before entering but kept his white socks. He took in the modest abode. "Love what you did with the place."

"Don't poke fun at it. This is the house where I lived as a child." Celene laughed. "I know it doesn't look like much now, but we'll fix it up as we go. It's valuable beachfront property. Besides, it's our wedding gift from my parents. We plan to make it our permanent home."

Jake pulled out a newspaper from his back pocket and handed it to her. "Thought you might want to read the news from your former home." He pointed to a headline. "It talks about your adoptive father."

Celene took the paper, sat on the sofa, and let Isis settle on her lap. The cat started to preen herself as Celene read.

Late archeologist Armand Dupres honored for his find of Anaz-voohri ship and artifacts vital in fighting off possible alien invasion. This important discovery will also help in the fight against the filovirus plague. The dig will be open to scientists worldwide to work on eliminating the Anaz-voohri threat.

A familiar portrait of Celene's stepfather illustrated the article. "I'm glad they decided to acknowledge his work. I wish I could attend the ceremony, but I can't show my face in Montreal right now."

"Oh?" Jake's eyebrows shot up.

"Can you keep a secret?" The question was rhetorical. Celene knew she could count on Jake. "Some very nasty government agency is looking for me. That's part of the reason I took back my birth name and I'm moving here."

"I see." He looked at her pointedly. "What did you do?"

"Jeopardize life on this planet, battle evil aliens, piss off some arrogant general, that kind of thing."

"Oh! That thing in Arizona? You were involved?"

"Yep. You can say that."

"Do your parents know?"

Celene nodded. "They know. They are good

people. All these years, they never lost hope and never stopped loving me as their daughter. The DNA confirmation was only a formality for them. They want to help."

Jake gazed out at the blue Pacific through the open window. "I can think of worse places to hide. Could be a good place for me to retire someday. Will you come visit me in Montreal after this blows over?"

"You can bet on it. You know I'll always travel a lot." Celene heard movement at the door. She picked up Isis and rose. "Mom? Dad?" The words still felt strange, but Celene liked saying them. Besides, it made her parents smile every time, like now. "Come in and meet Jake."

The couple in their late forties entered the living room. Celene's father, Palani Harrington, looked dark and rather plump, with a kind face and a noble forehead. Around his neck, he wore a *lei* of green *maile* leaves.

Celene's mother, Hawika, slim and light of complexion, had the same green eyes and high cheekbones as Celene. She wore an intricate orange *Pikaki lei* over an impeccably tailored burgundy *muumuu* and carried several flower garlands on her arms. She slid a fragrant *lei* of white jasmine blossoms over Celene's head before kissing her cheeks. "It's a happy day. You need cheerful flowers."

As she still held Isis, Celene returned the kisses and the hug with one arm. She loved the sweet woman. She held the cat for Hawika to see. "And this is Isis. She is Siamese."

"What a darling!" Hawika scratched the cat under

the jaw then kissed the feline's nose. "Welcome, Isis. We'll all take good care of you." Turning to Jake, Hawika selected an open *maile* strand and looped it over his head before kissing him, too. "Flowers are for the *wahines*," she explained, patting his arm. "*Maile* leaves are for men."

Palani offered Jake a wide smile and his hand to shake. "*Aloha*, Jake. We welcome any friend of our long lost daughter. In Hawaii, we still value family and friendship above all else."

Returning the handshake, Jake winked. "Even for a *haule* like me?"

Hawika frowned. "You are not a *haule*, Jake. *Haule* doesn't mean white person, it means a person without a soul. And I can see through your eyes you have a beautiful soul."

"Thank you." Jake smiled. "I've known Celene…sorry, Leilani since she was eight. She's been like a daughter to me, too."

When Celene deposited Isis on the couch, the cat stretched then curled up for a nap, a sure sign that Isis liked the house. Turning to her parents and Jake, who seemed to get along grandly, Celene offered, "Anyone for a drink?"

Jake winked. "I heard about something called *mai-tai* on the plane. But isn't there a wedding we should be going to?"

"Hang loose," Palani said jovially. "This is Hawaii. Things start whenever they're ready to start."

* * * * *

When Celene walked across the beach on her father's arm to meet her groom, she thought about her adoptive father. Armand Dupres would be proud of her today. She'd accomplished the mission he'd given her with his dying words, and the man who betrayed him had died. Now, he could rest in peace. Still, she missed him and wished he were here to share her happiness.

The beach reminded Celene of the familiar dreams she'd cherished since childhood. Had she been dreaming of her past all this time? Or of her future? It did not matter anymore. Celene had found her home. She belonged here. She could feel it in the grains of sand under her bare feet, in the roll of the breaking surf, in the trills of the cardinals in the palm trees, and in the breath of the trade winds playing with her long flowing hair.

In a black silk Mandarin robe embroidered with a magnificent red dragon, Kin stood by the *Kahuna*. The holy man, who had named her as a baby, would now bless their union. When Kin smiled, watching her walk toward him, Celene's heart leapt in her chest and she had to refrain from running up to him.

* * * * *

Kin had never seen Celene look more radiant than when she smiled and took his hand to face the *Kahuna*. Kin barely heard the sound of the conch announcing the start of the ceremony. He felt light-headed from the fragrance of so many flowers.

When the old *Kahuna* nodded and smiled, then

blessed their union in ancient Hawaiian, the ceremony unfolded in a blur.

"You waited a long time, but you found each other in the midst of the storm," the old man finally said in English. "Now is the moment of sweet *Aloha* when you pledge your love and seal it forever. Your ancestors are smiling upon you on this auspicious day. "Kin Raidon, do you promise to love this *wahine* with all your heart forevermore?"

"I do so promise." Kin's words flowed easily. He would never stop loving Celene. Of that he was certain.

When the *Kahuna* addressed Celene, she looked ready to burst with joy. "I do so promise," she blurted out, blushing.

Kin slid on Celene's finger a traditional Hawaiian wedding ring engraved with a scroll of *maile* leaves and plumeria blossoms. Then they exchanged flower *leis*. Kin took Celene in his arms and gave her the traditional kiss as the first notes of the Hawaiian Wedding Song, *Ke Kali Nei Au*, came floating on the breeze from the group of local musicians.

The guests gathered around the newlyweds for congratulations and buried them under piles of flower *leis* and kisses. The drums started beating to the rhythm of the ancient *hula*, and male dancers in grass skirts and *maile* leaves lined up on the shore.

"This is not the *hula* for tourists," Hawika commented for his benefit. "In ancient times, only men were allowed to dance, only men cooked the food. They were warriors. But things have changed. Hawaii is now a friendly, peaceful place."

Men were still warriors, and some women, too.

But Kin didn't share his thoughts. *No sense is spoiling such a peaceful gathering.* Celene glanced at him and held his hand as if she never wanted to let him go. Kin yearned for the moment when they would be alone. He had some good news he couldn't share in public.

The newlyweds watched and applauded as the cooks unearthed the roasted pig from the underground *imu*, where it had been cooking since early morning, wrapped in banana leaves, buried with hot stones and embers. Then the guests gathered at the tables set on the grass by the beach, to eat the shredded pig with sweet *poi*, papaya, pineapple, and *Mahi-mahi*.

Kin bided his time as the *luau* feast went on with *hula* girls swaying to the tune of *ukuleles* and Hawaiian steel guitars. The guests drank gallons of coconut milk, *mai-tai* and *Kahlua* cocktails. Soon the sun disappeared into the glittering ocean as a fire dancer took the stage, juggling live torches and blowing flames.

While everyone stared at the fiery show, Celene took Kin's hand. "Come."

Kin smiled with relief and followed her as they escaped into the shadows.

* * * * *

Celene led Kin along the beach to a small cove away from the guests. The beat of the drums still reached her ears. They sat on the sand, waiting for the first stars to appear. The trade winds had died out and the soft roll of the surf rocked their words.

Kin encircled Celene's shoulder. "So, will you

accept my job offer?"

"Did they agree?"

Nodding, Kin said, "As long as we work together."

Celene rejoiced at the good news. Mythos had rescinded the kill order, but she'd had doubts about their willingness to take her as an operative.

"Do you think we can manage working that closely?" He winked at her.

Celene played with the end of his *maile lei*. "You mean, without making out at every opportunity? It will take some getting used to, but I think I can do it. Can you?"

He grinned and kissed her with a passion that promised much more to come. They stretched on the sand and stared up at the evening sky. Above them, the Pleiades cluster came into view, followed by Orion the constellation of the hunter.

Kin pointed at the Orion belt. "See? The hunter can never catch the Pleiades sisters. It's written in the stars, like an omen, a symbol of your victory."

The musicians in the background intoned, *Sweet Leilani, Heavenly Flower*.

Kin smiled. "It's your song. The old *Kahuna* named you right. You really are a child from the heavens."

As they gazed at the stars, Celene understood her destiny. The tumult of the world did not seem to reach this island paradise, but she knew this was only a respite in the fight against the Anaz-voohri threat. And Carrick would never stop hunting her as long as he lived. She must fight to protect this innocent and loving island she now called home. But Celene didn't have to struggle alone. She felt loved and she knew that whatever happened from now on, her family would support her, and Kin would be at her side.

"Will you be all right?" Kin pushed a rebellious strand of hair back under her crown of flowers.

Celene smiled. "These people are teaching me to trust my human heart, no matter what the odds. In Hawaiian lore, the gods favor bold courage."

"Don't worry, you have plenty of that." Kin played with her fingers in the sand. "I wonder what our children will look like."

"Children?" Celene laughed. "Wait a minute. We still have time for that."

"I know. But think." He counted on his fingers. "They'll be Hawaiian, Irish, Chinese and whatever else in your parents' lineage."

"You mean chop-sui, like all true Hawaiians. They'll fit right in."

"I'd love to have a family of my own." He kissed her hand. "After we neutralize the Anaz-voohri for good, I hope we can raise our children in peace."

"Peace." How strange a word… But tonight, on this secluded beach, Celene believed anything was possible, even victory against the Anaz-voohri, even peace. "I'd like that, too," she said softly, nestling her head in the crook of Kin's shoulder.

THE END